Baddest APPLE

Melodrama Publishing
www.MelodramaPublishing.com

FOLLOW
NISA SANTIAGO

FACEBOOK.COM/NISASANTIAGO

INSTAGRAM.COM/NISA_SANTIAGO

TWITTER.COM/NISA_SANTIAGO

Order online at
bn.com, amazon.com, and
MelodramaPublishing.com

Baddest Apple - The Baddest Chick Part 7. Copyright © 2019 by Melodrama Publishing. All rights reserved. No part of this book may be used or reproduced in any manner whatsoever without written permission except in the case of brief quotations embodied in critical articles or reviews. For information, address info@melodramabooks.com.

www.melodramapublishing.com

Library of Congress Control Number: 2018957345
ISBN-13: 978-1620781029

First Edition: October 2019

Printed in Canada

Baddest APPLE

NISA SANTIAGO

DEDICATION

I want to dedicate this final book in *The Baddest Chick* series to all the people who continually go above and beyond the norm of an avid reader. These readers aren't "fans" to me; they're so much more, somewhat like family. They encourage and motivate me and are beacons of positivity regarding my works. They have helped push my Nisa Santiago brand forward in different ways—from starting and maintaining my Facebook fan page, updating other readers with my latest publication dates, and reviewing my book(s) on any of the online retail platforms without my having to ask. These little things are huge to me and mean so much. I am forever grateful. Thank y'all!

Your sistah-friend,

1

The rules to the street game were straightforward—don't get caught or killed. *So far so good,* Apple thought. It felt like the end of summer was going out with a bang—indignantly terrorizing New York City with a scorching heat wave that was becoming oppressive to the nine million people that populated the city. The urban city blocks were active with people trying to keep cool in the blazing heat. Hundreds of fire hydrants were opened and on full blast spewing cold water that flooded the worn, paved roads. Apple cruised onto the Henry Hudson Parkway, traveling north in her air-conditioned black and sleek Maserati while listening to her new favorite song—"Money." As she drove, the silence had her mind going to places she wished she could forget. Although the music helped distract her somewhat, the brain is so powerful that it would take more than Cardi B to pull her out of her funk.

The familiar road she traveled was an unpleasant journey, but one she felt she had to take. The heavy rainfall that began pounding against the roof and windows matched her mood: messy. Apple's Michelin tires hugged the newly paved Upstate New York road as she steered her pricey car to Clinton Correctional Facility in Dannemora, New York. Several blocks of towering concrete walls with barbed wire were indicative she had finally arrived, five hours later.

Apple turned left into the visitor's parking lot where multiple guard towers had a bird's-eye view of the vicinity. Clinton was a somber-looking structure—increased security after the recent prison escape of inmates Richard Matt and David Sweat. Apple hesitated to weigh her decision to be merciful. She wondered had she gone soft as she sat in silence, trying to get her mind right. She sighed and then got out of her car, opening her large umbrella before bolting toward intake. Her vintage Pumas splashed through puddles until her footwear and jeans were soaked.

Inside the cold, damp, stone building she reluctantly snaked through the tight-knit security without incident. Corey Davis sat with his back erect, body stiffened, and face in a hard frown wondering why he had agreed to let this parasite visit.

Apple made eye contact with the sixty-something-year-old senior and saw her beloved, Nick. Nicholas was a younger version of his father as if Corey spit him out. It pained Apple to revisit her feelings, but the pain was ever-present in her life; different day same shit. Corey was still physically fit, but it appeared he had aged since she saw him at the funeral, which wasn't *that* long ago for him to sprout all those new grays. Now he was mostly salt and a little pepper against his dark, chocolate skin—still no wrinkles, though.

Corey watched as Apple moved toward him with a tiger's stride—deliberate and untamed. He realized that she feared no one and noted she didn't fear him. He assumed that she would be all dolled up like most women who came on visits, but she was casual. Apple's hair was pulled into a messy bun, and her bare earlobes didn't have the sparkly diamonds she was accustomed to wearing. She wore no makeup, a long-sleeved shirt, jeans, and sneakers. At first blush, Apple looked no older than seventeen until you peered deeper into her dark eyes and saw a seasoned, and manipulative, grown woman.

She plopped down. "Hello again, Mr. Davis."

Corey absorbed her energy before he uttered something unintelligible. Apple watched as he clasped his large hands together, seeming to stop himself from lashing out. Finally, he asked, "What the fuck you want?"

Bluntly, she replied, "Absolution."

The blood drained from his face as he processed Apple's statement. "What the fuck you say?"

"You have every right to hate me, because the likelihood of Nick being alive had he not met me is high. He wanted to get out of the game, but I pulled him back in," she confessed. "His death is on me."

Thick veins bulged through Corey's temples as Apple confirmed what he already knew to be true. "Why are you here?"

"I came up here to . . ." Apple's voice trailed off. Instinctively she bit the inside of her cheek to stop the emotions swirling around her stomach, which were threatening to spill out. She swallowed to force the lump back down her throat, but it was too late. Her bottom lip quivered, and the tears came next. Within seconds she was blinded with salty reminders of the many mistakes of her past.

A strangled cry tumbled out of Apple's throat. "I loved him, Mr. Davis," she squeezed out. "I loved him," she repeated.

Corey sat there, unaffected and unmoved. Her tears wouldn't bring back his son. He leaned in and whispered, "I will kill you, Apple. Not by my hand, but you will die before I celebrate the New Year. I owe that to my son."

"Mr. Davis—"

"Please, call me Corey. You murdered my son; I think we should be on a first-name basis."

Quickly, Apple shut off her tears like she had shut off faucet water and said, "Mr. Davis, you can have a death wish for me, but I gotta tell you that that's not what Nick would have wanted. He loved me, he did."

"He was a fool."

"He was not!" Apple got agitated. "Nicholas was the smartest, most ambitious man I know, and he had the best heart. It's me; I think I'm cursed."

"Cursed?" He chuckled.

Apple shook her head and shot up from her seat. This visit was a waste of time. She knew what she wanted to accomplish, but this wasn't it.

"Sit down!" Corey demanded, and Apple glared his way. She was uncomfortable being told what to do. He lowered his voice. "Please, have a seat."

Apple sat back down and protectively folded her arms in front of herself. She felt vulnerable—a rare emotion for her. She was trying to remember a time when she felt normal; when she didn't have so much hate in her heart.

Corey asked, "What does cursed mean, and how does it pertain to my son?"

She wondered if she should let him in. Should she say her most private thoughts out loud to Corey? He was a stranger to her—an enemy. Corey was a man who wanted to take her away from her daughter, Kola, and the comfortable life she had created for herself. His cold eyes, etched in wisdom, gave her permission to proceed.

"On my drive back from South Beach I realized that so many people had died because of my choices, all people that I loved—and I don't love many—and I'm so scared, Mr. Davis, that the two people that I have left will die because of me and I'll have to live with it. But I won't. If something happened to my sister and daughter, I'd kill myself, but *only* after I avenged them."

Corey was glad he got her talking. So, she had a daughter and sister who if they were killed first would send this bitch over the edge.

"This doesn't sound like who you are." Corey's eyebrows raised and merged, forming a barrier of skepticism. "The woman that my son described was stubborn and strong-willed. This pity party seems forced. What's your angle?"

"You're not listening. You're judging."

"I'm listening, but get to the point. I want to hear about this curse."

Apple sucked in the air before forcefully exhaling. "There is something inherently dark hovering in and around my life that's been there since my early teens. I remember the first time I felt this powerful entity. We lived in Lincoln projects, and things were miserable. I'd gone to bed hungry, so I didn't sleep long, maybe a few hours. My eyes slowly lifted open, and the house was dark and still. I tried to get out of bed but couldn't. My whole body was paralyzed as I lay limp. The only movement was my eyes as they darted frantically around the room, so I screamed, 'Denise! Denise!' for my mom, but no sounds came out."

"And then what?"

"I told everyone what I'm tellin' you."

"Which is?"

Apple knew her story was bizarre, but she continued. "Have you ever heard of a witch ridin' your back?"

"Enlighten me."

"It's when you're lying in bed, and you want to get up but you can't—there's a force holding you down, an invisible, dark force—a powerful witch. You want to scream out, but you can't. You hear your screams in your head, but that's it. That morning was the first but not the last time that this occurrence happened."

"And this is your evidence of a curse?"

"It's a sign that a dark entity wants to hurt me and those I love."

Corey's eyes could bore holes in anyone except Apple. He stared her down, and she didn't flinch. Finally, he offered, "What you've described is a medical condition called sleep paralysis, when you haven't fully awakened. Your mind has, but the rest of your body is trying to catch up.

The terminology and explanation of a witch riding your back is folklore—an old wives' tale passed down through slave generations until the myth made its way to the mainstream."

Apple rolled her eyes. "That makes no sense whatsoever. I'm telling you what I feel—what I've alway—felt is a demonic presence. Why do you think I'm like this?"

"Like what? I don't know you."

She snorted. And then she slowly tossed out several adjectives she had heard her enemies use to describe her throughout the years.

"Heartless, angry, bitter, sociopath, vengeful, hateful . . . and mostly a crazy bitch."

"If you claim it, then it shall be."

Apple wanted to convince him of her theory. She wanted him on her side. She tried again. "It all started when I borrowed money from a loan shark and couldn't repay him. He ended up murdering my baby sister, and she was raped. Meanwhile, I fucked him, called him my man, and life went on for me. I'm still here. Can you see the curse now? She's dead because of my dark demons. How can you explain that? And because of me, my mother and Nick were both murdered."

"I'm trying to follow your supposition. The same people that murdered your sister, mother, and my son could have murdered you but didn't? You're still alive, yet you feel that *you're* cursed? You caught the raw deal here?" His voice dripped with sarcasm, and Apple didn't like it one bit.

"I'm not playing the victim here if that's what you saying!"

"Only you said it. Listen, you may have internal demons placed upon you by yourself. You will never have freedom until you stop caring what others think about you. Stop making this visit about how I think or feel about you. What is it that *you* want?"

"I wanted to affirm your feelings about the death of your son and also add a backstory to why things turned out the way they did."

"You have to let go of what was the past. Use it as a teacher and let that be it. But if you keep looking backward, you will miss things right in front of you. Plots, enemies, love, happiness could be sitting outside your front door and you wouldn't know because your eyes are fixed on your rearview. As I sit here in prison I pity you because you've allowed your mind—thoughts of things that happened in your teens, early twenties—to imprison you. Your past has you in bondage. You can either evolve as a person or repeat your mistakes."

Apple got his point. Nick's murder would be yet another reason added to her long list of explanations of why she robs, steals, and kills. She robbed because so much was taken from her. Apple stole because her mother never provided for her. And she murdered because her sister was killed. Corey was trying to get her to see she did those things because she wanted those things done.

"You hungry?"

"I could eat," he returned.

Apple pushed her chair back from the table and went to one of the many vending machines. She added money for two cheeseburgers, sodas, and two candy bars. There wasn't any nutritional value in the highly processed, carbonated choices, but it was fuel. As she placed the burgers in the microwave, her eyes scanned the room.

"Watch those hands, convict!" a corrections officer yelled to an inmate trying to finger fuck his girl under a table. "Try that again, and your visit is over!"

This place was depressing. Apple wondered how Kola could have survived both Miami and Colombian jails. Apple grabbed their meal and sat back down in the uncomfortable chair; luckily, her fat ass gave her some cushion.

"How was my son with you? What type of man was Nicholas out on the streets?"

Apple grinned. "He was a quiet storm, and I respected how he handled me. I mean, I can be a bit much with my foul mouth and strong will, but he would never lose his cool with me. He never went to bed upset, no matter how hard his day was. Oh, and he cooked."

"Shiit, you lying."

"On my life, he could burn. He never told you?"

"Our visits were mainly about the streets. How to keep my son alive."

Apple glossed over that and continued. "Well, he could make anything. Soul food, Italian, Asian, you name it. He was always planning his menu for his lounge, and every few days he would switch it up."

"I would have loved to taste his cooking."

"Nick was a big kid at heart too. He would play that *Fortnite* game until I was begging him to come to bed, which would cause an argument."

Corey chuckled. He liked hearing these stories about his son. Through Apple, he saw a side of Nicholas he hadn't met.

"So, Amir. That was you?"

"Amir went against the grain. He crossed me. He crossed my son. He had to die."

"Just like that, huh?"

Corey nodded.

"Fuck 'im," Apple replied. "I didn't like him. Nick's casket was hardly lowered in the ground before he was trying to holler at me."

Corey hated to admit this to himself, but he was enjoying his day with Apple. The young woman was troubled and had been through a lot, but she was fiercely strong-willed. He could see what his son saw in her just as Nick said he would. He killed Amir, his son was murdered, and he was pushing seventy and had no one. He wanted to see her again—if only one more time to hear more about Nick. However, Corey still knew a hard fact: Apple had to die.

"Let's call a truce, for now," he announced grandly.

"Done."

Apple looked left and did a head nod and then repeated that same movement to her right. Instantly, Corey's head swiveled over his shoulders to see who she was addressing. To Corey's right sat Drac, an old head from Harlem who had just gotten three life sentences in state court plus eighteen years in the feds for murders and racketeering. Nearing fifty, he had a long run out on the streets and had left a lot of grieving families praying for his demise. Drac looked worn and weathered, but he was everything but weak. The deep lines and battle scars in his face were like an old treasure map taking you to dangerous places and years of lascivious events.

The other man was Bubba, but you could never call him that to his face. Nowadays he went simply by Bee. Bee was a drifter; moving state–to–state, leaving bodies racking up in his yesterdays. He had a short but powerful run on the streets, and his hubris is what they said brought him down. Bee killed too many too quickly, leaving witnesses and snitches alive so they could tell his tale. His murdered victims weren't killed over turf, a drug deal went wrong, or the obligatory robbery. Most casualties of his war were because of a perceived disrespectful look, or talking too loud in his vicinity, or even accidentally bumping into him. His hair-trigger temper almost got him the death penalty, but a merciful jury had spared the monster.

Corey smirked. What the fuck was up?

"So, Corey, now is the time to tell you what the fuck I want." Apple snickered at his original question. "Your men, the ones who keep you alive in here, are now my men."

Corey glared. He was a cool dude and wouldn't erupt in anger or play himself until he knew who all the moving pieces on the chessboard belonged to.

"I know about the shooters, Whiz and Floco. And of course, you know they're both dead."

"Bitch, you drove up here to tell water it's wet?"

"Uh-huh," she said. "I also want to move forward. I'm back from South Beach, and I want to spend quality time with my daughter without worrying about you sending a limitless supply of paroled convicts at me."

"That's exactly what I'ma do. You think this shit scares me?"

"You're not listening, Pops. Can I call you Pops? I like it more than Mr. Davis or Corey." Apple smiled wide, and within a split second, her eyes turned dark, her nostrils flared, and a deep scowl emerged. "You have no power, old man. None! Your life is courtesy of my good heart. I've loaned today to you, maybe tomorrow. If I'm feeling generous, then you may make it to the New Year. Bottom line, you die when I say you die. I am your god!"

Corey's face darkened as he tried to sort through his options. Visions of getting shanked in the shower were all too real.

"Drac and Bubba, they on your payroll?"

"And the nearly twenty men you thought held allegiance to you."

Corey gave a nervous chuckle. "Money doesn't buy everything."

"But it does, though, and a million dollars and then some bought me your men's loyalty."

A bitch was handling the infamous Corey Davis, the legend who had come up with Nicky Barnes, Frank Lucas, and Bumpy Johnson. "I underestimated you."

"They all do."

Corey exhaled. Fuck it; he couldn't live forever. He asked, "How long do I really get?"

"You can live as long as you allow me in your life."

Corey was puzzled. His whole face showed his bewilderment. Apple continued to explain. "Your son wanted us to be close, and with him gone, I would appreciate it if you got to know me. You have no son; I have no parents. Maybe we could have each other?"

"I hate you! That will never change."

"Good, keep that same energy 'cause everyone loves a challenge. I could have never respected you if you had folded. I'll see you in a few weeks, Pops. I've left money on your books."

With that, Apple tossed deuces in the air to Drac and Bee and headed out of the visiting room.

Today, she would show mercy.

2

Touch sat at the poker table expressionless and glanced at the hand that he was dealt. He had ninety thousand dollars in chips riding on his latest hand—three of a kind. Seated across from him were three strong opponents who carried the same blank look as his because each man was skilled at high stakes poker. The high-end chips spilled across the poker table were a small fortune to most. It equaled a small hill of glittering gold, and every man at the table was ready to mine it all.

Touch had a lot of money riding on this hand, and though it was hard to read his adversaries, he felt he had a winning hand, and Touch was ready to call their bluffs and go all in—every poker chip he had on the table was on this one hand. It was now or never—no reward without risk. Touch had lost four hundred thousand dollars throughout the day. If he lost this hand, it would be over for him.

Touch mainly supported himself by playing in high stakes poker tournaments; it's what he was known for. It was instinctual for him, gambling—and over the years he had won big and he had lost big. Touch had flown to Las Vegas yesterday with the twenty-five thousand dollars buy-in. Ten hours later he was up nearly three hundred large until he lost most of it. A few hours of sleep and a quick shower, and he was back in the game.

His palms were itching, sweat beads trickled down his back, and his heart fluttered as he flipped each card. He was so close, and yet his fate could turn on a dime. Poker was a game of skill and luck, and on day two, he didn't feel lucky. Maybe he should have cashed out, but the million-dollar potential payday was similar to how Greek mythology described the sounds from the sirens luring the sailors to their deaths. He just couldn't walk away. There was nearly a half-million dollars in front of him that he wanted to leave with. All four men's cards were revealed. Touch's three of a kind was impressive, but he lost to a flush.

Fuck! he cursed to himself.

His ninety grand disappeared from his sight. Touch pushed back his chair, stood up, and removed himself from the table. He had a good run, but he still lost. What he needed next was a drink. He marched toward the bar with his head up and his ego still intact. You win some, you lose some was his attitude.

At the bar, he ordered a Whiskey Sour and downed it like it was water. He ordered another one. Losing nearly five hundred thousand dollars in one night, it would make a saint get drunk. But Touch knew that he would recoup what he lost by landing another job—and soon. He lingered by the bar for a moment and scoped out the area. Touch loved Las Vegas and its motto—what happens in Vegas, stays in Vegas.

The casino was packed like usual, filled with bright colors and loud noises. The slot machines were heavily occupied, with most players doing long stretches dropping their mortgage money and kids' college funds into those mesmerizing coin guzzlers. There were flashes, glows, beeps, and chirps coming from all directions. It was a Disneyland to many people, but the thrills were riskier.

Touch downed his third Whiskey Sour, and he spotted her nearby with her eyes on him. He wondered if she was following him. His first glance at the woman was at the poker table, watching him lose a lot of money. She was an R&B singer with a crossover pop following and had a hit song on the radio. Her moniker was Birdie, and she had a voice like Ciara, a body like JLo, and beauty like Beyoncé. She was the perfect package—a beautiful star. Touch knew her career, and he knew that she probably wouldn't go far because she wasn't Beyoncé.

Birdie was needy and insecure, and though she had a hit song on the radio, she was still looking for a come up. She needed a man with some long paper and a powerful presence because she felt she was getting fucked by her manager, her record label, and her producers.

Birdie had followed Touch around all night, thinking he was cute with an edge. She hoped he would notice her. She eyed him at the poker table and watched him lose tens of thousands like it was counterfeit. Birdie figured there had to be a lot more of it somewhere. He had to be wealthy.

Touch decided to shoot his shot. He walked toward the sexy songstress and asked, "Why are you following me?"

"Excuse me?" Birdie feigned shock. "I'm not following anyone."

"A nigga got eyes."

Birdie seductively bit her bottom lip. Her round, expressive eyes framed with long false lashes could grab any man's full attention. "Oh, yeah? What do you see now?"

"I see a lot of fun," he said thoughtfully.

"I see." She smiled.

Touch had started the spark, now he was ready to set shit on fire. He'd lost at the poker table, but he was winning inside the casino. Birdie was a pretty girl. She was the girl that a nigga would cut off his right arm just to have sex with. And he had her undivided attention.

"Since you're stalking me, why don't you buy me a drink?" he asked.

She chuckled. "Oh, I'm supposed to buy you a drink?"

"Why not?" He wasn't serious. He was just engaging in flirty banter and wondering if she would let him hit it tonight. "I figure all the money

I spent on my hair and nails to look this good should get me at least one free drink."

Birdie took a couple steps back and looked him up and down skeptically. She cocked her head to one side and finally said, "You look a'ight. You can order one drink—but not top shelf. Those cuticles are looking a little rough."

They both laughed.

Through the excitement and noise, Touch called the bartender over. His deep voice commanded attention.

"Yo, let me get a bottle of Veuve Clicquot Rosé champagne."

The bartender nodded.

Touch turned to face Birdie, and she had a look of sheer panic on her face. He could see that her mind was churning. All the seductive looks had come to a quick halt, and the diva came out. He was amused. There was no faster way to get a female's juices to dry up than by asking her to pick up the check.

"Why you so quiet?"

Birdie cut her eyes. "I'm not."

"I'm Touch by the way. What's your name?"

Dryly, she replied, "Birdie."

"What's your real name?"

"Birdie is all you need to know. I like to keep it casual," she snapped.

Her mood had done a one-eighty. Touch watched as she eyed the bartender like a hawk. He could tell she was trying to decide how she would handle the situation when the five-hundred-dollar bar tab came. Touch continued to try and engage her in chitchat, but she was less responsive. Birdie watched as the cork was popped on the bottle, placed in a chilled bucket of ice, and subsequently began making its way toward them.

"Birdie, did you hear me?" Touch reiterated.

"What?" she asked. She hadn't heard shit. Birdie was feeling played at the moment and hated that she couldn't ever find her voice to stand up for herself. She had less than sixty dollars in her wallet, and all her credit cards were maxed out. Maybe there was one card that might not get declined, but if it did, she was sure the situation would make it to The Shade Room. Birdie had one hit song and was on an independent record label. She had long ago blown through her advance, perfecting her celebrity image. The clothing, Benz, human hair weaves, lace front wigs, jewelry, thigh-high boots, stilettos, new apartment—a whole gamut of expenses. And then her record label sent her an exorbitant bill for studio time, beats, producers, album release party, vocal and dance lessons, publicity, and marketing. Financially she was worse off than before she became famous.

Touch thought he could see the color draining from her face. It wasn't that serious, was it?

Just as the bartender was placing the bottle in front of them, he felt Birdie about to take flight. Calmly he put his hand over hers while reaching for his wallet. "How much?" He could physically feel her acquiesce.

Touch pulled out his credit card and paid the tab, and instantly, the energy shifted. He filled both flute glasses and handed the lovely lady one. "So, Birdie, you sing, right?"

She grinned, showing the pearly whites. "I do. My album dropped last month. You buy it?"

"I did not."

"Well, what you waiting on? Take out your phone and download it from iTunes."

"Relax, superstar."

"You too cheap to pay ten bucks for a classic album?"

Touch chuckled. "Cheap?"

Within seconds, Birdie's champagne glass was empty. She took the initiative to refill her own drink. After taking another large gulp, she continued. "Yes, cheap. What does a girl have to do to get support in her career? Fuck for it? You should want to support a young, black female artist in a man's industry. All that money you lost and you make ten dollars an issue?"

This time Touch refilled her third glass. "Drink up. You seem a little thirsty."

Birdie allowed the quip to linger in the air momentarily. She was trying to decide whether this stranger had just insulted her. But the yummy champagne had her feeling less sensitive. By her fourth drink, she was ready to fuck. He was cute, charming, and he smelled nice. Touch was grown-man sexy, and she wanted in. Birdie had gotten lost in his smoldering eyes, thick eyebrows, and his strong jawbone. She did want him—maybe for life.

"What hotel are you staying in?" she asked. Touch's response would determine how she wanted her night to end.

"Bellagio suite comped."

"You get comped out here?"

He nodded.

"Because you're a professional poker player."

Touch shrugged. He was bored with her and the conversation. Birdie was pretentious and not at all how he thought she would be. Unwisely he believed the image she had created of this fiercely independent woman. Her hit single was all about female empowerment.

"Do you always play in million-dollar tournaments?"

"Birdie, I've been working for nearly two days straight. When I'm off the clock, I don't wanna talk about work."

Seductively, she asked, "Then what do you wanna do?"

Birdie was about to pour her fifth drink when Touch stopped her by gently placing his hand on hers. "I think you've had enough."

She jerked away. "I know my limit."

Touch nodded and stood. He hadn't taken a sip. "Enjoy the rest of the champagne. It was a pleasure meeting you."

She panicked. "Where are you going?"

"To my room."

"Well, I can go too."

"You come wit' me to my room, you're getting fucked."

Birdie grabbed the almost empty bottle into her small hand and stood up too. "Exactly."

Touch didn't smile or look thrilled when she agreed to go with him to his room. He carried that same straight-faced expression he had at the poker table. He walked, and she followed, like a sheep following the shepherd. Birdie had a hit song on the radio, but tonight, she felt like she was selling herself cheap for a potential shopping spree in the morning to a cute and intriguing man with deep pockets. It was a desperate move.

Touch wasted no time inside his casino suite, as he thrust himself against Birdie, taking her into his arms and kissing her passionately. She didn't resist. He was aggressive, but she was too. Birdie was horny and wanted to get fucked. As they kissed, Touch undressed her, removing her clothing piece by piece. Her body was remarkable—perfection from head to toe, and Touch could feel the beast inside his pants coming alive for her. He grabbed the lube.

"Come on now, don't insult me," she whispered. "My pussy stay wet."

Birdie stuck her two fingers into her wet cave and began pleasuring herself as Touch looked on. He was shirtless but still had his pants on. Quickly he pulled off his pants, and then his boxers as she masturbated. It looked like he had a tree trunk between his legs. Birdie gasped at the sight of his fourteen-inch erection. She was taken aback by his porno-sized penis.

"I know," he sheepishly uttered. "You sure you don't want the lube? It helps."

"I'm not some fragile bitch. I can take some dick."

Touch didn't know if that was true or if it was the alcohol talking. He reached for a Magnum condom and rolled it back until it stretched, looking like a fat bitch in spandex. It was the biggest dick she was about to fuck, and when Touch positioned her on her back against the bed and spread her legs, she took a deep breath and readied herself. And as expected, she had a hard time handling his massive erection. It felt like her vagina walls were stretched to the max, and her pussy was about to pop. She grunted and bit down on her bottom lip intensely as Touch slowly penetrated her.

"Aaaah . . . oooh . . . oh shit!" she cried out.

Touch could rarely lose control in the bedroom with many women, so over the years he had worked on this technique; soft and slow if he wanted to have an orgasm. He couldn't fuck hard and fast or else they'd scream, "Stop!" So he had to basically make love to one-night stands—which confused these women. Soon he had Birdie purring and grinding her hips, yearning for more of him.

"Fuck me," she moaned.

"Like this?" Touch asked as he sank deeper. His strokes were deep and gentle, and he wasn't even halfway inside of her yet. Already, she could feel his mushroom tip against the back of her wet cave with her legs clamped tightly around his waist. Touch was enjoying it too; the look of ecstasy on her face turned him on. Her soft moans and groans made him want to please her. And he did. Birdie had multiple orgasms and eventually called out his name in pleasure.

She exhaled, spent. Birdie was physically depleted as she cuddled under Touch's strong arm and drifted off into a deep, restful sleep. Meanwhile, Touch lay on his back and stared aimlessly at the ceiling, reliving how he'd fucked up each hand at the poker table.

With Birdie snuggled against him, Touch fell fast asleep.

Three hours later, his eyes popped open. He wasn't a man to sleep for long. It was his standard—three to five hours of sleep. Touch woke up refreshed and was ready to start a new day. He let Birdie sleep for a minute while he went to shower, washing away her scent from his skin. After he toweled off, he ordered up room service. Coffee for him and a full farewell breakfast for her. Touch prayed and then got dressed. An hour later, he pulled the cart into the room and tapped Birdie on her shoulder.

Groggily, she woke up with an instant attitude. She wasn't a morning person and needed from eight to ten hours of sleep. She was stirred awake, looked at him, and mumbled, "Baby, I'm not ready to fuck again yet. I need some time."

She rolled over to go back to sleep. Touch became annoyed. He tapped her again, this time rougher—a sterner poke and maybe she would get the hint. Her eyes popped open, and it was evident to him she was angry.

"Birdie, I ordered you some breakfast, and I would like you to eat it and then go," he said frankly.

"What are you talking about?" Birdie's scowl was deep as her eyes scanned the room and settled on the breakfast cart.

"I got a game today, and I need to focus," he lied. He hoped Birdie wasn't a drama queen.

"Are you serious, nigga? You can't be serious." She hoped he was joking—bullshitting her. There was no way he was kicking her out of his room—not her. Birdie? She was a pop star, and she had been nominated for a Grammy for Best New Artist, and she was voted New Artist to Watch by *Billboard* magazine. So, there was no way she was getting fucked, dumped, and kicked out of a hotel room all in one night. Birdie knew she was a wet dream to most men—a fantasy they jerked off to.

"I don't want any problems, Birdie. You know, I like to keep it casual," he said, repeating her remark from the night before.

"Keep it casual after you fuck me!" Birdie exploded and leaped from the bed with hostility. She was tired of being taken advantage of. "You know what? Fuck you! You should be lucky that you got to fuck a bitch like me, you fuckin' groupie! This is premium pussy right here." Birdie tapped her twat. "You trying to handle me like I'm some fuckin' one-night stand—like I'm some cheap fuckin' whore!"

Touch stood there unfazed by her hostile attitude and her angry words. He had heard it all before. Women were very complicated, and he didn't pretend to understand them. And he didn't force her to have sex with him; it was her choice. Nor did he make her any promises. Where was it written that sex came with cuddling for the night and future commitments?

Birdie continued to curse and carry on while she collected her shit. She was all in her feelings, and she wanted Touch to pay for her humiliation. The audacity of this nigga to use her—to put that humongous dick of his inside of her, and she took it, and now he was kicking her out with nothing monetary to compensate her for her time.

"I'm a fuckin' star! Only bitch-ass niggas kick out some good pussy."

Touch had four levels of emotions—charming, quiet, angry, and deadly. With Birdie, he already had done charming, and he was now quiet while she ranted and raved inside his room. He wished she would wrap this up.

When Birdie couldn't get Touch to react in any way toward her tantrums, it pissed her off even more. She charged toward him and slapped his face angrily. He didn't even flinch. Immediately, Birdie knew she had gone too far. Touch's cavalier demeanor transitioned into outrage, and he charged at her, grabbing a chunk of her long weave. He dragged her to the door in her bra and panties and tossed her out. Birdie kicked and screamed as he tossed her clothes behind her. Birdie found herself almost naked in the hotel hallway. One would think that she would be embarrassed and get dressed so she could tiptoe to her room and forget about the whole ordeal. Not Birdie. Her adrenaline was raging, and her ego was bruised. She banged, screamed, and cursed at Touch's door so loudly that she could have woken up the dead.

The hotel guests were aghast at what they saw—a bitter and angry and nearly naked celebrity in the hallway. It was scandalous shit for sure. Hotel security had been called, and they had to eventually drag Birdie away.

By the next morning, TMZ, The Shade Room, and many other social media websites had footage of Birdie screaming like she was a mad woman. Some details were correct; she had been kicked out an unidentified man's room half-naked.

3

Apple sat on the back porch with an ice-cold Corona beer in her hand. She watched her daughter Peaches playing in the backyard with Sophia and Eduardo Jr. They were in their swimsuits, splashing around in the pool with Kamel, who was giving them swimming lessons. Kola stood not too far away, making taco burgers on the grill. Apple had been there a few hours, and Kola said little; she was distant, her miscarriage still weighing heavily on her mind. Apple watched her sister. The way her eyes would squint low whenever she was in deep thought, or her nostrils would flare, spreading her thin, straight nose whenever angered were identical to her movements. Kola's body, from her size six feet to her toned thighs, was like having a living mirror in front of her who was similar in every way except her mind. The two never thought alike. Apple had to admit that having Peaches spread her waist and fattened her ass somewhat, but their differences paled in comparison to their similarities.

Kola's Westchester home was an active construction site. Kamel had hired several undocumented, unlicensed contractors to redesign the basement against Kola's wishes. The two consistently argued over the strange men coming and going each week. Kamel wanted to flip houses to supplement their income, finally tired of living off of Eduardo's money that was siphoned to his wife each month, and their home was his crash course. Apple knew her sharp tongue had played a significant role in him wanting to exert his independence again. Kola fretted about her husband filling the shoes of a general contractor—a position he had no experience in—and worried. She could afford to hire the best that money could buy, but he pleaded with her to allow him to do this his way. So she did.

The drywall, live wires, and exposed pipes gave her pause—the power tools, load-bearing walls, and gas lines made it seem like someone other than random men that Kamel picked up at the local Home Depot parking lot should be overseeing this project.

"Here," Kola offered her sister a slider and took a seat next to her in the wicker wingback chair. "You got any weed?"

"On me?" Apple smirked. "Nah. You should have told me you wanted to light up. I would have copped you an ounce."

Kola shrugged. "It's all good."

"Hey, what's wrong wit' you? You seem down."

"I'm fine for now," she explained. "But I think it's time for you to take Peaches to live with you."

"What? Why?"

Kola exhaled. "Because she's your daughter and she misses her mom."

Apple's eyes narrowed as she got defensive. "She has a mom! And a good one, Kola, you know that! But it's not fair to rip her away from Sophia and Junior. Let her stay throughout the year and then she'll be ready to come home next summer."

Kola was calm. "This isn't a negotiation. Peaches has to go."

"And those kids that aren't even your blood get to stay? How is that fair to Peaches?"

"I want them gone too."

Apple's eyes widened from panic. Something bigger than Peaches was going on with her sister. "What do you mean you want them gone? You're their mom."

"I'm not, though."

Apple wanted to scream at her sister, but she knew she couldn't keep causing dramatic scenes. She needed to get her adult on if she wanted to help solve whatever problem Kola was dealing with.

Calmly, she replied, "Kola, all three of their parents are rotting away in Colombian prisons. You and Kamel are their guardians. If you don't want them, where would they go? And don't look to me."

"I haven't thought that far ahead, but I don't want any children in my household. I've done my part, and I can't do much more. And maybe if you stop being selfish, you could take them for a year or two, at least until I figure this out."

Apple gasped. "Me?"

"We're all we got."

"Kola, what's really going on? I can't help if I'm in the dark, sis."

"First, I shouldn't have to explain to you why you need to take back your child. She's your daughter, Apple. I don't have to make that make sense to you. But if you really must know, since I got back from South Beach, I've been on meds."

"What the fuck?"

"Relax," Kola advised. The last thing she needed was Apple making her situation harder. The residue of losing Koke was still there at the surface of her heart. She couldn't brush it off, because she felt doing so would be to push away her son's memory. "I had too many bad days in a row, not able to get out of bed or stop crying. I want my son, Apple, and the pain was too much for me to endure. My therapist feels—"

"Therapist!"

"She feels that having the children around might be hindering my progress—triggering negative thoughts," Kola tried to explain her position. "And also, the medication I'm on has made me a shell of myself. Like, I'm here, but I'm not, and the kids are picking up on it."

"What's Kamel doing to help you?" Apple was already shifting the blame.

"Kamel isn't complaining. He's trying to be understanding, but I've hardly been a wife lately. My sex drive is gone."

"TMI, bitch."

"It is what it is."

Apple was silent. She felt terrible for Kola, she did, but this breakdown had come at the worst time possible. Apple had gotten used to visiting Peaches and had slept peacefully at night knowing that her daughter was in a loving two-parent home growing up with children who also spoke fluent Spanish. What could Apple offer? And she sure wasn't ready to take on that responsibility times three.

Apple nodded and allowed the silence to change the subject for her. Not that she didn't want her daughter, she just felt as though she should have some time to get South Beach out of her system. Apple still had pent-up energy and rage that needed to dissipate so she could be there for Peaches the way a mother should. She still hadn't processed the death of Nicholas the way she wanted, nor had she come to terms with not seeing the life drain from Citi's eyes. Apple was a warrior, and warriors wanted war. You can't just click a switch and be content with soccer runs and PTA meetings. And she hated to mention the obvious, but it was still summertime in one of the greatest cities in the world.

"I hear you, Kola." Apple felt that would wrap up this miserable discussion. "Before I forget, I went to see Corey Davis in Dannemora."

Kola gave her a quizzical look.

"He's Nick's dad."

Kola quickly understood why. "That was fucked up how he went out, but you can't blame yourself."

Apple shrugged. "I do, though. My nights are lonely as fuck, and I want my man back. I want his strong arms to hold me once again . . . his presence was enough, I had what I needed, and selfishly I pushed him to give me more."

"You did. It's who you are, but that's the beauty of growth. You can change and become a better, more thoughtful person, and it starts with you being a better mom to Peaches."

"Didn't I say that I would take my daughter soon?" That last line sent her over the edge. Apple gathered her things so she could exit. She screamed, "Peaches! Grab your things!"

"Huh, Mommy?" Peaches screamed from the pool. "Mommy, I didn't hear you."

Kola played right into Apple's hands. "Leave her here for now, Apple. I don't want you to take her while you're this upset. I'll manage my pain and place the kids first, but you should start looking for a three-bedroom apartment. Peaches starts school next year, so make sure it's in a top school zone."

"I live in SoHo. Even the public schools are tens. And what's wrong with my two-bedroom?"

"Sophia and Junior?"

"You were serious?"

"What the fuck have I been saying? You think mental illness is not to be taken seriously?"

"What I know about that, Kola? All I can do is be here for you, so I will take the children until you get back on your feet." Apple stood up and quickly embraced her sister. "But just not today."

Apple polished off a couple more sliders, played with the kids, and bounced. She told Kola to give her a couple weeks to get her affairs in order, and then they could continue this discussion.

"Two weeks," Kola warned.

Apple left Kola's Westchester County home and headed south toward New York City. She merged onto the West Side Highway, which had become thick with bumper-to-bumper traffic. No way could she ride this out until she reached SoHo. Apple sat and waited in what looked like a parking lot from W148th Street to where she ultimately exited on W135th Street. The icy cool of the air conditioner was a needed comfort. It was so hot outside that Apple felt she would melt if she had to walk anywhere in this heat.

She steered her Maserati onto the inner-city blocks, and immediately, her sleek hundred-thousand-dollar vehicle was stirring up attention as she slowly cruised through her old stomping grounds: the projects. Not too many pricey cars came around this part of town. The drug dealers would push Beamers, Lexuses, Benzes, and SUVs, but a Maserati was on another level, and this was her second one.

As Apple slowly rolled down the block with all eyes on her, she noticed a dark blue Tesla Roadster exiting the project parking lot across the street. Behind the wheel of the luxurious vehicle was a young woman with wild pink-and-blue hair and equally wild eyes. The woman noticed the Maserati, and she pumped her brakes to get a closer look at the driver—another fly bitch. Both ladies stared at each other aggressively, and there was an exchange of negative energy between them. The woman smirked, and then she simply went on her way.

Apple stared at the Roadster until it turned off the block. She wondered who the bitch was. Not seeing any recognizable faces in her hood, she headed home.

The next morning, Apple woke up in a foul mood. Her two-bedroom apartment was hardly kid-friendly. Her modern tables with their sharp edges and do-not-sit-on furniture were scarcely conducive for raising three active, loud children. Fuck, this sucked. Apple turned on NY1 news and was reminded that Harlem Week was still in effect. She hadn't attended the festivities since she was in her late teens. Maybe she was clinging to a time before she was a mom or feeling nostalgic about a time when there were fewer decisions to make, but she went. Apple had roughly two weeks to act a fool before she had to transform herself into mommy material. It was her turn. Kola had been holding her and Peaches down for years, so this was the least she could do.

Apple's hair was loose today, flowing past her shoulders. She wore a short, gold, Betsey Johnson dress that hugged her curves and gold gladiator sandals. Knowing that most streets would be closed off this afternoon, she hopped on the A-train to Harlem. Forty minutes later, she was on 135th street. As soon as she climbed the subway stairs, she felt at home. She could already hear loud music coming from the street level above, car horns, bus engines revving up, people hollering—life. The smells and sounds were invigorating. Apple stood at the top of the subway steps and inhaled the aroma of roasted nuts, sauerkraut, and onions. People were bustling around enjoying the festivities.

Harlem Week was flooded with thousands of people on the city blocks temporarily restricted from vehicular traffic. There was people, food vendors, and booths everywhere. There was also what could be described as a car show on one block where there was a Porsche, a red Ferrari, a yellow Lamborghini, a few Bentleys, a Maserati, and several Range Rovers. The ballers came out in droves to showcase their exotic cars and hug the crowded block with their swag. All the get money bitches were swarming around the hustlers and cars like bees buzzing around flowers. The stickup kids were out too, preying upon the weaker links with dozens of cops patrolling the event for everyone's safety.

As Apple snaked through the crowd, she ignored the catcalls, and it didn't take her long to spot a couple familiar faces in the fray. IG and

Baddest Apple

Hood were posted up on the corner directly across from the blocked-off avenue. Suddenly Apple felt a little insecure without her expensive whip. Quickly, she looked down at her clothing—yeah, she looked great.

"Oh, shit!" she heard. "Apple, is that you?"

Hood did a slow jog toward her and picked her up into a tight bear hug. He spun her around like they had history and then animatedly expressed how he missed her.

"Yo, I ain't seen ya ass in a minute." His grin was wide as his hands made many gestures. "You gon' live a long fuckin' time, yo."

Apple could smell the weed. "What you smokin' on?"

Hood grabbed her by her hand like they were boo'd up and walked her over to the corner where IG and Tokyo sat.

"Apple!" she heard.

"Apple, que pasa, mami!" IG yelled.

"What's up, y'all?" Apple replied. She knew everyone from Lincoln projects but hadn't seen Tokyo since she was a preteen. Tokyo was a few grades under her. Hood was the oldest, and IG grew up around her and Kola.

"Y'all smokin' out here in the open like that? Five-oh ain't doing shit?" Apple asked.

IG took a long pull and then passed his blunt to Apple. "Nah, they cool. They always chill each year as long as we keep the peace. Anyway, this shit 'bout to be legal."

Apple nodded. Things had changed from when she used to come strolling through. Everyone would smoke and drink, but you had to hide it or else you were getting dragged to the precinct.

"What brings you around here?" IG asked.

"I missed my hood," said Apple.

"Fo' real? We glad you back. We heard about that shit in South Beach.

You and Kola and that bitch from Brooklyn ain't no fuckin' joke. Y'all bitches know how to put in work."

"We ain't gonna be called too many bitches 'fore shit get personal," Apple sternly warned him.

"My bad. No disrespect to you, Apple, but from what we heard y'all got busy."

"You already know how we get down."

"True, true," IG agreed.

"Anyone else got the munchies?"

"I got you." Showing off, Hood handed Tokyo a C-note and told her to get them some snacks.

Apple felt right at home. She was posted on the hood of Hood's hooptie, enjoying her life. She was continually receiving praises, love, and respect by men and women, young and old. She deserved it. With the work she'd put in over the years and the people she had looked out for, it was good to know that her neighborhood hadn't forgotten about her.

4

Touch pulled back the throttle of his black-and-gold Ducati motorcycle, opening up the engine and accelerating to 85mph. The bike thrived on the highway; the thick tires were hugging the asphalt at high speeds with Touch in complete control. He crouched forward, his eyes focused ahead. His body leaned into a curve on the road as if his bike were an extension of him. He downshifted when he merged into traffic or a sharp corner, and then zigzagged between cars like a thoroughbred horse or NASCAR driver, hitting just the correct throttle to perfect a turn. The strong wind smacked against Touch's helmet as he accelerated. It was exhilarating. He felt alive on his Ducati—just him and his bike, the world zooming past him. Touch rode toward the festivities of Harlem Week, jumped his Ducati onto the sidewalk, and came to a slow stop in front of a residential building on 132nd Street. Touch killed the engine, removed his helmet, and climbed off before tucking his gun in his waistband.

He wore black cargo shorts, a *We Built This Joint For Free* t-shirt that hugged his slim, muscular physique, a pair of fresh Jordans, and a Yankees fitted. At thirty years old, Touch was eye-candy to the ladies with his smooth brown complexion; low-cut soft hair; a thick, shapely mustache and beard; and his deep, baritone voice. Most of the time, he was an introverted person, not allowing anyone to get too close. His issue stemmed from when his mother left his father, Jorge, when he was seven years old for his father's younger brother, and there were kids during the affair. So there were half brothers and sisters somewhere in the States who were also his cousins. The romance between his uncle and his mother was embarrassing to him, so he rarely talked about it. The awkward incident had cost him most of his childhood friends and affected his ability to commit to any woman.

At the end of one block, Touch came across Apple and some young associates of hers loitering around a few parked cars. Apple stood out in her gold dress; it wasn't too sexy, but she had that certain *je n'ais se quoi* that made him pause. She was posted up on the hood of a car and sipping something from a red plastic cup, most likely liquor. Besides looking remarkable, she was also the center of attention. The way she stood out amongst the hundreds of strangers moving about was a testament to her beauty. He liked what he saw, and he made his way over. Seeing Touch moving closer to her, Apple admired the lean, nicely dressed, and physically-fit nigga looking like a snack.

"Hood, whaddup?" said Touch as he walked over and gave him dap.

"Yo, my man," Hood blurted out, a little too loud. He was about one drink past drunk. "I'm glad you came through!"

Touch was facing Hood but looking at Apple staring too. "Let me holler at you for a moment." Both Touch and Hood walked to the side a couple feet away from the others.

"So what's up wit' shorty?"

Hood didn't even have to ask who. He knew what type of women Touch liked; always five-star beauties. If it wasn't some C-list celebrity like a K. Michelle or Keyshia Cole, then he was fucking some *Love & Hip Hop* reality T.V. chick.

"That's Apple."

Touch smiled. He hadn't ever fucked an Apple. "That's her man?"

Hood smirked. "Who? IG? Nah, she just came through. We ain't seen her in years."

"Shorty wifed up?"

"Why you askin' me? Go shoot ya shot, nigga."

Touch nodded.

They both walked back over, and within seconds, Touch was offered Hennessy and weed. He declined both.

Touch walked closer to Apple, invading her personal space. He gazed intently into her eyes without breaking his stare and asked, "You having a good time?"

"At this five-star resort? The blue sea and soft, cottony sand are just what the doctor ordered," she replied dryly.

He chuckled. "Nah, I know this ain't Cancun, but it's live out here."

"It's a fuckin' block party."

"True." Touch nodded. "What's your name? What you about?"

"What I'm about?" she repeated.

"It's not a hard question to answer. Hopefully, you're more than just a pretty face."

Apple smirked. "Look, you blowin' my high. If I wanted to be interviewed, I would apply for a job."

Touch's head quickly swiveled to make sure no one had heard her. Usually, when he pushed up, women responded to his advances. Touch tried again. "I'm just tryin' to get to know who you are."

"The feeling ain't mutual," she said. "Yo, Tokyo, any more brown juice?" Apple ignored Touch and had no issue bumping his shoulder as she pushed past him. There was cockiness about him she didn't like, as if his name was ringing bells. He was a nobody. Besides, she was still in mourning over Nick.

Touch took the disrespect. He figured those gladiator sandals had her thinking she had a royal title. And then he listened to the chitchat. Hood,

IG, and Tokyo kept giving her props for handling her business in South Beach. Touch watched as the conceited female grinned, drinking in all the adulation one person could receive.

Apparently, she did something great in Miami.

The caravan of glamorous vehicles made it look like a celebrity had just arrived. The display was a showstopper. Everyone turned and gawked at the chauffeur-driven Maybach and four matching onyx-black Range Rovers that came to a stop on 7th Avenue, where Apple and her people were lingering. It seemed like Harlem had frozen momentarily as the onlookers watched in anticipation to see who would get out of the car. To everyone's surprise, a slim male figure got out dressed in a black tailored suit. Hastily he made his way toward the rear door of the vehicle and opened it. Even Apple caught herself unable to turn away from the spectacle—her conversation with Tokyo came to an abrupt end.

A female climbed out of the vehicle, and Apple instantly realized she was the same woman previously in the Tesla. She was wearing a garish blue ensemble; tight skirt, blouse, and stilettos. She was short and thick in the right places, dark-chocolate, jet black curly hair with blue and pink highlights, but what caught Apple's attention was that she had heterochromia—one brown and one aqua blue eye. The blue eye had a tattooed teardrop that was supposed to represent murder in gang culture. Her face was small and pointy like a mouse, and some might say she had an exotic beauty.

Apple instantly felt the shift. The attention was no longer on her and her adventures in South Beach. She suddenly became yesterday's news as the crowd treated this woman like she was the mayor of the city—the head bitch of Harlem. Everything about this whore enraged Apple.

Her goons had grabbed people's attention too. They stood on the block wearing all black in the summer heat with blue handkerchiefs or bandanas dangling from their back pockets, which indicated that they were Crips.

When her men opened each hatch to the Ranges and removed cases of Ace of Spades champagne, Apple wondered, *Who is this bitch?*

Stranger after stranger was given a thousand-dollar bottle of bubbly like it was quarter water. It wasn't enough for this woman to show up on the block at Harlem Week looking like a rich bitch; she brought gifts for everyone. They passed out at least two hundred bottles.

"It ain't a partay until I come thru, right?" she shouted, and the crowd erupted in cheers. Simultaneously the Range Rovers blasted Despacito featuring Daddy Yankee, and her tiny frame was then hoisted up by her men, and she stood on the hood of her Maybach in stilettos and pranced back and forth like she was on a disco dance floor. Her feet were stepping quickly as her hips and hands moved in opposite directions. Apple assumed she was a Latina, from her looks, most likely Dominican, doing some sort of salsa dancing. She cringed at the spectacle but couldn't yank her eyes away.

Apple glared at the episode, gritted her teeth, and thought, *Why didn't I think of that shit?* When the song ended, the crowd erupted in cheers and claps, and the female was helped back down to eye level by her men. But that wasn't the only blow to Apple's ego; she turned around to see that Touch was gone too. She found him with this showy bitch all of sudden, in her face and downing champagne.

"Snake muthafucka," she uttered. "Our Henny and weed weren't good enough for this nigga?"

Finally, Apple caught her attention, most likely because she was glaring so forcefully. The two women exchanged hard, dirty looks. Apple wanted to drag her out her tacky outfit. She turned to Hood and asked, "Yo, who is that bitch?"

"You don't know Queenie? They call her the Queen of New York."

"Queen of New York?" Apple laughed.

"Yeah, it's a spinoff of her name," Hood added. "She's no joke."

Apple frowned heavily. Her jealousy was palpable. Right away, Apple felt resentment like she'd never felt before. Harlem was her turf—her playground, her territory. So who was this bitch infringing upon her legacy?

Feeling the heat emanating from Apple, Queenie made it her business to approach the girl with the attitude. She strutted toward Apple with purpose. Apple removed herself from the hood of the car and braced herself for a fight—if it came to that. She kept her eyes on Queenie. *Let this bitch try sumthin',* she said to herself.

She entered Apple's arena and said, "IG, introduce me to your friend."

"Queenie, this Apple. I know you heard of her."

Queenie shadily cut her eyes at Apple. "Not at all."

IG and Hood looked taken aback by her reply. "Word! Her name has been ringing bells since she was in high school. She put in work. You never heard of Apple?"

"Not even a whisper." Queenie shrugged. "Apple . . . nah, nothing."

"You better put some respect on my name when you speak it, bitch!"

Queenie gave a mocking chuckle, and then she walked away.

Apple intensely stared at the girl in silence. The mockery she was trying to make of her—of her name and reputation—it was uncalled for. Apple knew she was petty. She was ready to speak with her fists and not words. Apple clenched her fingers into tight weapons and was prepared to snatch Queenie out her fuckin' heels—show this bitch how a true Harlem bitch got down. But Hood stopped her. He grabbed her forearm, startling her for a moment, and he quickly and quietly said to her, "Another time, Apple. Not here."

Apple glared at Hood and then acquiesced. She knew he was right; it wasn't the place or the time to act ignorant.

Queenie and her crew of goons hopped back into their vehicles, and they sped out with her leaving just as extravagantly as they came.

One thing was certain, though. Queenie was now on Apple's radar.

5

The unassuming church on Castle Hill Avenue in the South Bronx, nestled between the fading mom and pop businesses on the commercial street, had become a steeple of faith, hope, and pride in the urban district. The church had been around for nearly a decade, and it had a growing congregation of almost a hundred members. Pastor Kenneth Foster, a local and esteemed clergyman, and his staff had founded influential programs such as *At Youth Kids* in the Bronx community that involved schooling, mentorships, and guidance. Their efforts included assistance for pregnant teen mothers, helping troubled kids defect from gangs, and guiding kids from abusive homes into becoming flourishing men and women. They were trying to turn their impoverished neighborhood into a positive image. The First Baptist Ministry and Pastor Foster had become pillars in the community plagued with gangs, poverty, drugs, police brutality, and racial discrimination. The South Bronx was reverting to a forgotten area—a haven for the undesirables and drug users, where the gangs felt they had control over the residences, the streets, and even the local authorities. And many individuals were finding the church an asylum from the burdens they faced out there.

Pastor Foster was well liked, educated, and admired, even by some gang members. He was one man that preached the hard truth and was unapologetic for his actions. Foster was an up-in-your-face kind of man—a black brother with a plan for his people. Foster stood a tall and proud guy; lean with a grayish goatee, low salt-and-pepper hair, and deep, dark, smoldering eyes. He was a handsome man who dressed handsomely too. He was unmarried but had a following of ladies that yearned to develop into his first lady of the church.

The night was growing late in the summer month. The traffic outside the church had grown sparse, and the church was finally empty. He was the last man standing. Earlier, it was a packed place with worshipers singing energetically and praising the Lord wholeheartedly. Pastor Foster had preached about answered prayers, how you must leave your troubles at God's feet and then have faith as small as a mustard seed to overcome adversity. He spoke on how people, especially young men and women, do not pray. "Prayer is the answer!" he announced unequivocally and passionately. "God is your provider!"

It was a powerful sermon, and it had many of the congregation lifting to their feet in agreement and clapping their hands. Pastor Foster was the truth. He was a man of the cloth and a man that the neighborhood needed. Foster cared for everyone, from the youth to the elderly. He was their pillar—their rock that was unmoving and unshakeable. He was the church's anchor.

Pastor Foster strolled through the sanctuary aisles, inspecting the pews and picking up trash left behind, trying to keep his church clean. He was a proud, content man and wealthy for a local Bronx preacher. The gold Patek Philippe watch peeking from under his shirt sleeve showed that.

The dimmed church and the quietness were welcoming for him. He needed the solitude. Finishing in the sanctuary, he moved to the hallway and made his way down into the basement. Though the church was mid-size, the basement was like a giant labyrinth—a place that more than a few have gotten lost in.

The pastor went to an iron door secured by a massive bolt lock. He opened it and stepped into a modest-sized dark room. Closing the door behind him, he turned on the lights and stared at what was being kept inside—chattel. Two young women, ages eighteen and nineteen, were gagged with thick cloths shoved into their mouths and flex cuffs around their wrists and ankles, restricting their movement. They were beaten and afraid. Pastor Foster approached them with a remorselessness that years of being marginalized and emasculated in his youth had formed. He crouched near the captives and said, "Soon, they will come for you."

Unbeknownst to everyone, Pastor Foster had been trafficking young women for profit. The church would be the last place anyone would come looking for them. He worked with a gang called the Lower Eastside Crips, and for nearly two years they had been moving women like cargo via pipeline routes from New York, passing through Toronto, and ultimately ending in Ontario, Canada. Human trafficking had high profit margins and risks lower than moving illegal firearms or drug distribution. Young girls and women were disappearing like magic acts, and no one gave a fuck. Sometimes an article or exposé would make the rounds through national media focusing on sex-trafficked women—which was an affront to all those who were trafficked for cheap labor. To publish an article of the voices of these women would open an old wound that right-wing conservative Americans like to gloss over: slavery. Free labor was what America was built on. Free labor was what they would sell these two migrant women for. And the profits that came from this helped finance Pastor Foster's lavish lifestyle.

Staring at the young and scared women, he felt no remorse for his dubious actions. It was business. The teary-eyed and afraid merchandise didn't speak one word of English. They were Asian, smuggled in by the Yakuza Japanese crime syndicate, who placed a large tab on each head in return for getting the women into the United States. If the tab wasn't paid off, then death would be imminent. The Yakuza was easy prey because their numbers were dwindling each year. The L.E.S. Crips sat back and allowed the Yakuza to do all the heavy lifting, which was getting the women to America, and then subtly snatched them up whenever the opportunity presented itself. They wouldn't be missed. They wouldn't be reported missing.

"Do not be afraid. Go with God, and He will make the way. He will give you courage during this time of darkness," he said to the girls, who did not understand his words. "God smiles down upon those who serve."

The girls cowered against the wall. Pastor Foster touched the frightened eighteen-year-old, but she cringed from him and whimpered. He wanted to lay hands on them and pray.

"Father God, surround your humble servants with a spiritual hedge of protection to get them safely to Canada with no outside forces stopping their journey, Lord. I know you're a God of miracles. You're a just God, the God who raised His son from dead . . . Hallelujah . . . Yes, Lord, sanctify His holy name. In Jesus's name, I say Amen."

He stood suddenly, pivoted, and exited the room. Once he locked the door, he heard an abrupt thud in the dark. It came from down the hallway—maybe it was something, perhaps it wasn't. The church always made strange and unwanted noises at night. Still, something or nothing, Pastor Foster inspected where the noise came from. He walked toward the sound, turning the corner, and saw that a wooden cross had fallen from the wall. The anchor holding the cross came loose somehow. He shrugged it off. It was an old building and an ancient cross. He picked it up and placed it nearby, somewhere to be found by a member in the morning and let them hang it back up.

"It's always something in this old building," he remarked.

He ascended from the basement and into the sanctuary. The pastor glanced at his watch; it was going on midnight, and they scheduled the men for a midnight pickup. Once their merchandise was handed over, he would lock up and leave the building with his payment in hand. To kill some time, he crouched next to the podium on the platform, reached inside the hollow area, and removed a silver flask hidden underneath the podium behind a few Bibles. He unscrewed the top and took a swig of brown liquor—something needed. He stood on the platform for a moment, looking out at the empty pews that were filled with his congregation hours earlier. They were engrossed in his sermon and hanging on every word he preached. Pastor Foster always had the gift of gab.

He chuckled at himself, knowing he had everyone fooled—the hypocrite he was. Earlier, he'd preached about the power of prayer, but he didn't believe that doctrine. He was agnostic. Sure, he prayed. It was his shtick. It paid the bills, and he was good at it. He loved hearing his voice, and his narcissism kicked in each time he saw how people responded to his sermons. The women throughout the years would pray out loud to be rescued to a God they couldn't prove existed. It was pitiful. He wondered how religion could last for as long as it had—how it could supersede logic and transcend all rational understanding. He sighed because he knew why. It was a hustle. And like all great hustles, it wasn't going anywhere. He took his 10% off the top of everyone's salary who parked their fat and skinny asses in his pews each week, and he had to do only what he loved most: talk and receive attention. He didn't even have to rack his brain coming up with the sermons. Thanks to YouTube and podcasts, he would listen to mega-church pastors like Jakes and Osteen and take a little here, combine a little there, and then perform. And the best part of this scenario was that the government—the most significant organized crime faction of them all—couldn't take one nickel of his earnings. Pastor Foster was living his best life.

He took another mouthful from the flask, and the moment he removed the bottle from his lips, there was another echoing sound. It didn't come from the basement, but nearby. Something was wrong, and Foster knew he wasn't alone; he had unwanted company inside the church. He placed the flask back where he'd removed it, and he went toward the noise. Foster took several steps into the stillness of the church with slight apprehension. He looked around, but it was hard to see in the dimness. The moment he stepped off the platform, it suddenly felt like he was being surrounded by darkness—a robust shadow that seemed to come from out of nowhere—a grave threat. Abruptly, a forceful arm violently wrapped around his neck and squeezed. Immediately his breathing became shallow, and a struggle ensued between the pastor and his attacker. The battle was brief, as the sharp knife violently plunged into his spine and twisted, profoundly penetrating through his flesh. He jerked riotously from the feel of the knife sinking into his skin—and then the blade paralyzed him. His attacker repeatedly thrust the knife into his back, and the pastor fell to his knees, quickly succumbing to his injuries.

His attacker towered over him and said, "You must atone for your sins, Kenny. You are a fraud and hell is waiting on you."

The pastor lay there on his stomach, dying slowly in the thick blood pooling around him. He could feel his soul being pulled away from him as he struggled to keep his eyes open.

The attacker stood over the body and stared without regret. Before leaving the corpse behind, he turned the pastor on his back and took his steel survival knife and gouged his victim's eyes out—a signature of The Huntsman.

6

"Remember who the fuck you're talking to, gwal," Queenie announced with authority into the cell phone. The person on the other end was pushing her limits. "Like I said, I don't got no fuckin' cash app, and if you keep pissing me off, then we're gonna have a problem—and you don't want any problems with me. Now all mi want are some lemonade braids!" She paused for a moment, waiting to hear the female's response, and then she returned, "I thought so. I'll be there next week."

Queenie ended the call and sat back, annoyed. "These Instagram dutty hoes really think they runnin' shit 'cause they got a few followers. Gwal runnin' down all her rules to me like I'm basic."

"Rules? For braids? Like what?" Pie, her driver, asked.

"You should have heard her. She was like, you need to make an appointment via text message only! Send twenty-five dollars to hold your spot via Apple Pay or any cash app one month in advance. One week before your appointment, you cash app a deposit of half the balance. You need to arrive fifteen minutes before your appointment time, and if you arrive later than that then you're canceled, and you lose your deposits." Queenie rolled her eyes, still heated. "As soon as this pussyclaaat finishes my hair I'ma slap the shit outta her."

"Didn't Regina refer you?"

"Yeah and that bitch tried to act like she didn't know who the fuck Queenie is!"

Pie chuckled at how petty women could be. "Did she have on her corporate voice when she asked for the twenty-five-dollar deposit?"

That remark made Queenie smile.

"You know she did."

The black Navigator she was in cruised north on the Gowanus Expressway during the evening hour. It was getting late, but the temperature and the humidity outside was still intense, feeling like the sun was still at its peak though it had long ago faded. Queenie sat in the backseat like the queen-bee bitch she was.

"How far are we?"

"We're about fifteen minutes out."

"Could you hurry up?" she quipped. "Maybe stop driving like some old fuckin' lady."

Pie nodded.

Queenie sat back and stared out the window, seeing Brooklyn from the elevated expressway that hovered over the city streets. They were nearing her destination, an industrial landscape in the southwestern part of Brooklyn. Fortunately for Queenie, traffic was flowing on the expressway, so Pie accelerated to 85mph.

Queenie was a unique woman who came from a complicated and troubled past. She was twenty-four years old and was a former drug mule who had transitioned into a drug queenpin. She lived on the Lower East Side of Manhattan and enjoyed the perks of being the boss.

Her wild looks ensured that she received around-the-clock attention from men and women. Queenie was often mistaken for being Dominican. Most of her life she pretended to be Latino—any origin would suffice. Sometimes she was Honduran, Colombian, Dominican, or her all-time favorite, Peruvian. Hispanic men and women would approach her and ask, "Habla español?" She was actually Trinidadian and white, but she was deeply immersed in Latin culture. Queenie had a thing for salsa music, and during her spare time, she would go dancing at nightclubs and bars. She felt she resembled Amara La Negra with her dark-chocolate skin and wild hair. Queenie tried desperately to learn to speak Spanish but could only pick up conversational words and little more. When she was angry, she went full Trinidadian patois, which often confused those around her.

There were so many layers to Queenie—too many to peel away. She was L.E.S. Crips and affiliated with gangs in Trinidad and Tobago when needed. She ran a profitable drug empire, yet, she would attend rallies against the U.S. Immigration and Customs Enforcement officers known as I.C.E. who used brute force to capture what they labeled as illegal immigrants. Queenie incessantly tweeted against building the border wall, she was at the front line marching hand-in-hand with the Latino community standing for undocumented immigrants against deportation, and she sent hefty donations to any campaigns that championed the civil rights of those in her "Latin and Hispanic" community. She followed Alexandria Ocasio-Cortez on Twitter and continually harassed her with tweets to throw her hat into the presidential race. Saying Queenie suffered from cultural appropriation would be an understatement, but the thing was, no one would dare say that because she was other things too; cold-hearted and ruthless. And one of her favorite ways to torture her enemies was to chain them to cinderblocks and drop them alive into the Hudson River at the darkest hour of night and let the dead drift away into the Atlantic Ocean.

The Navigator finally arrived at the abandoned warehouse on 5th Avenue in the industrial area of Greenwood Heights. The cover of the night made the streets ghost towns, as the local businesses were closed until the next day. The vehicle came to a stop in front of the one-story brick structure that was nondescript. Queenie climbed out the backseat and sauntered toward the rusted steel door as Pie remained in the vehicle. He was kept out of her day-to-day business dealings as he was a civilian. Queenie hired a bodyguard with a license to carry a concealed weapon who had been trained in his field. Pie vowed to jump in front of a bullet to save her life should the need ever arise, but that was a promise she never wanted to take him up on.

The door instantaneously opened for her, where her right-hand gorilla, Lord, was there to greet her.

"We good?" Queenie asked him.

"Yeah, we good."

"What about what went down with Kenny? You got any leads on who put the hit out on him? His murder is fuckin' with my money."

"Five-oh saying The Huntsman has taken credit."

"What mi look like trusting intel without verifying it beforehand? I want this solved."

Lord nodded. "I'm on it."

Inside the spacious structure stood her other goons—Rehab, Killer Mike, Stone, and a computer nerd who they actually called Nerd. He was a whiz kid, a skilled hacker that Queenie was paying good money for, and he was worth every penny. Nerd sat at the folded table with his high-end laptop; he stood out amongst the fierce thugs. He was the only anomaly inside the room.

It was time to get down to business. Queenie's Fendi pumps click-clacked against the concrete floors, cutting through the silence that filled the massive structure. Her tight jeans accentuated her apple bottom as her hips switched with authority. Queenie took bold steps and looked each individual in the eyes as she quickly scanned the room. Standing in one line were twenty females hoping to get hired. Queenie would drug mule these girls, mostly young women that needed a job. They would either swallow balloons containing coke or heroin for flights, drive cars with kilos concealed inside secret compartments, or they would fasten drugs to their body and board a Greyhound bus headed out of state—anything for a return on her investment.

Parked inside the warehouse were six modest cars, each equipped with a full tank of gas, hidden compartments, and kilos of heroin.

Twenty girls were ready to fill twelve positions in her organization. The girls were quiet; Queenie's presence was intimidating. Her weird eyes stood out in the room. It was something most people had never seen before—and the teardrop was a statement. When she spoke, everyone knew to shut the fuck up and listen.

"Qué pasa, amigos?" she cheerily yelled. And then her face turned to stone, and her voice dropped several octaves. "Y'all chicas got only one job, and that is to transfer my product from point A to point B, no bullshit. You do this shit correctly, and we won't have any problems. Do y'all understand?"

Her tone was harsh and demanding.

The twenty girls understood. The majority had worked for her before, knowing the ropes. Her speech was aimed at the new girls—the newbies that yearned for a quick payday. Each female inside the warehouse had their own reasons for becoming a drug mule. Though it was a risk, word had gotten around town that it was easy money.

Queenie insisted that the girls travel two deep; two heads were usually better than one. The ages ranged from nineteen to thirty-five years old. But there were requirements to getting the gig. Some trips were longer than most, so Queenie needed someone able to drive the long distance. Most importantly, they needed to have clean licenses and not be girls who would light up a blunt or drink while driving. Queenie was running a professional organization, so she warned against fucking her clientele at the drop-off point. A roundtrip drive from New York City to North Carolina was $2,000, from New York City to Virginia was $1,500, from

New York City to Philadelphia was $850, and from New York City to New Jersey was $350. It was good money, especially when most had no or low income.

One of the new girls was Bambi. She was a former stripper who needed the money to move into a new apartment. She'd filled out a questionnaire and was confident that she would get hired. Queenie stepped closer to Bambi and stared at her with intensity. The look in Queenie's eyes made Bambi nervous. Having Queenie standing threateningly closer to her made Bambi cringe where she stood. It seemed like something was wrong.

"What I expect from y'all is absolute honesty—no lies. I fuckin' hate liars! Lying can jeopardize my operation, and things will turn up if that happens," Queenie made known with her eyes still trained on Bambi.

Bambi swallowed nervously as Queenie's eyes were cutting into her. She wanted to divert her attention from Queenie, but that would have been rude.

Queenie continued. "Are there any liars on deck?"

Unbeknownst to Bambi, Queenie already knew the truth about her. Nerd had hacked into the Department of Motor Vehicles, and he ran her license. It was suspended. Queenie raised an open hand and slapped Bambi in the face so hard, her neck snapped. The other women gasped. Bambi held the side of her face that stung painfully and endured the abuse. Queenie was petite and looked breakable compared to Bambi, who was thick and stood tall. It was a sight to see Bambi get slapped and not retaliate, but that's what happened.

Queenie right away announced, "The next gwal that lies to mi is a dead gwal. Period! So, it would behoove you bitches to be up front and real 'bout your shit or leave now."

The girls were silent for a moment; Queenie was giving them something that she rarely gave anyone: a second chance. A few strippers stepped out of the line, and they hastily exited the building, knowing that the dishonesty card was the wrong card to play. They didn't want to die. Queenie waited until the room thinned out because Bambi wasn't the only female who lied about having a legit license. Finally, she announced, "Now, let's get back to business, chicas."

She had merchandise to move.

Queenie was forced to split up the remaining girls and have them drive solo. It was something she didn't want to do, but she didn't have a choice—time was money, and money was time. She paced back and forth in front of the girls, and while she talked, Lord was handing the females burner phones—for emergency use only.

Queenie gave the remaining women a pep talk.

"I used to be exactly in your shoes," she stated. "I was once a drug mule, but mi was smart, and I worked my way up and became a boss bitch. I run the show here, while bitches are selling pussy to the highest bidder. Women are getting fucked in the strip clubs for two tacos and a grape soda and wonder why they ain't got shit to show for it."

Some of the girls shifted their weight from leg to leg looking uneasy, because for one, they had heard the same speech from her before, and two, it was true.

Queenie continued to pace back and forth, and she said, "This shit here is easy money to be made, as long as you don't break my rules. But let me school y'all. I got in this game when I was thirteen, stuffin' coke in mi pussy for transport before my cherry had been popped. I was robbed, shot at, pistol whipped, and betrayed, but through it all I survived in a man's world."

Queenie loved telling her story; she wanted them to know that she came from nothing and now had everything.

While Queenie talked, one female stood there looking bored. Her name was Kassy, and she was a new but older mule who had seen better days. Kassy was only there in support of her daughter, Elise, who needed

Baddest Apple

this steady gig to pay her way through community college. Kassy seemed irritated by Queenie's lecture. She rolled her eyes and sucked her teeth and then mistakenly spoke out when she was supposed to listen.

"Stash cars been around for nearly thirty years, so why was a minor hiding coke in her pussy? And how much coke can a thirteen-year-old pussy hide?" Kassy sarcastically uttered. "But it was an impressive speech, though. I'll give you that."

There was a pregnant pause as Queenie stopped to address the female who dared to speak so disrespectfully. These countless seconds were uncomfortable to the others. They all wondered why this old broad couldn't just keep her big mouth shut so they could move forward and get paid. Kassy stared at Queenie like she was supposed to be that bitch in charge of things, her jealousy overpowering her common sense. She was annoyed that a young bitch—little older than her daughter, Elise—could hold down this type of organization.

Everyone, except her squad, expected Queenie to bitch slap Kassy as she had done Bambi. However, she smiled at Kassy and said, "Please don't interrupt me again."

Kassy smirked at the girl and rolled her eyes. Queenie overlooked the continued disrespect because she had merchandise to move.

"Let's get this fuckin' show on the road, mi amigos," Queenie said.

On her orders, the men inside the warehouse got to work. The vehicles were previously loaded with tight and neatly packaged kilos ready for transportation. In the glove compartment of each car were the registration and insurance cards. Each girl had a cover story for her visit into that state if they were pulled over by the police. Everyone was good to go, and the majority of the young women had made the trip at least a dozen times.

Kassy and Elise both walked to the remaining two cars that the men had prepped for them: a white Chevrolet Cruze and a gray Toyota

Corolla. Queenie subtly looked at and nodded to Lord, and Lord glanced at Rehab and Killer Mike. Without a word being said, Killer Mike and Rehab methodically walked up behind mother and daughter, raised their pistols to the back of their heads, and fired—*Pop! Pop!*—executing the two females right there on the spot. Their bodies dropped where they once stood against the concrete ground, their blood thickly expanding around them.

Queenie marched toward their corpses in her heels and crouched near Kassy's body, the loudmouth bitch. She grabbed a chunk of the mother's tacky weave, glared at the dead woman's face, and uttered, "Badras bummboclaaat! Don't you ever fuckin' interrupt me again. Okay, puta? When the Queen speaks, the commonwealth listens." She chuckled. And then she added, "You should see your face. You look so fuckin' stupid right now."

She stood up and focused back on her business. She clapped her hands loudly and shouted, "Let's get this show on the road. I got money to make."

The cold-blooded murders of a mother and daughter didn't faze Queenie one bit. She went over to Lord and said to him, "Dump these bitches in the Hudson River."

Lord nodded.

The cleanup was instantaneous. Rehab and Stone grabbed the bleach and plastic tarps kept on deck for situations such as these. Duct-tape, plastic gloves, flex cuffs, chains, cinderblock—a whole crime scene cleanup and murder kit was stocked and ready. The bodies were wrapped up and tossed into the trunk of a car with Killer Mike in the driver's seat.

As Mike slowly drove out of the warehouse, Queenie then asked her remaining goons, "Now with that out the way, I need to know something. Tell me 'bout this Apple bitch. Mi don't like her."

Her crew found this odd. The twins' names rang out in Harlem.

Lord spoke first, "You already know who she is. She's a twin—Apple and Kola."

Queenie had heard about the twins for years, and she even admired their handiwork. But with a straight face, she responded, "Never heard of them."

Lord assumed that she was lying. It was impossible to be in her position and not know about the twins, notably Apple, who turned out to become the most ruthless twin.

"Apple? She used to fuck with Supreme and then his man, Guy Tony. You don't remember her?"

"Ay dios mio! You see this and this?"—Queenie dramatically pointed to both her eyes— "They never saw that gwal."

"A'ight, we hear you. So now what?" Lord played along.

"We wait."

"For what?"

"A challenge!"

She was a weird one. Lord knew it and her team knew it, but they never questioned her about her unusualness. Lord also knew that Apple had piqued Queenie's interest, and that wasn't necessarily a good thing for their business. From Lord's understanding, Apple would be hard to kill if the two factions ever went to war.

Spanish Harlem called Apple *La Cucaracha* because she was hard to extinguish, and Harlem titled her *The Baddest Chick* ever. Her twin was nicknamed *Cocá Kola* because she moved so many kilos throughout the streets and she was connected to the cartel. Lord knew that if they went after Apple and were fortunate enough to take her out, then most likely her twin, Kola, would come seeking revenge. And it was still rumored that Kola had the full backing of the Colombian cartel.

Lord exhaled. They were into August and summer was almost ending. But with Queenie questioning him about Apple, his gut instincts told him that his boss was about to bring the heat. The trouble they didn't need.

7

The quiet of the morning was interrupted when Apple clicked on NY1 news coverage. She had woken up feeling a little depressed. She missed Nicholas. Last night she went to sleep in one of his t-shirts that still had his scent on it. After he was murdered, she gathered the items she wanted to keep and placed some of his shirts in Ziploc storage bags for clothing, which preserved his scent. If she could turn back time she would, because in the end, what did she accomplish? She had no proof other than Kola's claim that Citi was most likely dead. Translation? Nicholas had died in vain. And that reality had her adding Baileys into her morning coffee.

As she sat there puffing on her cigarette and deep in thought, the news reported another murder allegedly committed by The Huntsman. He had been active throughout New York City for nearly three decades. Apple had been hearing about this vigilante since she was a child, and he still hadn't been caught.

"Damn, this nigga had a long run," Apple said to herself.

This time it was a local clergyman murdered for allegedly using his church in the Bronx to traffic immigrants. It was a shock to the community as two Asian women with a translator told news reporters at a press conference a horrific tale about the Yakuza, kidnapping, and how close they came to being sold into a life of indentured servitude. The news coverage stirred up negative feelings for her because she could relate. Apple clicked off her T.V. because she needed to get her mind right. This afternoon, Kola was coming to meet with her and bringing the children so they could discuss this transition. Apple wanted to make the argument she needed more time—which she did. She would need to search for a three-bedroom apartment, furnish their rooms, enroll them in daycare, and ultimately change her lifestyle. Kola kept hinting that she felt Apple should move to a suburb, but Apple felt differently. She loved walkable neighborhoods. Apple felt there independence is instilled early on when you have to walk to school, learn how to travel on various trains and buses, and shop the local supermarket with a shopping list and shopping cart unassisted by parents. A hot real estate market had emerged in Brooklyn, where she could be close to Cartier, but Apple knew she would be a fish out of the water in that borough.

Apple got dressed in a pair of leggings, stilettos, and *Cheapiana* t-shirt. She wore hood chic for the long day she had in front of her. Her mood had improved thanks to the Irish cream in her coffee, and as expected, her sister texted her promptly at one o clock. Come Down Now.

"You sure this is the address?" Queenie asked Killer Mike as he steered her Navigator into a parking space that had just opened up.

"It is," he said as he placed the SUV in park. "Nerd said it's her last known address. She's had a lot of them, so we'll see if she still lives here."

Queenie's eyes scanned the tree-lined SoHo block and thought it felt inauthentic to the woman she had heard about a good portion of her life. It was too quiet and family-oriented for her taste. It was a side block that got little foot traffic and had a few Noise Ordinance Curfew signs on poles. Queenie unclasped her seatbelt and opened up the Spanish takeout she had just bought.

Mike asked, "So how long we gonna sit here?" What he really wanted to know was why they were there. He knew that Queenie asked him to drive her because Lord wouldn't be down and would have talked her out of this, whatever this was. He didn't like it, but she was his boss. Nor would she just take her driver, Pie, when stalking a lethal nemesis such as Apple. She needed a street goon like Killer Mike who would know what to look out for should things jump off.

"Mi don't know. Just chill."

In silence, Queenie tore into her arroz con pollo dish, stuffing her mouth with large spoonfuls of rice. Mike watched as she wolfed down her meal like she was an inmate in prison with a couple minutes for chow time. His stomach churned as he listened to her smack her tongue against the roof of her mouth while she ate and repeatedly lick her fingers. Her eating etiquette was often talked about behind her back because it was just nasty.

"I'm not sweating this bitch if that's what you're thinking," she finally spoke to break the silence. Her cheeks were puffed out, stuffed with an unreasonable amount of food. She looked like a hamster storing its cheek pouches for the week. "Mi don't trust her. She's a sneaky one and it ain't a coincidence that I've seen her twice in twenty-four hours."

"You think she tryin' to make a move against you?"

"Maybe," she surmised and addressed her paranoia. "What I know for sure is that now that I'm blowing up, I peep this puta stalking me at Lincoln projects and then the next day at Harlem Week. Once, it's a coincidence, but twice it's a problem. You know how the stick-up kids do."

"Stick-up, kid?" Mike smirked. "That's not on her résumé."

"Why it ain't?" Queenie pulled the Pepsi from a straw and let out an "aaaahhhh" before continuing. "What you think that shit was in South Beach? She don't push weight. Apple and her goons be lying in the cut like all those other lowlife, thieving muthafuckas. Bitch ain't gonna get me, though."

"Nah, I think she do fuck wit' them scales." Mike's voice reflected his uncertainty. Throughout the years he had heard so many tales of the twins he couldn't remember everything. He wasn't Apple's biographer to affirm what was and wasn't true. But it was interesting that Queenie was, after swearing otherwise.

"You gettin' her and her sister mixed up. It's Kola who moves them ki's." Queenie had polished off her soda but kept pulling from the straw to get every last drop until the air bubbles were making an awful sound. If she kept this up, Mike felt he was about to snap. "That bitch ain't gonna catch me slippin'."

"Could you stop, please, Queenie?"

"Stop what?"

"The soda. It's gone."

Apple came out of her building and quickly scanned her block for Kola sitting inside Kamel's Range Rover with all the kids. But that's not all she saw. Midway down her block, Apple spotted the black Lincoln Navigator trying to blend in. She stared at the vehicle like a hawk and saw the wild afro. Apple looked at Kola. Her sister instantly recognized the fear in her eyes and reached under her seat for her .45 and tucked it in her waist. Before Kola could get out of her truck and ask Apple what was up, through her rearview, she saw Apple marching down her block.

"Junior, I want you, Sophia, and Peaches to stay in the car and do not get out for any reason. Do you understand?"

He nodded.

"Say you understand!"

"I understand."

"You're in charge, okay? I want you to look after my girls and keep them safe." Kola handed him her cell phone. "If I don't come back in ten minutes, you call Kamel and tell him to come and pick y'all up from Auntie Apple's."

"Where are you going?"

"Just down the block, but if I don't come right back, that means that I'm doing something good and Kamel needs to pick y'all up."

"But I thought we were going to—"

"Just do as I say," she snapped. At this time, Apple wasn't out of view. Kola bolted out of the car and yelled, "Lock the doors!"

As soon as Queenie realized that she had been spotted by Apple, she felt she had no other choice than to get out of the car, especially when Apple came barreling down the block toward them. Mike suggested that they leave.

"And let this bitch think I fear her?"

Queenie knew there was a small possibility they could get spotted, but she felt the chances were so slim because they had parked some distance away, they weren't driving in any of her two luxury vehicles, and also because why was this bitch home this time of day?

Queenie exited her car with Killer Mike steps behind her and leaned against her hood for support. Apple's deathly stare was shooting holes through her body. Outnumbered, Queenie thought her adversary would be squirrelly in her presence.

Boldly, Apple asked, "What the fuck you doin' here?"

"This my block."

"Your block?" Apple wasn't sure if she was speaking literally or figuratively.

"Yeah, I own this block, this area, and the sky above it. Anything from the Lower East Side through Midtown is L.E.S. Crips territory. You too far south for my comfort, so I'ma insist that you take your Harlem ass back to Harlem."

Apple looked at Queenie's triggerman and thought of her daughter a half a block away. She didn't want to bring the heat and endanger the children. She did something she thought she would never do.

"Look, I don't know what this is, but I don't got any beef wit' you—"

"Shut the fuck up!" Queenie demanded. "I'm puttin' you on the clock. You got three days to get the fuck out of my barrio before you no longer have a life, cabrón."

"Don't do it!" Kola said as she placed the barrel of her .45 to Killer Mike's temple. He saw the threat through his peripheral too late, as Kola had stealthily snuck up behind them. "Two fingers please. You know what it is."

Slowly, Mike pulled his 9mm out of his waist and handed it to Kola, who placed it in her Gucci clutch. She was hardly dressed for a gun battle in a dress and heels, but she was ready. Kola stayed ready.

The moment Apple knew her sister had Mike under control, her fist smashed into Queenie's face repeatedly. Her head snapped back so quickly it felt like it was about to pop off. Queenie swung wildly into the air, never connecting with the intended target. Apple took one hand and grabbed a firm grip on Queenie's hair while pulling her into a headlock. Apple's fist slammed into Queenie's face until her eyes swelled up. Queenie scratched and clawed at Apple's arms and tried to bite into Apple's side, but Apple had full control over her in the headlock. Apple wasn't done as she dragged Queenie out of her heels, scraping up her knees, elbows, and back. The hot concrete ate off layers of Queenie's skin. The drug queenpin yelled out in pain until Apple's foot came smashing down on her face, silencing her.

Mike wanted to do something, maybe swing on Kola to save his boss, but he knew it would be suicide. In broad daylight, he watched in horror as Queenie's body became limp, she was unresponsive, and her face looked like ground beef.

"Yo, that's enough, yo!" he called out aggressively.

But Apple didn't stop wailing on Queenie until she was ready. Eventually, there was no fight left in her opponent.

"App," Kola called out for short and then nodded toward Killer Mike.

Apple glared for a few seconds and then shook her head. Kola was ready to body Mike and Queenie, but Apple didn't want the heat on her block, especially with her daughter not too far off.

"This shit ain't over," Apple warned.

She grabbed Mike's gun from her sister's clutch, and they both backpedaled to Kola's idling SUV.

A pissed-off Mike scooped Queenie into the backseat and sped off to the nearest emergency room before getting on his jack and calling Lord.

"Yo, we got a fuckin' problem."

8

"Aaaah, Poppo, come and get us!" screamed Eduardo Jr. through the Bluetooth connection to a now worried Kamel.

"Junior, what's happened? Where's Kola?"

"She's gone," added Peaches. "She left us all by ourselves."

"We been here forever, Papi," Sophia announced and cried. Sophia's tantrum triggered the emotions of everyone, and within seconds Eduardo and Peaches joined in on the hysteria.

"Sssssssh," Kamel consoled. "Don't worry; I got y'all. Junior, be a big man and tell me where y'all at." Kamel was already running out of the house shirtless with only ball shorts and his .357.

"I don't know where."

"Look around. What do you see? Where y'all at?" Kamel asked again, his voice slightly elevating.

"We in Nar-r-r-nia," offered Sophia, through sobs.

"Narnia?"

"We are not, stupid!" Peaches corrected.

"You stupid!" said Sophia.

"No, you stupid!"

"Peaches, let Unc know where Kola left y'all."

"We at my mommy's house."

Both Apple's and Kola's adrenaline had escalated to high levels as they speed walked back to Kamel's Range. When they entered the car, it was full-blown hysteria. Sophia and Peaches were arguing, Junior was crying, and Kamel's voice was sheer panic.

"Oh my god, what's going on?" asked Kola.

"Kola?" said Kamel relieved. "Where the fuck you been?"

"We're at Apple's. I went upstairs real quick to use the bathroom," she lied. Kola swiveled her head toward each child and glared.

"What I tell you 'bout leaving them alone? Why the fuck you ain't take them wit' you?"

"Watch your mouth, Kamel."

"Think!" he continued. "You can get locked the fuck up for leaving kids alone in the car!"

Kola rolled her eyes. Her husband was overprotective of the children, which was alien to her. Denise didn't smother her, Apple, or Nichols, so his constant bitching just added to the weight that was already pushing her down.

"These big-ass kids?" Apple challenged. "You can't be serious. Shit, when Kola and I were their ages we food shopped and playground hopped."

"Apple, I'm speaking with my wife!"

"A'ight," said Apple. She just had exerted all her energy, so she had zero left to argue with her brother-in-law.

"You're right. It won't happen again." Kola folded. "Love you. I'll be home later."

"Love you too."

As soon as Kamel hung up, Apple's head turned toward the backseat, where Eduardo and Sophia were still whimpering while Peaches had her lips poked out. Apple smiled. Peaches had her fiery temper.

Apple asked, "What's with all the drama?"

Wiping his tears, Junior said, "Kola left us alone. She's always leaving us alone."

"I do not!" Kola snapped. "That's a lie!"

Apple gave Kola the side-eye. Her response was a little too aggressive, but she deduced that the recent event had set her off.

"Peaches, why were you cryin'? You know Auntie Kola was comin' back, right?"

She shrugged, looking sheepish.

"That's not an answer."

Peaches thought for a moment. "Because Sophia started crying first."

"No, I didn't," Sophia wailed.

Both Apple and Kola took deep breaths. Sophia was a crybaby, always whining for attention.

"What did I tell you about being a follower?" Apple didn't have time to coddle Sophia. Right now was a teachable moment for her child, and she needed to seize it.

Peaches sternly said, "I'm not a follower!"

"That's my baby girl."

Apple turned back around and faced front, staring out the window. She was ready to focus her attention again on her nemesis, but Peaches wasn't done arguing her case. "I'm not a follower 'cause when Sophia told Uncle Kamel we were in Narnia, I was going to say that we were in Wakanda, but I didn't wanna follow her!"

Apple and Kola burst out laughing, which caused the children to do the same. From the outside looking in, you would never know how much drama had just unfolded.

"Yo, those twin bitches are about that life," said Killer Mike. "I watched as Apple handled Queenie with ease. She put those paws on her like she could go pound-for-pound wit' a nigga! And that bitch was in heels."

"Nigga you dick-riding a bitch?" said Lord, who stood with his hands stuffed deep in the pockets of his sweatpants. His eyes were darting back and forth as they waited impatiently in the emergency room of New York Presbyterian Hospital. His fitted hat was pulled low, slightly camouflaging his menacing eyes. "And expound on how you let a female get the drop on you again? Because you know when Queenie wakes up, shit gonna get really real."

Mike knew that he had some explaining to do once he had to face Queenie. Real talk, he hoped she wasn't ill-equipped to deal with the reality that she got her ass beat. It was a fair fight, Apple laid two hands on her, and it wasn't unprovoked. Queenie went looking for trouble, they were on her turf, and they both got caught slippin'. If he were man enough to accept that a bitch took his burner, then Queenie needed to embrace her truth too.

Queenie's henchmen were huddled outside the triage area politicking about what was ultimately coming—a war.

"This is fucked up," Rehab deduced. "Queenie gonna go ape shit as soon as she's discharged."

"Look, if Queenie wanna go to war, then that's what we do." Killer Mike was always down for whatever, and he also knew that he had a lot to prove. He was ready to get his hands dirty because if he hedged again, then Queenie could easily give the order to have him hit.

"Nah, that's exactly what we *not* gonna do," said Lord, speaking for Queenie in absentia as if he was the shot-caller. Everyone knew he was second in command—her right hand—but he was overstepping boundaries.

Killer Mike frowned. "How you figure we gonna sit this one out?"

"Easy. Queenie didn't green-light no hits, so we gettin' ahead of ourselves. Most importantly, I got a bad feeling 'bout those twin bitches—"

Mike interjected, "You talking 'bout feelings and emotions like we ain't L.E.S. Crips, nigga!"

"Where was ya blue bandana when those bitches stepped to you? Nigga, don't ever play me like shit is sweet 'cause I'll push ya fuckin' wig back," Lord threatened.

"Y'all niggas chill," said Rehab. "We ain't each other's enemy."

Lord nodded. "We all know that when Queenie comes out of that room, her ego will be banged up and she'll want revenge. But we just don't need that type of heat over no ass-whooping. I gotta make her see that; we gotta make her see that shit."

"Lord, no disrespect, but we've been to war before. You need to break down why this shit is any different."

Lord bit the inside of his right cheek, straightened his back, and took a pregnant pause before speaking, something that he usually did when he was contemplating weighty decisions. He said, "We all havin' a good run. Our dope is flooding the streets, our connect has the grade-A product, and nobody fucks wit' us! We're respected on these streets, and most importantly, we're feared. But and however, I did my research. Apple is lightweight. Her man got murdered, and she don't got no thoroughbreds on her team, so she wide open."

Killer Mike was thirsty. "So, let's get at her tonight."

"Chill, Mike," Lord's voice boomed louder than he would have wanted in such a populated, public area. "If we get at Apple, then we gotta add more shooters on the payroll for Kola."

"Word? Who's shorty's man?" Rehab wanted to know.

"She's married to some twin nigga whose name rang out for a minute. I heard he put in work, but he's not the problem. Kola is under the protection of a Colombian cartel, and the cartel has an unlimited supply of shooters. So that kinda heat ain't worth it. When you at war you can't make your bread, and I need to eat. A nigga got bills, my woman likes nice things, y'all feel me?"

Killer Mike and Rehab both nodded.

"How we gonna convince Queenie?" Mike asked.

"Let me handle her."

Kola drove quickly to Central Park so the kids would have open space to run off their energy and also to give her and her sister time to discuss the obvious.

"What was that shit about back there?" asked Kola.

Slowly Apple's head rocked side to side as she wondered how she always found herself in precarious situations. She didn't go looking for beef, but it still ended up at her front door.

"That crazy bitch got heart," Apple admitted. "All I know is her name is Queenie. We had a run-in at Harlem Week; she came through stuntin'. She got some paper, some goons, and a slick fuckin' mouth."

Kola whipped out her phone and called Kamel back. She placed the call on speaker so Apple could hear whatever he had to say. Kola knew her husband still kept his ear to the streets even though he'd been out of the game for a while now.

"Babe, have you heard the name Queenie?"

"Why?" Kamel said.

"K, why does everything have to be twenty-one questions? Just run it down if you have intel and I'll fill you in when I get home."

"You a'ight?"

"I am."

Kamel knew that his wife asking about a female of Queenie's caliber and with Queenie's reputation ultimately had something to do with the problem child, Apple. No matter what the circumstance, all roads would always lead back to Apple being mixed up in something dangerous—some beef that she would drag his wife into that would trickle down to him and could inevitably place their children in danger. They didn't need that exposure. Kola was still healing. He knew she was in a transitional chapter of her life, and he worried greatly. Ever since she came back from South Beach, she had been acting strangely—different. She was leaving the kids unsupervised for long periods, so much so he limited how often and how long he left their residence. He knew that she was taking medication, but he wasn't sure he liked the effect it had on her. Her sex drive was gone, and he could feel her slipping away. Kamel knew better than to come between the sisters, especially a twin. He knew firsthand the bond that twins share. However, Apple was a bad seed, an anchor pulling his wife down, just as Jamel had smothered him with his erratic, drug-induced behavior.

"Queenie's a young broad, L.E.S. Crips. She's been expanding her territory, making power moves."

"Power moves?" said Apple.

"She doin' a'ight for herself. Nobody knows who her connect is, but I know she mainly pushes heroin."

Apple hung onto each word Kamel spoke. Her body stiffened with each compliment and she could only listen, question, and then ultimately plot.

"What is she? That bitch looks crazy wit' those eyes and hair, and she said *cabrón* as if she's Hispanic or some shit."

"Yeah, I heard she a mut. Some say she's Spanish, some say she's West Indian, and some say she's mixed. You know how the streets be runnin' their mouths. But the one thing consistent is she's no joke. A couple years back some Blood niggas tried her with a home invasion and she bodied them niggas all by herself. Streets said each year she sent a body part to a different family member and told them in twenty years they should have enough parts to fill a casket for a proper burial."

"That's bullshit." Apple quickly shut Kamel down.

"It could be. But all I know is that Queenie's making too much noise so those alphabet boys are either on her or will be on her. Stay the fuck off her radar."

"That bitch should have stayed off mine!" Apple was less than comfortable with how Kamel knew Queenie's highlight reel. "This broad done bumped her fuckin' head if she thinks she can go up against me! She runnin' round calling herself the Queen of New York, had a straight face when she said she never heard of Apple like my résumé don't stretch long and wide like I-95 out this bitch! And then she comes to my front door with a shooter?"

"Apple, don't make this personal," Kola warned.

Apple sucked her teeth. "Too fuckin' late."

Kamel had heard enough. He had the confirmation he needed, and as soon as his wife got home, then they needed to discuss what came first— her household or helping her sister with her unlimited supply of enemies.

"I'm out," Kamel said and hung up.

Apple looked at Kola. "I didn't make this personal. She did."

"I'm not here for it, Apple!" Kola snapped. "I told you I got my own demons that I need to handle; therefore, I can't have your back."

"I don't need you."

"Like you didn't need me for South Beach?"

"I told you not to come!" said Apple. "You didn't do that for me; you did it for you. So don't lay that at my feet and expect me to pick it up and run with it."

"App, please, let this shit go! You glanced at this bitch, and she was at your front door within the first forty-eight. You need to move. Better yet, come and stay with us for a few days until you find a new place."

"Kola, stop worrying." Apple's mind was already in combat mode. "I got this."

9

Apple gripped her cell phone and wondered if this was fate or misfortune. The authoritative voice that boomed through the line was Manolo Santiago. He was summoning her to meet with his boss, Caesar Mingo—who also was the connect of her enemy, Citi. Caesar, who was a top supplier in New York City, set the meeting place at a Spanish restaurant in East Harlem on 116th Street. Apple paused momentarily only to consider Peaches and the promises she had made to Kola. Apple reasoned that if he wanted her dead there would be no courtesy call, so this meet had to be about business. Apple agreed to meet with Caesar and understood she had two choices: she could either go and keep the peace or refuse and possibly ignite a war. As she drove her sleek car north on the FDR, one nagging thought wouldn't go away. She called Kola on one of the burner phones that they always kept for emergencies so that she could speak freely.

"What's up?"

"Real quick. I'm on my way to meet up with Citi's connect."

"Caesar Mingo? Why?"

"I don't know why, but I'm going."

"Again, why?"

"Because you don't say no to a man like Caesar."

"Oh, please, Apple. I know you ain't gonna start moving ki's again, especially when you know what you've promised!"

"Who said anything about moving weight? We killed his bitch, so I suspect he wants answers."

"You love this type of shit."

"I don't have a choice, Kola. You know that!"

"There's always a choice, even if it's a tough one."

"Anyway," Apple ignored her, "I don't wanna walk into a trap. Are you sure that Citi is dead? I don't want to walk into his place of business and she's sitting there with her pistol trained on me."

Kola exhaled to bide her time. She wrestled with whether she should finally come clean. What if this was a trap? "You know the game. You're supposed to always think the worst, so I know you're strapped, right?"

"No doubt."

"You need me?"

"Nah, I'm straight."

"So to answer your question, I already told you that Citi shouldn't have survived her injuries. Her body ate up a lot of heat, but crazier things have happened. Just be careful."

"I will."

Apple arrived at the restaurant with her gun concealed inside her designer handbag. As she walked inside, her eyes darted around cautiously, drinking in her surroundings. Apple examined faces and body language and took note of the rear exit. Busy staff fluttered around taking orders, and chitchat filled the air as customers enjoyed their meals. Apple sat at the bar and ordered an Appletini and just waited, as Manolo didn't leave specific instructions. Apple stared out the large, tempered glass and took sips of her tasty alcoholic beverage. It didn't take long for her to notice a Chrysler minivan pulling into the reserved parking spot. The door opened, and the man who emerged couldn't be Caesar Mingo, the head of the Mingo cartel. This family man wore a sight-blinding tie-dye t-shirt, cargo shorts, and orange Crocs. There was a hint of a beer belly and a jovial, upbeat twinkle in his eyes reserved for people who hadn't crossed over to the murderous side of life. And his complexion was off. Apple had heard that Caesar was Mexican, and this man had dark-chocolate skin and a massive amount of jet-black, curly hair. His smooth skin glowed in the distance, and Apple wondered why she couldn't take her eyes off of him. Who was he to park in the reserved spot?

When the back door slid open and out popped a toddler and a plump white woman exited the passenger's seat, Apple lost interest. She finished her drink and ordered another one.

"I'll have it sent to the back," the bartender replied.

She was perplexed. "The back?"

"Mr. Mingo is here," he nodded toward the minivan trio. "Edenia will show you to your table."

Apple was impressed. When she had arrived she hadn't spoken with anyone, so how could they know who she was or who she was waiting on? It was then that she looked, *really* looked, and saw the shooters. She could count at least nine goons, and most likely more, with the restaurant under their protection.

"Ms. Evans, please, this way," Edenia said.

Hearing her last name sent a chill down Apple's spine. As far as levels, this was "other."

The waitress was gorgeous. Her thick hair was flat-ironed straight, parted down the middle, and fell past her shoulders. Her makeup was tasteful, as she needed little. Her uniform—black pencil skirt, white shirt, and black heels—couldn't take away from her natural beauty.

Apple was led through the restaurant to a private area in the back closed off from patrons. Seated at a decorated table were a man, a woman, and a child. Apple still couldn't believe this man was the infamous, alleged megalomaniac head of the Mingo cartel.

"Please, Apple, siéntate."

"Caesar?"

"Sí, yes, of course." His self-assured voice boomed throughout the private area, and before her sat a confident man, a man who commanded and demanded respect. Caesar sat upright in his chair with his legs spread wide like he had an elephant trunk between his thighs. "And this is my wife, Lena, and my son, Oscar."

"Pleasure to meet you," Lena said.

"You're pretty," Oscar said.

"Thanks," was all Apple could say because she felt she was being punked. This dark-chocolate, curly-haired Mexican who was claiming to be Caesar Mingo invited her to have dinner with his wife and child? Why?

Subtly, she slid her hand into her purse and gripped her 9mm pistol. Apple would ask questions, and if she didn't like the answers, then she would shoot her way out.

"So," Apple began. "Why am I—"

Her line of questioning was cut short when the Heckler and Koch met her temple. Apple looked up to see the dainty hand of Edenia gripping the weighty pistol. No longer did Apple see her beauty, but a stone-cold killer. Apple could recognize the eyes of a murderer because Edenia's eyes were like hers—lethal. "I'll take this," Edenia reached down and took Apple's clutch. "You'll get this back when you leave."

Apple was humiliated. She felt naked and played, but she would not allow anyone in that room to see her sweat.

"You were about to ask why you were invited here, no?" Caesar said.

Apple nodded.

"First, let's eat. Order whatever you would like."

"I'm not hungry."

Caesar waved Edenia back over to take their orders.

"Ms. Evans will have another Appletini and seafood paella."

"How do you know my last name!" Apple demanded. She was also unnerved that he knew her favorite Spanish dish was seafood paella, but she didn't want to give him too much power.

"Tranquillo, please, Apple," Caesar pointed toward Oscar. "My son."

Apple stared at the round-faced cutie pie and fell back.

"And I'll have the Caesar salad, hold the croutons." He patted his robust stomach. "I'm watching my weight."

"Would you like a Corona draft, Mr. Mingo?"

"Sí, and have Chef Avila make Oscar a cheeseburger and fries and bring him a Coca-Cola."

Lena couldn't wait to order. Her impatience was written all over her face. Quickly she ran down her food requests. "For my appetizers give me the Calamares Fritos and the Tortilla Española, and for my main course, I think I'll have the seafood paella too. Tell Chef Avila to make sure to add extra lobster in my dish. Make sure he uses at least three large lobster tails. Did you get that?"

"Of course, Mrs. Mingo."

"And tell him that I want a to-go bag—a couple of medium-rare steaks with those spicy mashed potatoes he makes, and the garlic shrimp—"

"Lena, we have a guest. You can order that later once I've finished my business meeting."

His wife didn't look too pleased about being interrupted, but she sped things up. "I guess I'll have to wait to order dessert," she remarked dryly. "Edenia, just bring me a Diet Coke."

"Yes, Mrs. Mingo."

When the drinks hit the table, Caesar picked the conversation back up where they'd left off.

"Your actions. When you waged war against one of my top earners, Citi Byrne, you left distribution in Manhattan and the Bronx wide open."

"And?"

"And you're a reasonable woman, smart and motivated. You understand the fundamentals of business, sí?"

"Keep talkin'."

"With distribution open, you will oversee two territories, Manhattan and the Bronx, and your coconspirator, Cartier Timmons, will distribute the Brooklyn and Queens areas."

"And what if I say no?"

"You won't."

"But what if I did? Have you ever heard of free will? I do what the fuck I want."

Caesar didn't like Apple. The way she had disrespected his son with the foul language and around-the-way girl attitude had him reevaluating his decision to add her to his team.

Caesar did a subtle nod to the two waiters guarding the doors. Instantly they walked over and surrounded her like a bishop and a knight on a chessboard guarding the queen. "Then, you die. Not tonight, not tomorrow, but right here as you sit at my dinner table we will watch as life is strangled out of you and continue on with our meal."

Apple could see the waiter on her left slide a telephone cord from out of his pocket and tightly wrap the wire around each hand and then pull tightly. The wire ominously snapped. It was moments like this that she wished she had brought a second burner.

"I don't owe you shit, Caesar," Apple said defiantly. "The beef between Citi and I was personal."

"Why do you disrespect me so?"

"You've just threatened my life, and you feel disrespected?"

"Your foul language, in front of my only son. I've already warned you and yet you continue to not respect my authority." He turned toward his wife. "Lena, what do you suggest I do with her?"

"I'd cut her fucking tongue out."

Caesar smiled grandly. "Yes, my señorita, you would."

Apple wanted to smack that fat bitch in her fat face, but she was on his turf, surrounded by his men. She could feel the seconds counting down on her life expectancy. She looked directly at their son and spoke.

"Oscar, I apologize for my slick mouth. I have a daughter not much older than you; I should know better. Can you forgive me?"

"Um-hmm." He nodded his head while quickly drinking his soda. Apple had to admit he was adorable. When he finished, he repeated, "She so pretty, Papi. I like her."

"I like you too."

"So, are we clear? If so, all I want to hear you say is, 'yes, Caesar.'"

Apple had been down all along, but what her ego couldn't get past was his ordering her back into the game. She was a boss bitch, the worst chick Harlem had ever seen. Apple had put in work and then some. He should be kissing her ass and telling her what an honor it would be if she joined their team.

She said, "Yes, Caesar," and rolled her eyes.

"I see you are still angry? Why?"

"I'm not some—" she had to choose her words—"I'm not a newbie at this, and I don't appreciate the way you're handling me. I've earned my respect in this drug game. If you know enough about me to know my last name and the food and drinks I like, then you know about how I had the heart to go up against the Gonzalez cartel, and most recently the work I put in down in South Beach. My name rings out, and I should be treated accordingly. Now, I don't have a problem. In fact, I'm ready to have the

Mingo cartel as my connect. You actually rang at the perfect time, but treat me with the same respect you do your men, and it should make this transition that much easier."

"Your problem," Caesar sat forward in his seat, cracked his knuckles on his large, powerful hands, and stared at Apple with ice-cold, dead eyes, "is that you think you still matter. Your past wars, your past beefs, are inconsequential to today. The only time your past matters is when you're dead, and then it becomes your legacy. What matters is what you do today moving forward. Do you want to know why?"

Apple shrugged.

"Because humans have short memories. Any memory that can make a person larger than life is quickly forgotten because it's a constant reminder that they can't measure up; makes a person feel inferior. But a dead man, those stories are immortalized because a person can't compete with a ghost. I personally have to murder someone by my own hand each week. It's a code that I live by because my men need to see me get my hands dirty. If not, then they will forget why I am who I am and think that they can take my place."

Apple thought about how quickly everyone at Harlem Week lost interest in her South Beach tales when Queenie came through. Maybe Caesar was correct; she needed to make new street stories.

"I got something to pull your coat to. Cartier ain't gonna be down with this. She's out of the game and has no intention of getting back in. I don't mind covering her territories too."

Apple was thinking big. She wanted it all.

"Cartier is not your problem."

"I'm just saying the obvious."

"Say nothing more."

The food was finally at the table, and the two waiters were ordered to stand down.

Lena didn't hesitate to tear into her meal, unfazed by the guns and unaffected by potential violence.

Everyone ate, including Apple, who felt like she had just found a new spot. The seafood paella was the bomb and the drinks were the perfect blend of strong and sweet. Soon the conversation drifted away from the business, and Apple was shocked to discover that Lena was an attorney and Caesar was a former professional baseball player.

"I've had my law license for nearly two decades," Lena said. "I have a modest practice; clients who've I've worked for over the years. Of course, I don't work for the money. Caesar and I have more than we could ever spend. We would need a couple lifetimes to spend our money."

Caesar turned to face his wife. "Lena, my money isn't ours, sí?"

"I don't need your money, Caesar. My practice does very well. Too well," she embellished.

"And yet you have hardly any clients."

Apple could feel the underlying marital tension and knew there was trouble in paradise. She hated when couples brought their issues to the light in front of guests. She changed the subject. "I can't believe you were really legit."

"I was." He explained that he played Major League Baseball for three years for the Texas Rangers. "My son will play too. He already has a pitcher's arm."

Oscar beamed with joy as his father spoke fondly of him.

Before she left her one last question was nagging her. "Can I ask you a personal question?"

"Sí, yes, you can always ask."

"Are you Mexican and African American?"

He chuckled. "I am not. I'm Dominican born in Mexico."

Apple nodded. Made sense.

10

Queenie was a few days out of the hospital when she called the mandatory meeting her men knew was inevitable. Lord, Killer Mike, Stone, Rehab, and Nerd all converged in her gaudy living room and waited for their boss to finally emerge from her bedroom. Everyone stood around and hoped this wouldn't take long. They hated being there; there was something ominous about her apartment. It felt like a museum or funeral home—dead and dark. Her living room walls were painted black with a vast, blue-and-white L.E.S. Crips mural written in graffiti. A matching custom blue leather couch and chairs, ornate glass and gold-trimmed coffee and side tables, a large zebra print rug, and the oversized crystal chandelier made for a tasteless combination that none of her goons found attractive. African masks with strong features carved into pine wood hung on the walls. Two shelves of Santeria dolls were placed directly above an altar of white and blue candles she lit daily, and a statue of Jesus Christ on the cross and an oriental jade waterfall was next to the sage leaves. The cross-pollination of religions was a testament to what was going on inside her head: confusion.

The large apartment felt cramped with the oversized furniture taking up precious real estate. You couldn't walk inside without banging a knee on a sharp table or a toe on a hard object. And to add insult to injury, your nostrils were instantly assaulted when you exited the elevator on Queenie's floor. The strong stench of cat urine permeated throughout the hallway, causing all of her neighbors to complain to members of the homeowners association. The H.O.A. of Queenie's condominium had initiated an eviction process, which Queenie was fighting.

Within seconds of being inside, Nerd's eyes began to tear up and his nose started to run. Queenie knew he was allergic to cats, yet he was summoned.

"Yo, I wish she'd hurry up," Rehab said. His eyes angrily scanned the room and landed on two of her cats, Cersei and Jamie Lanister, who were perched in her window. Queenie was obsessed with the HBO mega-series *Game of Thrones*. The other three cats—Tyrion, Daenerys, and Jon Snow—were chasing each other throughout the apartment, amped up off catnip. Her men's nerves were about to ignite if she didn't come out soon. Like a match to a stick of dynamite, their anger was a slow burn about to erupt.

Tyrion came running across Killer Mike's Timbs, and he didn't hesitate to give him a reactionary, swift kick.

"Me-oooow!" Tyrion's high pitched yowl expressed his pain as his body went crashing into the wall after somersaulting in the air. He landed on his feet and took off running toward Queenie's bedroom.

Finally, Lord yelled, "Queenie, what's good? You comin' to politick or what?" They all were highly agitated, and once Nerd itched, it started a chain reaction. Each man used their strong fingers to dig into their skin to relieve the imaginary itch that needed to be scratched. It seemed like a zillion cat hairs were floating in the air, getting clogged in their throats, and blocking their airways.

She didn't respond. Lord hollered again, "Queenie!"

Heavy footsteps could be heard thundering down the hallway. Queenie had something to prove. She appeared in full combat mode—

army fatigue pants, Timbs, bulletproof vest, and a Walther PPK tucked in her waistband. But what gave these grown men pause was her attempt to cover up her bruises with makeup. Four days in, and the swelling around her left eye had ballooned to an almost inhuman size. The discoloration had progressed to a deepened red and a darker shade of blue-black. Her brown eye had several blood vessels inflamed, and they looked like red vines that had almost absorbed the remaining white of her eye. Her busted, split upper lip now protruded over her thin bottom lip, and it now appeared as if she had an overbite. Her men could only imagine how fucked up her body felt.

When Queenie spoke, the words came out muffled. Her mouth twisted to one side as she squeezed out sentences. It looked like her jaw was wired shut, but it wasn't. She did have nine stitches though, a consequence from when Apple's fist smashed into the side of her face, causing her to chomp down on the inside of her cheek.

"That . . . bummboclaaat . . . dies . . . tonight." Her words were delivered slow and with great pain. She pointed toward Nerd, who looked like he needed an EpiPen, and continued. "Find . . . where . . . Kola lives . . . She's next."

"Queenie, chill," Lord began. "We got this. Let us handle this beef."

Queenie's heat was permeating; circulating throughout the room, strangling anyone who dared to go against her. Her nostrils flared as she gritted her teeth. It hurt to talk, and this nigga was undermining her in front of her henchmen.

She looked at Mike, who was on borrowed time. He owed her his life as he stood before her. Killer Mike was on payroll to protect her, and he allowed her—his boss—to get her face smashed in. For each stitch sewn into her body, she thought of new ways she wanted Killer Mike killed. But now wasn't the time. Queenie was about to ignite a war that the streets of

New York hadn't seen in a long time. For now, he lived because she needed all the firepower to go up against the twin-faced bitches.

To Mike, she said, "Let's . . . go!" Surely he would jump at the chance to redeem himself—a second chance to right his wrong.

Mike hesitated, debating on whether he should follow the orders of the second-in-command, which was to avoid this beef by any means, or his boss. He looked at Lord, and Queenie peeped this. Before Lord could respond, she pulled out her gun, outstretched her arm, and fired, *Pop!* and Killer Mike dropped with one to his right temple.

"Fuck, Queenie!" Rehab said and jumped back, not wanting any blood splatter to get on his new kicks. His vintage edition Gucci sneakers were fresh out the box. He looked at his man and knew he was gone.

"Let's . . . go!" Queenie repeated, now to everyone, and so they did.

Queenie's Lincoln Navigator held Lord in the driver's seat, she sat shotgun, and Rehab played the backseat with Stone. Nerd was left at Queenie's apartment with dead Mike and her cats, which felt like a death sentence. They rode around for hours looking for Apple at all the known spots, continually circling her block while listening to Queenie keep demanding, "Shoot . . . on . . . sight!"

Lord was in deep thought. He'd fucked up and felt that Mike's death was on his hands. He wanted to stop Queenie and try to reason with her, but right now she was out of control. His boss was a runaway train with no brakes ready to cause mass destruction.

"Yo, Queenie, we been out here for a minute. I'ma breeze through this bitch's block one more time and then we gotta bounce. We have been at this shit for hours. Mike's body gonna be a problem—"

Simultaneously, they all spotted the black Maserati pull into an open parking spot. The passenger climbed out and surveyed her surroundings.

As the Navigator came to a rolling stop, Queenie hopped out before Lord could place it in park and took off running down the block.

Bak! Bak! Bak! Queenie's heart raced as she ran with her eyes trained on her target, Rehab and Stone a few paces behind her. Instinctively, Apple reached under her driver's side seat and pulled out her 9mm and reached in her waist and gripped her .45. Apple had prepared for this. She did a *Matrix* spin, extended both her arms and busted off numerous shots.

Pop! Pop! Pop! Pop! the guns blared back as she backed both assailants off of her.

Apple took fire from all angles as she took cover behind her pricey car. She heard, "ting, ting, ting!" as bullets ate through each vehicle parked on the high-end block. Glass shattered, and she could hear Queenie screaming obscenities. Apple could see she was outnumbered, as Lord had now joined his crew. Rehab tried to inch closer, and Apple pushed him back again.

Pop! Pop! Pop! Pop!

She had only one opportunity, and she took it. There was a steel basement door that the superintendent was supposed to lock each night at nine p.m. However, he never did. If she could get to it and bolt the door, it could save her life.

Apple's clips were nearly empty, so the time was now or she'd die. Skillfully she shot out the street light to give her cover from the darkness and then returned fire.

Pop! Pop! Pop! Pop!

Apple snaked through several parked cars and then darted down the basement steps and kicked the door. It flung open, and she slammed it shut. The large bolt was quickly locked, and Apple raced underground through the massive corridors, up one flight of steps, and out the front door, which exited one block away.

She was safe.

11

The noise from the visiting room was just slightly above what most would consider loud. Several children sat across from fathers, mothers sat across from sons, and wives sat across from husbands. Ironically, Apple sat across from Corey, a sworn enemy. Their unconventional relationship was moving along nicely. She woke up some mornings looking forward to their visits, eager to hear his wisdom and to look into his familiar eyes. Apple wanted Corey to meet her daughter, and she wanted to introduce him to Kola, but what she thought about was his freedom. She figured he could be a real asset on the streets.

"Have you ever thought about hiring an attorney to look into your case to possibly get your sentence reduced from life to time served? The Rockefeller Drug Laws were reformed, right? Weren't sentences commuted?"

Corey looked into Apple's eyes and saw a mixture of concern and hope. He had weaseled into her heart without even trying. He knew the ghost of his son played a huge part in her trusting him. That was the thing with women; they always got attached the moment a man showed kindness. It was a flaw—sometimes a fatal one.

Corey shrugged the question away. He had so many bodies on his résumé that even if the drug charges got reduced, he still would have to die twice before he could be released. "I've done my due diligence, and I'm okay with the choices I've made."

"But you should at least try. I can help you with lawyers if you want. I'd pay for your appeal," Apple offered.

"Just drop it," Corey replied curtly.

"Done."

Sitting across from Apple was reminiscent of having visits with his son. He knew something was bothering her and whatever it was, the problem involved the streets.

"What's on your mind?"

Apple wanted to share her issues with him. She had thought about confiding in him since the incident. However, for just a fleeting moment, she wondered if it was fair to burden him with her troubles. Apple wanted an organic relationship with Corey, so she didn't want their visits to be reduced to her being the receiver. If he saw just a hint of usury in her, then he would never accept that she loved his son. And to Apple, that was important. Even with Nicholas being dead, she wanted his father's approval.

"Just a little tired after the drive."

Corey could extract the truth from almost anyone. Sternly, he said, "Don't bullshit an old man. Give it to me straight. What's up?"

"I took some heat the other night," Apple said. "I barely made it off my block alive."

He understood. "Does this involve my son's murder? Is this the same beef that got him killed?"

"Nah, this some new shit. Twice now I was ambushed by this young, weird bitch named Queenie."

"L.E.S. Crips?"

"You've heard of her?" The inflection in Apple's voice was pure disbelief. His response stung like a million bees attacking her pride, ego, and overall self-importance. She knew that the streets knowing of Queenie was to be expected; she drove flashy cars and was gang affiliated. But when your reputation transcended through the cement walls and iron bars of correctional facilities, then that was validation.

"I have."

"Had you heard of me?"

Rapidly, his head shook. Each time Corey's head swung left to the right, it felt like a knife shredding what was left of her baddest chick status. Apple felt gut-punched. Was she really now officially a nobody?

"How will you handle this?" he wanted to know.

"She came to my front door," Apple said. "She's dead."

"I understand," Corey said. "But I suspect there's more at play here. You want more than just the death of your enemy. You want respect? Adulation? Infamy? It's the reason you hunted your prey in South Beach."

"It's not like that, Corey. She came at me."

He nodded. "You know, if you kill her, you won't get what you want. I'm trying to make you see that. All you'll have is blood on your hands. This situation will be just a placeholder until you find someone else to scratch your itch."

Apple was confused. "You know better than to suggest that I'ma sit this one out and let this nobody have my crown."

"The advice isn't to bench you. It's to suggest that you dribble the ball for a while before you go for the layup."

A puzzled look was her response.

Corey continued. "A fool and her money are easily parted, and before you ask for clarification, that means that you should take everything she has before you kill her. That way, you don't have to keep going in search of satisfaction. You'll get what you want. The streets will call out your name because you'll have put in the work. You want the crown? Take it, but if you take it, everyone will know you didn't earn it."

This wasn't exactly the advice she thought she would get, especially after a lingering beef had resulted in his son getting murdered. "The game says that I kill her. She's a liability, and those are the rules."

"Make her pay a toll before she passes through to the other side. Listen to me, young blood, or else you won't be able to retire your name from the game anytime soon. Get your numbers up, make noise, and make them take notice. If you murder Queenie now, you'll just be the nobody who took out a somebody. Force the culture to remember that you're a formidable adversary."

"I'll need some triggermen."

"Buy them."

Apple's thirst to be the baddest was clouding her judgment, and her promise to Kola to take the children while she worked on her sanity quickly took a backseat. Before Apple left the visit, she gave Corey a tight hug, and although unplanned but still satisfying, she gave him a quick kiss on the side of his cheek. The gesture didn't go unnoticed by them both. Corey smiled sheepishly. A row of bright white teeth showed his gratitude.

"See you soon, Pops."

"Be safe, Apple."

Corey went back to his cell and had to stuff his feelings back down the dark hole they crept out of. It was too easy manipulating Apple to go against the L.E.S. Crips. As much as she had chipped away at his tough exterior, he swore an act of vengeance to his only son at his funeral. Corey tried to counsel Nick that women destroyed men, but he wouldn't listen. He was pussy whipped. Corey Davis was an old head. He had seen what had happened to his son happen to countless men.

It was time for Apple Evans to go to her grave. How that would transpire was out of his hands, but he took comfort in knowing he was the catalyst that would cause her demise.

12

If Apple wanted a strong, loyal team on her side, she knew exactly where to start. She drove to Lincoln projects looking for Hood and IG. It was a chilly, autumn day when she parked across the street from the corner bodega. There was a confrontation ensuing, and Apple noticed that Tokyo was in it. She was arguing with a few other girls. Three girls against one, and that one was Tokyo. But Tokyo was undaunted by them and their threats. She heatedly stepped toward the three girls with a fierce attitude. She yelled, "I wish y'all would try me!"

"Ain't nobody scared of you!" one girl screamed.

"What you gonna do, bitch?" Tokyo taunted.

It didn't take long for the heated argument to transition into a violent confrontation. Tokyo threw the first punch, and that set it off. The three girls returned blows; angry fists and strong kicks stomped Tokyo to the ground, but she kept getting back up. The fighting was intense with punches being thrown so forcefully, Apple could hear each fist connect to the skin from across the street. One opponent was built like a linebacker, a husky broad with a wide back and thick waist, and she had the most energy. She wanted to make a statement. The female had wrapped her strong hands around a chunk of Tokyo's hair and repeatedly smashed her in her face. A crowd gathered, watching and egging on the violence. Tokyo was face-up in the melee going at every last one of her enemies with all she had. Tokyo was fighting like she belonged in the UFC. But it was still three against one. She tussled with these bitches taking hits and kicks to her face and side. So, to even the numbers, Tokyo quickly pulled out a razor, and the linebacker-looking bitch didn't see it coming. The slash against the girl's face was subtle and swift. It wasn't until the girl felt a coat of blood trickling down her face that she flew into sheer panic.

"Yo, that bitch cut me!" the girl shouted frantically.

The side of her face had opened like a zipper. Things went from a fight to a vicious assault, and her friends quickly paused to see if they were cut too. Tokyo gripped the box cutter tightly and continued to swing, hoping to do additional damage.

"Back the fuck up, bitch! You bitches thought y'all were goin' to just fuckin' jump me? Fuckin' jump me!" she shouted.

It was time for Apple to intervene. She removed herself from her vehicle and did a slow jog across the street. She approached the confrontation with authority in her stride—with determination and purpose. The bystanders thought that the trouble was about to escalate with Apple's sudden presence, but it didn't. She was there to defuse the conflict.

Apple looked at Tokyo, whose face was lumped up. Her chest was heaving up and down, and Apple could see that at any second she was about to burst into tears. She whispered, "Don't let them see you shed one fuckin' tear. Swallow those emotions."

Tokyo nodded, gritted her teeth, and fought to hold back her tears. She continued to seethe, though. She wanted to do more damage with her blade, making them all feel as fucked up as she did.

The young girl with the ghastly slash across her face was howling and crying, clutching the side of her face and vowing revenge.

"That fuckin' bitch cut me," she continued to rant.

It was serious. It would require stitches and maybe surgery.

Apple reached into her pocketbook and pulled out a wad of hundred-dollar bills. She gave the cut girl nearly three thousand dollars for her pain and suffering.

"Keep this quiet, you understand?" she ordered. "Take care of your bills, and I'll bless you later."

The girls were stumped. But they knew the code of the streets: keep y'all mouths shut, no snitching.

Tokyo was still fuming. The box cutter was still clutched in her tight fist, and it looked like she wanted to keep swinging away and cutting.

Apple said, "Let's go."

Apple made Tokyo toss the weapon down a sewer drain, and she handed the girl a napkin to wipe the blood from her hands. Tokyo followed Apple to the eighth floor where Hood lived. She banged on his door like she was five-oh.

"Yo, Hood, open up!" She banged again. Apple was impatient. She wanted to handle what she came to the projects for and then head out to Kola's to see Peaches. She turned toward Tokyo and asked, "Do you know if he's home?"

Tokyo shook her head. She was trying to keep her composure, but now she wanted to curse Apple out. Just a couple moments ago she was jumped, so all she wanted to do was go home and nurse her wounds. All she kept thinking about was her face. How fucked up was it? She could feel the scratches running down her cheeks. The open wounds stung and one of her eyes felt different as if it were about to get puffy.

"You did good back there. You know how to handle yourself. I like that. I respect that," Apple complimented the girl.

"Them bitches had it coming," Tokyo said, rubbing her forehead.

The girl had fire, and she was pretty too, with flawless brown skin and natural soft black hair she always kept in a bun. Tokyo only wore black catsuits that showed off her starter curves.

"Call Hood." Apple gave the order, and she listened. Tokyo reached down for her phone when Hood and IG exited the elevator. Both men paused, seeing figures in front of Hood's door and then quickly acquiesced.

"Yo, Apple, you gonna live a long time. I was just talking 'bout you. What's good, baby girl?" Hood said.

"Can we talk inside?"

Hood led everyone inside his three-bedroom project apartment. His great-grandmother, Annabell, who raised him and his two brothers, was knocked out asleep in the back bedroom. She was old-school sixty-six, so although she looked no older than forty, her body felt like she was well into her eighties. Hood was the only surviving sibling. Both of his brothers were murdered. His mother lived in Baltimore and hardly ever came around. Apple looked around his apartment at the dated furniture, dingy walls, roaches scattering about, and a smell that referenced unsanitary hygiene habits. It was all too familiar—this was her situation about a decade ago. Apple would never forget where she came from, so she didn't put on bougie airs. She took a seat on the worn sofa and was ready to get down to business.

"Damn, what happened to your face?" IG asked Tokyo, finally noticing her wounds.

Tokyo still had her lips poked out and was more than eager to give a recap of her latest squabble. Apple desperately wanted to interrupt. She hadn't come here for the spotlight to be on Tokyo, but she let the young girl live. Tokyo told her war story while Hood passed out glasses of Henny and lit up a couple blunts. He took a pull from one of the blunts and passed it around.

When it was time for Apple to speak, she got straight to the point. Apple's eyes were low; she was faded but still focused.

"I need some shooters on my team—thoroughbreds that if shit got thick, I would feel safe with my life in their hands."

"Whatever you need, you know I gotchu," said Hood. This was an opportunity of a lifetime. For years he tried to come up on his own only to repeatedly fail. His hands saw no success, and he caught a few cases. Hood knew how to hustle and also had a skilled trigger finger, but he also needed guidance. Some people were born leaders; that was Apple. And some needed to be led. Hood knew he was the former and wasn't ashamed to admit his shortcomings. Working with Apple, a hood legend in her own right, could ultimately be a big payday.

Apple looked to IG.

"You already know what it is. Let's make this paper," said IG.

"I need a team to watch my back, but my enemy may be a friend. Things could get ugly—no, things *will* get ugly. So, I need to know where your loyalties will lie."

"A friend? We don't got friends if it will interfere wit' us makin' our paper," Hood said and gave IG a dap. Both men knew they would kill each other if pushed. It was just a silent fact in the hood that was never spoken.

"Good, but full disclosure: it's Queenie."

"Queenie?" IG repeated. His response lingered in the air as everyone either pulled on a blunt or took a sip of brown juice.

Apple said, "That bitch came to where I lay my head at night and tried to murder me."

IG shook his head. Queenie always had heart since she was a young girl, but her downfall would ultimately be her inability to control her jealousy. He spoke, "So this is a hit? You want us to handle her for you?"

Hood jumped in. "How much you payin'?"

"Nah, that's not what this is. I'm back to moving weight. My connect has that premium white powder, 97% pure. I need skilled shooters to help me move it through Manhattan and the Bronx, and maybe in the future, expand to Brooklyn, Queens, and Staten Island. With this crazy bitch on my ass, my re-entry into the game will not be unopposed."

Hood and IG thought quickly about what this meant. They looked at each other, and their eyes were speaking the same language.

"Why don't we just body her? I mean, Queenie is cool peoples, but fuck, we gotta eat," said Hood.

"We will. But for now, Queenie lives. We move on her when I say and not one day before." Apple looked sternly into their eyes so they could see the seriousness of her direct order. "But, we need to send her a message. Let her know that my team is stronger than ever. Y'all know where she lives?"

Both thought this was a mistake, but she was the boss. IG answered, "Nah, but she does own a restaurant."

"That'll do."

Eventually, Tokyo spoke. "Do you think you could find a position for me? I mean, I've sold drugs before—nothing major, but I know the game. And I could really use the money."

"How old are you?" Apple asked.

"Nineteen."

Apple looked to Hood and IG. "Y'all vouch for her?"

Without hesitation, IG said, "We do."

Apple looked at Tokyo. "Don't let me down."

Apple climbed out of her vehicle on 135th Street and walked toward Hood's project building. Lincoln Houses was a dangerous neighborhood, but it had birthed her and Kola who were like gods to the locals—not to be fucked with. She strutted confidently through the grubby looking lobby and stepped into the pissy elevator. Using her thumb and index finger, she pinched her nostrils as she ascended to the top floor. Apple exited and knocked on door 15D, and the round slot in the door quickly slid back for the occupant to see who was there. The reinforced steel door flung open, and Apple walked inside.

She smiled at what she considered a white Christmas. Snow had arrived early—fifteen kilos of cocaine spread out across the wooden kitchen table. It had arrived directly from the Mingo cartel in hidden compartments of several vehicles. The kilos went from various tractor trailers out of Zacatecas across the Mexican border into El Paso, Texas heading east. The cocaine was then transferred to awaiting transport vehicles. Hood and IG, Apple's lieutenants, were at the meeting point to collect their portion of the two thousand kilos smuggled into the United States.

Apple nodded toward one of her newly minted workers in the trap house and said, "Get me the purity kit so I can test this product. See if it really is as good as Caesar says."

The young goon obliged his boss and lifted his ass from his chair and grabbed the supplies. The worker stood in front of the table and pulled out a small pocket knife. A small slit was cut into one of the packaged kilos, and he extracted about 15mg of cocaine. The coke was placed in an ampoule with clear liquid and shaken. Everyone focused on the results of the test, watching the transparent liquid change colors. Instantly, the bottom layer turned dark like coffee, indicative that the product was 97% pure.

Apple grinned. This product would monopolize the streets and cement her claim as the baddest chick that had ever done it. She was the rightful Queen of New York, and she was ready to make niggas and bitches bow down to her.

"What we waitin' on?" Apple said. "Let's get this coke street-ready."

Apple's workers jumped into action, processing a part of the cocaine into cooked crack rocks. The remaining ki's were to be sold at massive profit margins to local distributors in Manhattan and the Bronx. Apple lit a Newport and inhaled, enjoying the sudden rush of nicotine as it entered her system. Apple and her lieutenants walked out of the kitchen, allowing the workers to do what they did best—cook coke and bag up crack vials. They went into the next room to politick. There was a problem. In the drug game, there was always opposition.

IG set the tone. "Once this shit takes off we wanted to pull your coat to a possible threat. You haven't been to Lincoln in years, and this is now L.O.E. territory."

Apple grimaced. All these acronyms were annoying. What happened to individuality? The days when a singular person held shit down like Nicky Barnes, Rich Porter, Corey Davis, Cocá Kola, and, not to brag, but Apple—The Baddest Chick. "Who the fuck is L.O.E.?"

"Lincoln Ova Everything gang, not to be confused wit' the Lower Eastside Crips. They ain't puttin' in the work we 'bout to do. They're low-level but still dangerous."

Apple rolled her eyes. "The first lil' nigga from that crew that's bold enough to give a stern look, grit his teeth, clench his jaw in the direction of anyone under our umbrella y'all make an example out of him. Don't call me to approve the hit, just do it. Do it fast, quick, and messy. Make a muthafuckin' statement that we're not to be fucked wit'. Understood?"

IG and Hood nodded. This is how they wanted to get at L.E.S., but she was the shot caller.

13

The sleek vehicle double-parked on the busy Midtown street, and Tokyo coolly exited from the driver's seat and came around to open Apple's rear door. Apple climbed out of the Maserati wearing a red Balmain bodycon dress that complemented her figure and a pair of strappy YSL heels. Pulling up directly behind the Maserati were Hood and IG. Both men had dressed for the occasion in designer suits that Apple had paid for.

El Tempo's in Midtown looked like a star-studded occasion. It was the perfect venue for the most sophisticated Latin celebrations, and it was conveniently in the heart of Manhattan. The long city block was inundated with high-end vehicles being valet-parked—Bentleys, Maybachs, Porsches, Benzes, Beamers, Ferraris, and Lamborghinis.

Apple strutted toward the venue flanked by Hood and IG. Tokyo remained posted up outside. She would be Apple's eyes.

Standing outside of the venue were two stunning females—models, dressed sexily in mini dresses. One was a tall and slim Puerto Rican female, and the other was a tall and slender white female. Together, they guarded over a list. They smiled politely at the approaching guests and checked for their names. Poised nearby was an ominous looking man dressed in a dark suit and dark shades. He was muscle—a gunman.

Apple stopped midblock and inspected the area. She knew she was taking a chance by showing up to the event unannounced and uninvited. But this is who she was: someone who always took risks. Apple knew to tread carefully. Therefore, she sent IG ahead to the front entrance of El Tempo's to see if he could bribe their way in.

IG moved with conviction. He approached the two ladies and tried to initiate conversation with them. He was quickly dismissed. IG was told that they weren't allowed inside if they weren't on the list. The two women found the incentive he tried to offer offensive. There were too many influential people inside, and anyone slipping into the event uninvited could be a threat.

IG marched back to Apple with the news. "Shit is tight, Apple, and they ain't taking no bribes."

Apple stood there expressionless. She was determined to make her way into the building—where there was a will, there was a way. The last thing she wanted to do was involve her sister, but there wasn't another option.

"What is it, Apple?" Kola answered indifferently. She was having a hard day.

"Question, Kola. I'll make it quick. Could you call Eduardo and ask if he could get me plus two into an event here in Midtown? It's a birthday celebration for Kiqué Helguero."

"Oh my god, you fuckin' partying right now?" she said. "When you gonna get ya fuckin' kid!"

Kola was in a mood, and Apple wasn't ready to deal. Her sister's outburst had surprised her. Apple's first inclination was to curse Kola out, but a smarter mind prevailed, and she knew she had to placate her.

"Stop yellin' and stop worrying! I didn't update you, but I found a three-bedroom for us. We can move in three weeks," she lied.

"That's a month away!"

"I'm doing my best, Kola. You just sprung this on me, but I'm ready. You can count on me this time. Please, call Eduardo."

"A'ight, I'll see what I can do. Give me thirty minutes." Kola's voice sounded almost hoarse, like she was fatigued. Apple noticed immediately, but her concern had to take a backseat. Kiqué was the last piece to the puzzle, a necessary step for the takeover, so her sister had to come through for her.

Eduardo, with his Colombian cartel connections and money, had a cell phone inside his prison that didn't have to be hidden. He called Kola regularly when he wanted to speak to his children. Apple just hoped that Eduardo's reach extended to the Helguero cartel.

Forty minutes later, Kola called back. "You're in."

"Let's go," Apple said to Hood and IG.

They coolly walked toward the front entrance of El Tempo's, and Apple looked into the eyes of the two models and gave them the name, "Apple Evans."

The Hispanic model scanned the electronic list for the name and right away found it—Apple Evans plus two. It was a go. They were allowed inside the extravaganza, and IG and Hood were impressed. They felt there wasn't anything Apple couldn't do.

Inside was packed. The who's who of the underworld was in attendance. Members of drug cartels and their wives and mistresses, drug lords, and drug dealers mingled amongst each other. The décor of the place was magnificent with towering marble columns, soaring ceilings, luxurious inlaid custom floors, and gorgeous chandeliers. Authentic Bolivian cuisine was served, and no expense was spared.

Flanked by her two henchmen, Apple moved around the party casually. There were faces she knew, but she remained withdrawn so far. Her primary purpose was to search for Kiqué. It wasn't hard to find him.

She knew he would be the most guarded man there. Apple told IG and Hood to fall back while she tried to see if she could get a quick face-to-face with him.

She observed her surroundings first. Kiqué was seated at a table flanked by five individuals—four men, one woman. The woman was dressed in an all-white, frilly lace dress with bright red lips and heavy makeup on her aging face. She had a massive amount of thick hair flowing wildly with a red rose pinned just above her right ear. The female looked tacky and was undoubtedly his wife. The table was cordoned off with a black velvet rope, and two armed gunmen stood in front as gatekeepers. The music was loud, Latin, and making Apple's head want to implode. There wasn't any way she would be staying long.

Apple approached Kiqué's security guards, who stared straight ahead, looking past her. Both were ready to shut her down and shove her to the side if need be to let Mrs. Helguero see them rough up this whore trying to get close to her husband.

Apple said, "Tell Kiqué my name is Apple Evans and that Eduardo vouches for me."

Eduardo was one of the very few who only needed his first name to be spoken, like Cher or Madonna, and still command respect. The henchman nodded and relayed the message to his boss. Apple watched as Kiqué's eyes looked toward her and then gave a subtle head nod. She was allowed through. One of his men moved, and she took a seat in the plush velvet chair.

"This is my wife, Brunilda," Kiqué said, making the introduction.

Apple smiled politely and then gave respect. "Hello, Mrs. Helguero. My name's Apple. Nice to meet you."

The aging woman had a cold stare that could kill on sight. She was familiar with young, ambitious girls like Apple wanting to fuck their way up the ladder. Brunilda was a powerhouse in her own right and had murdered more than a dozen of Kiqué's mistresses.

Brunilda nodded but didn't speak.

Apple shifted her body toward Kiqué. He was an average sized man with naturally tanned skin and a sleek, jet-black ponytail and matching mustache and goatee. He was dressed impeccably in a tailored suit with custom crocodile cowboy boots and a pencil tie. Kiqué wore a custom diamond rosary of St. Jude, the patron saint of lost souls and a diamond watch flooded with so many diamonds it weighed his arm down.

"Out of respect for Eduardo, I added you to my guest list when he called," Kiqué said. "What is it that you want? What's so important that you interrupt my party?"

"No disrespect, Mr. Helguero."

"An interruption is a sign of disrespect."

"This was the only way I could get your attention. But I'll leave." Apple stood to leave, and he gently placed his arm on hers and pulled her back down. She was beautiful to look at.

"Please, tell me, how can I help you?"

"I need a connect for heroin, and I hear you distribute the best."

"You are correct. My Bolivian heroin is premium quality, but why is it Eduardo isn't your supplier? This makes me nervous."

"It's not like that. Eduardo and my sister, Kola, have a thing. He's like family, so mixing our personal lives with business doesn't work."

He was listening. "What territories?"

"I'd like to start off with Manhattan and the Bronx."

"No!" Brunilda snapped. Apple looked at her sideways. She had no idea the bitch was ear hustling. "We've already vetted someone for those territories."

"Whoever he is, I'll guarantee to move more weight."

"Tsk, tsk, tsk," Kiqué said. "You sound like an amateur. Who guarantees in our business?"

"I will."

He shook his head. "I'm sorry you traveled all this way, but no. We will not be doing business. But stay, have drinks and food, celebrate me."

"Or not," Brunilda said. "Adios!"

Apple tried again. "The men I rub shoulders with in this business trust me because I've earned their respect. It would be easy for me to move that white and brown powder through Eduardo, but a bitch like me don't do shit easy. I get my coke through the Mingo cartel, and I would like my heroin to come through you. Please, ask around about me before you make a decision."

His interest was now piqued. Eduardo *and* Caesar? Maybe she was someone to consider. Apple knew little things while sitting at the negotiation table, and one was that the Helguero and Mingo cartels had been fighting over territory for over a decade. The Mingo cartel only pushed white powder, so Kiqué's organization monopolized heroin in the five boroughs and as far north as Massachusetts and as far south as Florida. Kiqué would consider giving her those areas because now he wanted to eventually pull her from Caesar so she would cop his heroin and cocaine. He wouldn't decide on his birthday. He would first need to do a thorough background check on the ambitious drug dealer.

"I will consider you. Now, please, leave so I can enjoy my wife and my party."

Apple stood. "Pleasure meeting you both."

Apple, Hood, and IG grabbed a table, and then they ordered buckets of champagne and food. The unlimited supply of food and liquor was all free. Initially, she had planned to leave directly after she spoke to Kiqué, especially since Tokyo was sitting outside waiting on them. But why was she rushing home? No one was there waiting on her. Besides, this party was drenched in the underworld. There was no telling what additional connections she would make.

The deejay played Migos, mixed in Lil Yachty, and gradually played the music they actually wanted to hear. The party was turning out all right.

Hood whistled. "This shit gotta cost a grip. At least a million."

"You see his jewels?" IG asked. "Shit, he got that drip niggas will body him for."

"They could try," said Apple. "But it won't be no smash-and-grab type of jux."

"True," Hood agreed.

IG said, "Yo, App, this gonna be us! Mark my words. This time next year, the city gonna belong to us."

Apple loved that they were all on the same page. When the champagne arrived, Hood asked Apple if she wanted him to text Tokyo to tell her she could leave since it appeared they would be staying.

Apple smirked. "I placed her outside for a reason—to watch our backs. It may seem we in here in vacation mode, but don't ever sleep. It could always jump off at any second."

"Speak of the devil," Hood said and nodded toward the front door. Apple's head turned on a dime and she watched as Queenie, Lord, Stone, and Rehab came through. Just then Apple's text lit up from Tokyo, warning her of the obvious. Apple hit her back and told her to be on high alert.

Queenie ran directly to the dance floor the moment the deejay switched back to Latin music. The salsa music blared throughout the nightclub, and Queenie and one of Kiqué's men, Arturo, were about to dance the night away. Spiritedly they glided and slid across the dance floor in perfect harmony. Tonight Queenie was glowing in her sexy blue salsa dress and clear stilettos. They danced through several songs. Arturo grabbed Queenie from behind and twirled her around and then he lifted her into the air, and she came back down without missing the beat. They did shimmies and spins and rapid moves, each keeping up with the other.

She was a natural, as this was her element. Queenie was having an amazing time until she spotted Apple.

"Look at this blue bitch with the blue eye."

"What you want us to do?" IG asked. "You want us to chill, right?"

Apple nodded. "That bitch knows better than to disrespect Kiqué with her bullshit. He's implemented a strict no-fire zone within the ten-block radius. Anyone who disrespects his party will have to deal with him. But watch my back."

"With my life," said IG.

Queenie was taken aback that Apple was at the event, but she kept her cool. She tapped Lord and gave him the heads-up and all mingled as if things were copacetic—as if they hadn't tried to murder Apple a few weeks ago. Lord did have an uneasy feeling that she was flanked by Hood and IG. It wasn't fear he felt; they were just someone to consider—another layer standing in front of successfully murdering Apple. Lord knew that being second-in-command meant that Queenie's life was in his hands. If he was being honest, he had to admit that things had been going well for them for a minute. No one had tried them in some time, which he felt was evident and embarrassingly humbling. Four shooters—him, Rehab, Stone, and Queenie—weren't able to kill Apple at the shootout. They were rusty. To now have to go up against Hood and IG—two dirty, thirsty niggas starving for a come up—would test their resolve.

He had to admit, even if Queenie didn't, that Apple was a movement all by herself. The way she pulled out both burners and backed down four shooters was impressive, like she was born for this life. Killer Mike had described how nice she was with her hands, which only affirmed what the streets had been saying about her for years.

Apple remained unruffled. The only thing exchanged between the two ladies was a hard glare. The red dress Apple wore stood out. It was a direct contrast to Queenie's blue gown. Red was in honor of Apple's name, but it irked Queenie because it was the color that represented the Bloods, the Crips's main rivals. Apple wasn't in the Bloods gang, but the color didn't sit well with her foe.

Queenie was a simmering pot of anger. *How the fuck did she get in?* she wondered, as her paranoia kicked in. Queenie felt that Apple had stalked her there, tearing a page from her playbook.

Lord approached Queenie, and she whispered in his ear, "I want that bitch thrown out of here, but mi don't want to make a scene. You think I could ask Kiqué's people to kick her out?"

"It will be a bad move on your end," he warned her.

She contested. "Mi want that likkle redbone bitch gone!"

"You'll look weak, Queenie, and besides, this party isn't about you. This not your shit. Apple's not a threat right now, and there are too many important people in here for you to worry about her," he said. "Let's handle business, and forget about that bitch . . . for now."

She gritted her teeth and scowled. Lord was right. It wasn't the time or place to make a scene.

"This party earns her a few hours of amnesty, but mi want you and Rehab back on her first thing tomorrow. I have a couple cinderblocks wit' her name on 'em." As Queenie spoke, she felt some regret about killing Mike. He was easier to handle and rarely challenged her authority as Lord did. Mike wouldn't have given her order to have Apple thrown out a second thought. He was just as petty as she was.

"You already know we're gonna handle that," Lord affirmed. "I think we should also find out why she's here. It could be a problem if she's connected to the Helguero cartel too. I told you about her sister and the Colombians. This shit don't smell right."

"Get. Off. Her. Dick!" Queenie took her index finger and poked Lord in the head with each word. Her disrespect was on full display, and as a man, Lord's first reaction was to knock her the fuck out. It took full restraint, something that had to be built up over time, to not get his Ali on. Queenie didn't appreciate that Lord had kept her alive on more than one occasion and that he was fiercely loyal to the gang—his brotherhood— over his own self-respect. But laying hands on him in front of his peers had diminished his resolve to murder her archenemy. If Lord fell back and allowed Apple to take out his boss, it would leave her operation wide open for him to fill her shoes.

Lord's voice was even when he said, "Please don't touch me again."

Queenie craned her neck to look up at her underling. "Know your place, Lord. Mi won't warn you again."

As the night progressed, Apple was no longer in a festive mood. She had been ready to leave but didn't want Queenie to think she had run her out of the place. And then she saw him again. The guy from Harlem Week had just entered the party and approached Queenie. Apple noticed how Queenie became overly animated toward him. The two hugged, and it looked like they were flirting with each other from Apple's viewpoint. They chatted briefly, and then Touch walked away. He wanted to mingle.

Apple had watched the interaction between Queenie and Touch like a hawk. She observed Queenie's eyes following Touch around the party. Queenie had a thing for him—it showed in her face, and although Apple was once disinterested in him, suddenly she felt differently.

"Who is that nigga again?" she asked Hood.

"Who?"

"Your six o'clock."

"Oh, that's my man Touch. You want me to bring him over here?"

"Nah, what for? I was just asking 'cause he keeps showing up at all the events. He moves weight?"

"That choir boy?" Hood chuckled. "He's some big-time poker player out in Vegas."

"Poker?" Apple said incredulously. That was different.

"He's doin' something right. He travels the world and shit, getting paid," said Hood.

"What's up with him and that bitch?" she asked.

Hood shrugged. "Ask him."

Apple went to the ladies room alone on more than one occasion to try to get Touch to notice she was there. Finally, she and Touch made eye contact. Apple kept it moving back to her table, and egotistically felt he would approach her just as he had done before. But he didn't. When she saw him exiting, she realized maybe it was time to do the same.

"Let's bounce," she announced.

As Apple, Hood, and IG snaked through the crowd and made their way to the exit, she saw that Queenie, too, was having a sit down with Kiqué and Brunilda. What stood out the most were the smiles and hugs exchanged between the women.

Apple had a bad feeling that the man she assumed was being vetted for the Manhattan and Bronx areas was a woman. And that woman was her archenemy.

14

Touch woke up before the sun and immediately started his morning routine. One step was to bow down to Allah in scheduled prayer, one of five prayers each day. He made sure that his body and his place of worship were clean of dirt and impurities.

While standing, he raised his hands up in the air and said, "Allah Akbar." Still standing, he folded his hands over his chest and recited the first chapter of the Quran in Arabic. Touch raised his hands up again and said, "Allah Akbar," once more. He bowed and then recited three times, "Subhanarabbiyaladheen," which meant "Glory be to my Lord Almighty," before concluding his prayer.

Next, he worked out doing mostly calisthenics for about an hour. Afterward, he finished a bottle of water and made himself a breakfast of eggs and waffles with a cup of green tea. Touch was physically fit and healthy, and he trained his mind daily to focus on only what gave him joy. He spent an hour each day playing memory building games, Sudoku, jigsaw puzzles, and online chess to sharpen his short and long term recollection. His father, Jorge, taught him at a young age how to discipline himself and control his thoughts, so he was perplexed as to why he was struggling to keep her out of his psyche. Last night at El Tempo's he had seen Apple; her beautiful face couldn't be overlooked even amongst all the revelers. He wanted her. He wanted her time, and he wanted to make time for her.

Touch had watched as she glided across the room, slow paced and sensual. She obviously was a woman who knew her curves, knew what men liked and how to please. It took all his strength to not approach her, especially since he saw her with Hood and IG, but he would not play himself. Not when she had made known that she wasn't checking for him. Being in the same club and trying to avoid her was a balancing act he wouldn't attempt, so Touch left and didn't look back.

He glanced at the clock. It wasn't even seven a.m. and he'd been up for hours, prayed, exercised, and had eaten while most people were just starting their day. He opened his computer and logged into his email account and had only one message. He only needed one, especially after the lousy games he'd played in Vegas.

Touch was a private, cautious man, just like his father. He used a secure network and took many precautions to not leave his online footprint. His router was encrypted, and he also used Tor's server, a virtual private network which hid his IP address and allowed him to surf the web in anonymity from any location he chose. He could pick Russia, Germany, Atlanta, California—anywhere in the world—but he never chose his current location. His computer was scrubbed daily, and he didn't do dumb shit like click links sent to him. He took most of his calls on burner phones through encrypted phone apps such as Signal or WhatsApp to converse with most, but the fact remained that he didn't have many attachments.

He quickly read the email and exhaled. It was a murdergram.

Touch quickly walked back into his bedroom where two large hutches sat. At first blush, one would think they contained his designer clothing. He swung open the double doors of one of the hutches to reveal a treasure trove of guns and ammunition. The second hutch held similar materials.

Touch carried each weapon from the first hutch into the living room, doubling back for the contents of the second one.

His apartment had few amenities—just essential items to get him through his days like a coffeemaker, television, couch, bed—shit like that. There weren't any personal touches or things a man his age might have in a bachelor's apartment like artwork, family photos, or sports memorabilia. Touch sat erect in the stiff kitchen chair and carefully removed each piece of weaponry he owned. Within a short span of time, he had his whole life's collection displayed across the table—two .38 Specials, a black .45 ACP, four 9mm Berettas, three Glock 19s, three Smith & Wesson SW99 9mms, and a stainless .45. It looked like he had committed a smash-and-grab from a gun shop.

Touch was also the proud owner of two of the most powerful guns ever manufactured: the Barrett M82 and a Remington 700 PSS. Both could blow baseball sized holes in muthafuckas. Touch marveled at his FN Tactical Police 12-gauge and Mossberg 500 12-gauge, along with a Heckler & Koch G36C 5.56mm, a SIG SG 552, and a Heckler & Koch HK91A3.

Touch started life in a single-wide trailer in the woods of the Deep South, where his father trained him to be a marksman. Back then, it was just a hobby to pass the time. When they moved north to New York, he kept up his training at the shooting range.

It was bound to be a long day for him. Touch was determined to properly clean his guns before his next job, taking care of his arsenal like they were his children. He had all the tools he needed in front of him: a bore brush, cleaning solvent, a cleaning rod, lubricant, and cotton swabs.

He grabbed his now-vintage iPod and scrolled through until he found his Prince playlist. Prince's smooth yet sultry voice crooned "Purple Rain," and Touch found the strum of the guitar strings relaxing.

One by one, he looked through the barrel of each weapon from front to back to confirm there were no live rounds stuck in the chamber or barrel. Touch dismantled the guns—which was complicated work of removing firing pins and barrels from each gun before ultimately reloading it.

Nearly five hours later, every gun was cleaned, functioning, and looked brand-new. Touch was ready to put them to use.

Touch worked for an agency called GHOST Protocol (Gather Humans Only to Slaughter Them). This was one of the better-known establishments in his line of work. There wasn't age or sex discrimination, and they placed no real restrictions on their hired guns other than complete discretion and professionalism. Touch's services weren't cheap, and his funds were directly deposited into his secure account within a day after he carried out a hit. Touch was vetted and then hired a week after his eighteenth birthday. To this day he had no idea how his recruiter had picked him or even known he existed.

His assignment was Haruto Takahashi, the head of the New York Yakuza crime family. Haruto was from a small town in China and had worked his way up the ladder traveling throughout Asia as an enforcer before being promoted to move West. The bosses back in Japan were disappointed with how he was running his faction in New York City. Takahashi had lost many shipments of cargo containing the Asian women sent to the United States to work off their debts to the Yakuza. These women were ultimately stolen under Takahashi's watch and sold as slave labor by rival drug organizations. To make matters worse, one of the Yakuza members had accused Takahashi of informing on fellow gang members to local authorities. GHOST Protocol was hired to dispose of Japan's problem.

He had one week to complete his assignment.

The air was thin and dry on Humphreys Peak near Flagstaff, Arizona. The high elevation forced him to take slow, deep breaths while his lungs adapted. At nearly eleven thousand feet above sea level, he could develop altitude sickness or pulmonary edema, so he was ready to put the wheels in motion to end this. His head swiveled left and right. The hidden cabin nestled in the woods was eerie and empty like a sacred burial ground or New Orleans cemetery. Haruto Takahashi had fled with his family after he had gotten wind that a contract was put out on his life and was hiding out in the small cabin.

Touch waited in the dark, controlling his breathing and keeping a keen eye out for threats. The living room was illuminated by the shimmer from the T.V. playing in the night, and eventually, Takahashi exited his side door in his boxers and a t-shirt carrying two large trash bags. The Beretta to his ribcage told him he had gotten too relaxed too quickly.

"Do as I say and your family lives," Touch instructed. Takahashi looked at the shadows inside his home where his wife, Emiko, and his son, Banri, were and complied.

It was just under an hour's drive to the burial site in Arizona. Touch steered the stolen car near a secluded section of a sprawling cemetery, tucked away from the community. It was pitch black out there, and it took some time for his eyes to adjust to such darkness as he killed his headlights.

Takahashi's final resting place was already dug; he just needed to get in. The full moon above gave Touch enough illumination to handle his business. Touch parked close to the grave and forced a resisting Takahashi out of the trunk at gunpoint. A cloth was wedged into Takahashi's mouth, so his angry pleas and cries were muffled. His small wrists were bound tightly, and his t-shirt and boxers were disheveled. Takahashi had to be dragged to the open grave as he refused to make shit easy for Touch. He squirmed, kicked, and tried to head butt his captor, but all his efforts were made in vain.

The butt of a Beretta suddenly came crashing against the back of Takahashi's skull. He collapsed to his knees, dazed from the blunt force trauma.

"Stupid muthafucka," Touch said.

Takahashi groaned loudly. The rag shoved in his mouth made him sound like a wounded animal. He didn't want to die, that was certain, but he had no choice. He had fucked up.

Touch grabbed Takahashi by his collar and dragged him some more. He was now at the foot of an open grave. Takahashi's impending fate allowed him to shake off the dizzying blow and he was once again trying to fight for his life. He wiggled, squirmed, and even tried to crawl away from the inevitable. Touch felt remorseless.

"You Yakuza, Takahashi," Touch stated the obvious. "Take this shit like a man!"

His words made Takahashi hang his head in defeat. He was Yakuza, and he felt he deserved an honorable death. Haruto Takahashi was born in the year of the rat, and that was precisely how he would die.

Touch and Takahashi locked eyes. "This ain't personal."

The Beretta was placed on his temple, and a bullet slammed into his frontal lobe. The bullet's impact sent Takahashi flying backward into the unmarked grave.

Touch outstretched his left arm toward Takahashi and fired two more shots into him.

Poot! Poot!

Touch covered the grave and hovered over the body like an omen. He showed no remorse for killing a family man. It was his assignment.

Quietly, Touch hugged the darkness and drove off into the night. He had a redeye flight he needed to catch.

The next morning Touch's plane was taxiing to his JFK gate when his cell phone vibrated. He reached into his overnight bag and grabbed one of his three mobiles and opened a text message from one of his many bank accounts. The remaining balance for the hit had been transferred in. He could buy into his next game in a couple of weeks, but he needed some action now. He knew exactly where he would go.

15

The Lincoln projects trap house was Apple's most prized possession in the drug game. She had the whole floor on the payroll. When she won, they all won. All parties had a vested interest in making sure her product was safe, and they kept their ears open for snitches and their eyes open for any ambushes. The apartment was also heavily guarded with armed thugs and a high-tech security system. Several henchmen took shifts on the building rooftop as lookouts, each equipped with a police scanner and walkie-talkie for instant communication. From up top, you could see the whole perimeter down below; 360 degrees of the territory was monitored. Any police raids would be spotted in real time, giving everyone a chance to evade capture.

Apple's organization was running smoothly. Years of being in the game had prepared her to run an operation of this magnitude without Kola or Cartier. And speaking of her friend, she had received a panicky call from her a few weeks ago giving her the heads up about Caesar. Apple asked her to come through, but she hadn't. Word on the curb was that she was having man troubles again—something they had in common.

Inside the two-bedroom apartment turned trap house were the most lethal killers on Apple's payroll. Each man had "executioner" seeping through his pores. They stunk of death and destruction. They greeted

Apple with respect, but Apple was only concerned with the shipment of heroin from the Helguero cartel. She addressed IG.

"Where is it?" Apple asked.

"We put the heroin in the back bedroom, El Jefe," IG said. "We wanted to keep it separate until you came through."

"El Jefe?"

IG nodded.

"I like it."

Apple entered the bedroom that held no bed, no dresser, and no comforts and saw fifteen kilos of heroin, a street value of at least a million if packaged correctly. The apartment also contained stacks of cash and a few firearms.

Hood asked, "What we gonna do wit' this? I mean, I never moved heroin."

"We move this right here one package at a time. Cut it up into bundles of twenty at twenty-dollars per package. We got that pure heroin, grade A quality those fiends gonna love. Don't step on my shit and watch how quickly we flip this. Put Easy on design duty for me. I want this stamped, '*Queen of New York.*'"

"Done," Hood said.

"A'ight, y'all niggas get to work," Apple ordered her crew. "Y'all know what to do."

Touch felt her presence before she entered the room. It was as if his soul was pulling him toward a sparsely populated area of the casino. He was puzzled as to why, and then he saw her. She glided into his view with purpose, her silhouette even more alluring then he had remembered. He wanted her—every inch of her. He couldn't explain it. Why her? What did she have those other women didn't? What was it that caused his heart to beat differently when he saw her? He had heard all the sordid stories about her past and foul tales about her present, and he didn't care. Touch would never ask her or want her to change. She was probably more woman than he deserved, but he'd never know if he couldn't get her to go out with him.

Touch stood with his hands stuffed in his suit pants pockets and observed the beauty from across the room. He wanted to turn around and go to his room—leave, just as he had done at El Tempo's—but he couldn't. He was risking all his cool points, but he figured no risk, no reward. If she shut him down again, then he would blame it on the alcohol. Apple was at the bar when Touch came up behind her and whispered near her ear.

"Can I buy you a drink?"

Apple turned around to see who had violated her personal space and it was him, the guy from the block party. The man who had quickly lost interest in her when Queenie came through was standing before her. Apple's eyes scanned him quickly—fitted suit pants, Louboutin hard bottoms, and a fresh haircut. Touch was on trend with his full beard and mustache trimmed low. His cologne, Dubai Emerald by Bond No. 9 New York, was one of her favorite scents on men. On him, it was like liquid pheromones.

She finally responded, "It's your money."

"What does the lady drink? Champagne?"

Apple smirked and rolled her eyes. "Bor-ing." She did drink champagne, actually loved an expensive bottle, but it was fun torturing him. She wanted him to work for it—earn her time.

Touch needed no time to contemplate his order. He waved the bartender over.

"Let me have two ginger beers and two shots of whiskey."

Apple crinkled her nose at his drink choices.

He saw her face and said, "Trust me."

His sleepy eyes almost lulled her into a trance, hypnotizing her to let her guard down. When the drinks came, Touch poured the shot of whiskey into the large glass of ginger beer and handed it to Apple. "Ladies first."

Apple took a sip, and surprisingly, it was so good. She grinned her approval, and he liked the way her top lip stretched across her perfect, white teeth. Within minutes she was seemingly different than the stuck-up, distant woman he had met at Harlem Week.

"It's good, right?"

"Very," Apple said.

"What brings you to Atlantic City?" he asked.

Apple was in South Jersey because she was summoned by Kiqué Helguero, who had given her the Manhattan and Bronx territories. Apple and Kiqué had a few formal sit-downs and he broke down the particulars, which included a lot of threats of what would happen should she not meet his expectations. It was all monotonous to Apple, and she was more than beleaguered by his commands and demands, but he had that good shit, so she obliged. When Apple and her crew left the meeting this time, it was late, so Hood suggested they stay overnight in Atlantic City and drive home in the morning. The foursome spent hours gambling until Hood and IG hooked up with some women and went to their rooms to fuck. Tokyo went to her room too; she wanted to watch television since she didn't have cable at home.

Apple still had some energy to burn off, so she ended up at the bar, which was where Touch had found her. There wasn't any way she would speak of her business dealings, so she said, "I'm here for the same reason as everyone else."

"And that is?"

"To gamble away my daughter's college tuition."

"You think everyone here is here to gamble?"

Apple didn't care why people were there. She was just making small talk in an attempt to curb her smart mouth. After Touch ignored her at Kiqué's party, she figured that she should be a little nicer this go around. "Well, why are *you* here?"

Touch cocked his head to one side, and with a burst of nervous laughter he said, "To gamble."

Apple chuckled.

"You don't have an addiction, do you? You are in Atlantic City at two in the morning."

"So are you," she pointed out.

"True," he said. "But, this is what I do for a living. I play poker, and I do it guilt-free because I don't have kids to lose their college tuition."

"Are you any good?"

"I am," he said thoughtfully. Apple was impressed that he seemed like he was stating a fact and not leading with his ego.

"So, Apple, I have to admit that I've thought about you since Harlem Week when you shut me down. I want to get to know you."

"Not much to know," she said evasively.

"You have a man?"

"No."

His eyes were like lie detectors searching for her truth. "How long you been single?"

"A while." Apple took another sip of her drink. She didn't like where this conversation was heading, but he didn't seem to pick up on her discomfort.

Touch thought about that. "Oh, you're celibate? I understand if you want to take it slow."

"I'm not celibate," Apple snapped. She didn't like the way women used that word, almost from a manipulative angle. That Steve-Harvey-wait-ninety-days wasn't who she'd ever been. Apple fucked who and when she wanted, and right now she didn't want to fuck him. "And what am I missing here? Take what slow? We don't have shit going on."

Her response made him a little jealous. She had a nigga sharing her bed that she wasn't claiming. "Then keep me in the friend zone until I can earn more."

His voice was calm and self-assured, and Apple realized her outburst didn't unsettle him at all. Sometimes she could be too sensitive, too emotional, or too explosive for no reason. She needed to chill. Apple stared at the poker player with the smoldering sleepy eyes, deep baritone voice, and athletic body and knew he was a heartbreaker. His skin was flawless, his lips were juicy, and his hands were enormous. Apple eyes scanned him up and down once again and—hold up—did she see a dick print in his fitted slacks? She sucked her bottom lip in between her teeth and then bit down as her mind went places it hadn't gone in a while.

As he and Apple sipped slowly, it was as if everyone around them had disappeared. There was an intensity in his eyes she hadn't noticed during their first encounter. He had a way of making her feel like she was the only person that mattered when she spoke, like he was dialed in to every word.

She finally answered his "friend zone" proposition. "A'ight. That's fair."

"I wanna see you again. Can I take you out?"

Apple was a woman, so she was entitled to change her mind. She no longer wanted to keep this platonic. "You can take me to your room."

Touch nodded. They finished their drinks and walked silently to his room, exchanging flirty glances the whole way there.

As soon as they entered his suite, Touch couldn't help but wonder how Apple would take being asked to leave his room in a few hours. He decided that he'd deal with it when that time came. Apple stood before him and began peeling off her clothes. He wanted to help, but she took a step back and continued to unbutton her blouse to reveal a lacy bra and a flat stomach. Her belly button was pierced, and an apple charm dangled seductively from it. Slowly, she unzipped her pencil skirt and stepped out of it and stood before him in her bra, thong panties, and heels. Her French-vanilla colored body was perfectly toned, curvy, and thick in all the right places.

Apple had turned him on with her striptease, and he wanted more. "Take off your bra and panties and leave your heels on," he whispered.

She complied. Touch undressed quickly and tried to hide his penis with his hand, but it wasn't easy to conceal. He expected a reaction from her like all the previous women about how large he was, but she said nothing. Instead, she crawled onto the bed and then flipped over to lie on her back.

Touch went down low, sucking on her pussy and gliding his tongue against her fat clit, enjoying the way she tasted.

Apple wrapped her curvy thighs around him and began to grind her hips, expressing her pleasure. "Ooooh, fuck," she moaned, biting her bottom lip.

Touch's tongue slid deep inside her, causing waves of pleasure to wash over her. She had made a wise choice. He licked and nibbled on her sensitive button and felt her body shudder, her moans turning him on. Touch slid his fingers inside her wet hole, causing her body to buck. He used his lips and tongue on her wet clit as her body moved to its own rhythm. Touch wanted her to explode in his mouth.

"Aaaaah, please, don't stop. Ummm, hmmm . . . ooooh, don't stop. Right there." Apple grabbed his head and held it to her neatly waxed mound, not allowing him to move at all. Apple exploded, her wetness dripping on his tongue as he continued to taste her juices.

"You like that?" he asked, and Apple moaned her approval. Touch began moving north with soft, wet kisses on her stomach, making his way to her breasts. His tongue flicked on her dime sized nipples until they were both erect. Touch rose up and reached for a condom from off the nightstand. He rolled the Magnum back onto his massive length and girth and looked into Apple's eyes to make sure she was okay with what he had to offer. She noticed that he had hesitated, so she opened her legs wider, giving him an invitation to fuck the shit out of her. Touch was ready to feel her, to enter her and see if they had a connection. He pushed the mushroom tip of his dick in her pussy, and they both cried out. Apple closed her eyes and began grinding her hips, and he slowly inched his way inside. Her pussy gripped his dick as her nails dug into his skin.

"Oh, shit," she purred.

"You want more?" he whispered.

Apple nodded.

"Say it," Touch coaxed. "Say you want more."

"Fuck," Apple murmured. "I want more . . ."

Touch got into a slow and steady rhythm, opening up her tight, deep cave with his girth.

With her eyes closed, Apple purred her approval, as her legs tightened around his waist. Apple knew he was holding back and whispered, "Now fuck me."

Touch placed Apple's legs up over his shoulders and began thrusting himself in between her open legs, allowing his full length to hit the back of her cervix over and over again. Touch could feel he was about to erupt. He opened his eyes and saw a glimpse of Apple's pleasure faces and fell in love. With each deep penetration, Touch felt his orgasm bubbling up, ready to be released. Apple cooed beneath him, her pussy pulsing nonstop around his thick dick. She, too, felt her orgasm brewing.

They came simultaneously as Touch collapsed on top of Apple. He lay inside of her totally spent before finally pulling out. Both drifted off into a much-needed sleep. Touch woke a couple hours later, and Apple was gone, leaving her cell number on a napkin. Cute.

16

The potent *Queen of New York* heroin had spread like a virus in impoverished areas of the city but had mainly infiltrated the South Bronx community. The effects of those addicted had quadrupled in numbers seemingly overnight. Former recreational users were now full-blown dope fiends with a thirst that couldn't be satiated from a bag or two. New users were holed up in their apartments for weeks, only coming out to make drug runs or commit crimes to pay for their habits. Corner stoops were littered with men and women engaging in the obligatory drug-fiend-lean, a slow head nod that took you from ninety to a forty-five-degree angle and back without ever toppling over. There were overdoses running rampant throughout the city; young or old, rich or poor, black or white, heroin wasn't a selective drug when choosing its victims. Anyone with a pulse would do. The brown tar-like substance didn't discriminate, but it did dominate.

The Range came to an abrupt stop in front of Blue's West Indian restaurant on the lower east side. The driver and passenger doors opened, and two ominous looking men climbed out of the SUV. The rear door subsequently opened, and a third man exited the vehicle. He looked unimpressed by the other two niggas he was with. They escorted him into the restaurant, which was semi-crowded with customers. These three men moved through the eatery, snaked through the kitchen, and eventually ended up in Queenie's office.

Queenie sat behind a modern, white lacquer desk with a tufted leather high-back office chair. Her sharp black fingernails briskly tapped the keyboard to her Mac desktop as she did her best impression of a legit corporate businesswoman. Stone sat in a chair off to the far right fumbling around with his new iPhone. Lord, Rehab, and Philly Jack folded into the small office and waited to be acknowledged.

Queenie glanced up and greeted Philly Jack with a cold, foreboding stare, but her fingers kept their rhythm as she took this opportunity to ignore the man she had summoned. Philly Jack leaned on the wall and propped his left foot against it for support. His wheat-colored Timberland boot would definitely leave an imprint on her clean, white wall, but he gave no fucks.

Two tense minutes went by as three sets of eyes focused intently on Queenie. A deep voice finally boomed through the tat-tat-tat-tat keyboard clacking as Philly Jack announced, "Yo, Queenie, I ain't got all day. What's this about?"

Queenie's brown and blue eyes slowly scanned Philly Jack from his Timbs to his massive mane of dreads. He was arrogant like most hustlers getting money and answered to no one. His crew was expanding, and he was trained under one of the most lethal kingpins Philadelphia had even known, Haitian Fritz. When Fritz's badly decomposing body was found with three gunshot wounds to his face, the streets called for mutiny. Fritz's operation felt that only someone he trusted could have gotten close enough to murder him inside his home. A lot of names were tossed around before finally settling on Jack's. The heat in his hometown had nearly scorched him, so Philly Jack made his way north. Queenie didn't like him. He was a man who could never be number two.

"Philly, where you been, nigga?"

"I been doin' me," he said and rubbed his chin.

"So you out the game?" asked Queenie. "Is that why you stopped buying my product?"

"I came here out of respect, but I ain't on your payroll nor are we partners! I stopped copping from you 'cause there's a better product out on these streets that moves quicker. I'm a businessman, not your bitch. Don't ever fuckin' summon me again."

Queenie would overlook his disrespect because he had the information she needed, also because Philly Jack was Crips and Bloods affiliated. He got mad love from both sides, so if he were murdered, there would be retribution.

Queenie wasn't here for his slick mouth, though. She looked to Lord, and he subtly shook his head. Lord was always levelheaded when it came to putting his murder game down. He thought eight steps ahead of Queenie, as she was reactionary.

"Who's your new distributor?"

"That high-yellow Harlem broad, Apple. She got that good shit those fiends going crazy over. Her shit 98% pure." Greed danced in his eyes as his brain recalled how quickly the dope was moving. He needed to re-up every three days, which was the fastest turnaround he had ever known. "She don't be stepping on her shit."

Queenie's heroin was 90% pure, but that was before she stepped on it a couple times being greedy. By the time her product made it to her customers, it was about 65%, if that.

"That stick-up bitch is selling heroin?"

"*Queen of New York* is her stamp. It's red lettering with a crown over the city. These fuckin' fiends can't get enough of it. I'm surprised you haven't heard about it. You got competition."

"What the fuck are you talkin' about, '*Queen of New York*'?" Queenie looked at Lord and asked, "Lord, what the fuck is he talkin' about? Have you heard about this?"

He responded, "Nah, but makes sense. Apple was at Kiqué's party. I told you to find out why she was there."

Queenie frowned. "And mi told you to get that bitch thrown out," she replied with conviction. "The next time mi ask you to do something, you fuckin' do it!"

Lord didn't respond. Sometimes he questioned Queenie's rise to the top because she lacked restraint, forethought, and an ability to be calculating before delegating. She was deadly and odd—a woman who had killed her way to the top—but he knew that she wasn't thinking about staying there. To Lord, Queenie was thinking small, like an amateur with no mind for expansion. He had tried to warn her to question Apple's attendance at Kiqué's birthday celebration. Lord assumed that her presence meant Apple had ties to the Bolivian cartel, but now it was clear that Kiqué was her connect and that was why the Helguero cartel refused to do business with the L.E.S. Crips and give Queenie the Manhattan and Bronx territories. Queenie's connect was Diego Guzmàn, who ran a small fraction of the Los Zetas cartel. His heroin was good, but Queenie wanted the best; she wanted Kiqué.

Philly Jack didn't know how a man with Lord's pedigree would ever allow this weird little bitch to speak to him as she did. Philly Jack turned his fitted from the front to the back and got serious. He used his foot to push him off of the wall and took a couple steps forward while adjusting his jeans that hung dangerously low, exposing his Versace boxers. He said two words, "I'm out."

All men exchanged daps as Philly Jack exited. He'd find his own way back home. Queenie and her henchmen obviously had pressing issues to sort through.

Queen of New York embodied the zeitgeist of the eighties era that addicts didn't realize that they were nostalgic for until Apple brought it to their front door. This feat, although abhorrent, was something that Queenie hadn't accomplished.

Queenie spoke, "I thought my business's infrastructure was built on solid ground—that it was unfuckwitable, but now mi hear this? Are we not L.E.S. Crips?"

It was a rhetorical question, but one she needed to answer. For years, Queenie and her team went unchallenged. They had murdered many during her rise to the top, and then the violence greatly diminished. Those that were killed were usually drug mules or insignificant corner boys. Now she was going up against a boss, someone who had paved inroads into enemy territory and lived. Apple was flagrant and abrasive, but so was she. The audacity of Apple to put Queenie's moniker on a new product and flood the streets spoke too loudly to her soul. It said, "I don't fear you! You are nothing!" Queenie felt like this was a stickup, like she was being robbed in broad daylight, and the event was being streamed live on Facebook. She was humiliated but couldn't show it. Queenie wanted bloodshed. She'd come too far for some clandestine organization to creep up from behind and try to take over what she put her blood, sweat, and tears into. Queenie put in work to ensure her reputation was solid—that she was feared. *She* was the Queen of New York—no one else.

Queenie needed to shake shit up, keep her men on their toes. Lord wasn't earning his title as her right hand, neglecting all the requirements that title came with. She wasn't selling hand-to-hand on corners or hugging the blocks. Queenie was running a multi-million-dollar drug operation with a few legal businesses she oversaw. Between that and always looking over her shoulder and trying to have a personal life, she knew she couldn't do everything. What good was paying Lord to keep his ears to the streets if he didn't? It was Queenie who recognized that her clientele had fallen back. Had she not requested today's meeting, she would still be in the dark about *Queen of New York*. Lord's insubordination was an executable offense.

Queenie began rapping "Notorious Thugs" lyrics about buying and cooking coke. The melody and beat were off, but they listened intently.

Lord and Rehab knew the lyrics to Notorious BIG's hit song, but they were perplexed as to why Queenie was rapping in the middle of a meeting. It was random.

"What's that supposed to mean?" Lord asked.

"It means that if mi have to do everything to keep my business running—shit that you get paid for—then basically mi don't need you, now do I? I should just pay myself to keep my ears to the streets, murder Apple, and also vet our buyers as to why our product isn't selling. Isn't that right, Lord? In between my meetings with connects, drug mules, kingpins, hustlers, and keeping our legitimate holdings above board, should Queenie also do Lord's job?"

The fact that she spoke about herself in the third person and spoke as if he wasn't in the room was quite disturbing. Lord said, "A'ight, I heard you. We can move on now. I said I'm on it."

His tone triggered something insatiable inside her: her thirst to kill. Queenie stood up and walked around her desk; her heels click-clacked on the dull wood floors. She sat catty-corner on the edge of her desk and allowed one foot to dangle, and the other was planted firmly on the ground. One hand was placed on her thigh, and the other rested close to her waist where a .45 was snugly held.

Queenie's goons recognized the murderous look in her eyes, a look that she had when she had earned her first tattooed teardrop at fourteen. Queenie had dropped several bodies since then, and she was wise enough to know that if she added a teardrop for each kill, then she would no longer have a recognizable face, and she was too pretty to be inked up to that degree.

Rehab took a couple steps toward his boss because he felt that at any second she would drop Lord where he stood, and he wanted no blood splatter to get on his new Yeezys. Lord drew in a sharp breath and recoiled. He removed the bass, sarcasm, and pure disdain from his voice. Rehab and Stone stood protectively near Queenie, their cold stares aimed at Lord. Their trigger hands rested near their waists too as body language shifted from friend to foe.

Lord was in survival mode when he said, "You got every right to feel that I fucked up. I should have known about *Queen of New York*, but I'll shut it down. Kill all her runners, goons, Hood and IG, and I'll personally bring her to your door alive so you can do you."

Queenie was unimpressed. It was too little a little too late. However, she still needed him, so his life would be spared today.

"Rehab, you're in charge. You're my number-two. Get shit done."

The demotion almost felt worse than what he expected a shot to his head would feel like. Lord gritted his teeth and looked firmly into Rehab's eyes. He didn't want it. He wasn't ready. Lord steeled himself to accept the disrespect so he could live until he was willing to exact his revenge.

Queenie's orders were unequivocal. "We gotta shut this shit down, cabrón."

Her men nodded.

"But in the meantime, mi have a plan of my own."

"I'm listening," Rehab replied.

"I want our peoples to replicate the stamp of *Queen of New York*. Make our stamp blue and we flood the streets with our own product in their name. We'll sell a good product at half the cost of the original stamp. Drive her sales down," she remarked. "And don't step on our product for now. Once her sales start dwindling with the Helguero cartel, they'll go looking for a new distributor. Kiqué will come crawling to me to start moving his heroin, and we'll be ready."

Rehab smiled. Queenie was smart and ruthless, one of the many reasons she was respected, he killed for her, and he followed her lead.

17

The money was flooding in. It felt like the levees had broken in Louisiana and Apple's Hurricane Katrina was named *Queen of New York*. The cocaine from the Mingo cartel was doing exceptionally well, as anticipated. But the heroin was doing numbers they hadn't expected. Crackheads were morphing into dope heads, and the two-step crackhead dance was replaced with the obligatory dope-fiend-lean. Shit was crazy.

Hood came out of his project apartment with his Louis Vuitton knapsack stuffed with cash. He, IG, and Tokyo were about to ball out of control; make it rain down those hood trappings that every drug hustler chased. Hood had on a pair of army fatigue pants, Timbs, and a new *I'm Allergic to Broke* hoodie—no jacket. His .45 was tucked in his waist, and he walked like a new nigga with new money.

IG and Tokyo were in the lobby waiting on him with their own knapsacks.

"Damn, nigga, we been waiting down here for a minute," IG complained. "Who you gettin' pretty for?"

"You know I stay fresh."

Everyone gave daps and loaded into his SUV. "So what's our first stop?"

Tokyo's stomach was doing somersaults. She had nearly fifty thousand dollars on her person, and she couldn't be more grateful to Hood and IG for vouching for her. They always treated her like a little sister, and because of them, she finally got out from under the oppressive environment she was in. Tokyo could do or buy whatever her heart desired, and it felt fucking great. She spoke, "Let's go to the Diamond District first and get that out the way, and then we can hit Northern Boulevard."

Both men nodded.

Joseph knew a drug dealer when he saw one, and these three individuals were about to make his slow-moving morning more profitable. He greeted them with warm smiles and respect as they approached his booth. He had two goals: the first was to not allow them to walk away to his competition, and the second was making a sale.

"Hello, my friends," he announced grandly as if they were lifelong customers. "What can I help you with today?"

All three were already eyeing the expensive showpieces inside the display cases. Everything was beautiful under the fluorescent lighting. The dazzling diamonds mesmerized anyone who dared lay eyes on them, hypnotizing potential customers to spend all of their money no matter the consequences.

IG looked at the Hasidic Jewish man with his yarmulke and curly sideburns and smiled back. "We wanna look at some watches."

Joseph didn't even have to ask which brand. He jiggled the keys on his massive key ring and went straight to the men's Rolex watches. He pulled out a case that held eight gold and platinum watches and beamed. Both Hood and IG rolled up their sleeves. This was a dream come true, the ultimate initiation into the big-boys club. They had finally made it.

Hood and IG both picked out gold watches flooded with diamonds. Joseph carefully placed watches on the men's wrists and began to sell.

"These here watches represents status—they're showstoppers," Joseph said. "You won't find anyone else in the city with either one of these watches."

Hood wanted clarification. "No one got these joints?"

"No, sir," he lied. "Rolex is a premium company. They made these one-of-a-kind watches for only the most elite customers."

Both Hood and IG beamed. IG was already sold, but he liked hearing the history of the watches so he could repeat it to any and everyone he would come into contact with.

"Yo, how much?" Hood asked.

Joseph paused for dramatic purposes. He'd been at this a long time and knew how to play these naive fools. "Are you both going to buy these?"

They got amped, looking for a deal. "Yeah, and she gonna buy a watch too," Hood replied.

Joseph eyed the young woman in her catsuit and smiled pleasantly. He exhaled. "Okay, then I could let these go for one hundred thousand each. And that's only if it's cash."

Hood felt that was too high. "Nah, man. We spending a lot of money wit' you. You gotta come better than that."

Joseph scratched his head and pretended to be flustered. "She's buying a watch too?"

Tokyo spoke up. "Yeah, but I don't have as much money as them. I can't go over twenty stacks."

"Okay, if she's going to spend twenty thousand, then I can let these go for ninety apiece, essentially giving the beautiful lady her watch for free."

It went over everyone's head that Joseph knew what twenty stacks translated to. But he was well-versed in street vernacular.

"Done," IG said, but Hood wasn't done negotiating. He didn't want to seem petty, but IG had made them look thirsty. He shot IG a hard scowl, but IG didn't care. There wasn't any way he was removing the Rolex from his wrist; the bling, weight, and an aqua-blue crystal was every hustler's dream.

It was now Tokyo's turn. She picked out a gold presidential Rolex with a salmon-colored crystal and diamond bezel. The eighteen-carat gold against her dark-brown complexion popped. And within seconds she cried tears of happiness.

"What the fuck?" Hood said. "What's wrong?"

"Nah, I'm just so happy. It's something I always wanted."

Now both IG and Tokyo had Hood looking stupid. He looked at Joseph and said, "Pardon us for a moment."

He walked IG and Tokyo a few feet away with Joseph eyeing them intently. The watches weren't paid for yet. Hood said, "Yo, I can't take y'all anywhere. Y'all actin' like y'all ain't used to shit. You cryin' in front of this cracker! All this money we 'bout to spend in here, he should be the one fuckin' cryin'! From here on out, let me do the talkin'. Shut the fuck up if y'all know what's really good."

The trio walked back to the case and Hood and IG wanted to see the diamond chains. They wanted chains that hung as far south as possible. Whatever Joseph had that rested not too far from their dicks was what they wanted times two. As he threatened, Hood did the negotiating. No drug dealer's makeover was complete without diamond earrings, so Joseph suggested they peruse his vast selection. IG passed. He wasn't into men wearing earrings, and his ears weren't even pierced, but Hood was ready.

Tokyo's eyes yearned for a pair, but she had something more important to do with her money, which was buying a whip. Her pitiful look didn't go unnoticed by her big bros, so they chipped in and bought her a five-carat pair to ball out in. She wanted to cry her appreciation but chilled this time. Overall, they spent a grand total of $520,000 with Joseph. It was more than double what an average consumer would have been charged. But what did they know?

They pulled up to the used car dealership stuntin'. Their newly purchased bling had all their heads swollen. They had money, and they wanted everyone to know this. The buffet of luxury vehicles on the lot had them salivating. They almost didn't know where to begin. Should they test drive an Audi? Does the CLS 400 speak to niggas? Or, is the Range more practical in their line of work?

The overweight car salesman did a rushed trot over to the potential buyers before any of his coworkers got wind there were drug dealers on their lot. This trio stunk of cash buyers from a mile away. George greeted them with a wide, toothy grin. His cheap suit was ill-fitting, and his sensible shoes leaned despite his making a good salary each year. George's money was poured into the large home he'd purchased in Amityville on the water and his most prized possession, his boat named *Kick Rocks*.

Introductions were made, and George summed up who he felt they were. He walked Hood and IG over to two custom Range Rovers just off lease with hardly any miles on them. He showed Tokyo a Lexus. It was sleek and sexy. When they all rejected his choices, he was visibly surprised. Perspiration trickled down the sides of his cheeks because there were ten other dealerships in the three-block radius.

He walked IG and Hood toward more exotic cars—an Audi R8 and Maserati—and he showed Tokyo a convertible BMW M8. It took hours of test driving before Hood, IG, and Tokyo ultimately settled on his first choices. He would be remiss if he didn't feel the small sting of aggravation.

Hood traded in his old SUV and jumped in his new black Range. IG exited in his white Range, while Tokyo drove off the lot in her very own midnight blue Lexus. She was a bad bitch.

18

Blue's West Indian restaurant was a trendy spot for dining and takeout. The Jamaican cooks worked their magic in the kitchen, creating authentic dishes the locals craved. Some of the most popular dishes were the beef patties with coco bread or oxtails with rice and sweet plantains. The décor was average, hardly on par with the owner's net worth or the substantial amount of money she laundered through her books. The walls were covered with outdated wallpaper of scenic areas in Jamaica, and the wooden tables and chairs had names, penises, or gang signs carved into them. The flooring was ceramic tile, and the tan grout lines were so dirty they now were jet black. The ceiling fans circulated hot, dry air from the kitchen, so the front doors were usually left open during warm months, which invited flies to enter and have a meal too. Yet, it was always packed. There was dining indoors and outdoors, and during summer months it was a local hangout for gang members.

Queenie's men, those who loved West Indian food, ate there at least twice a day. They were street dudes, so going home for lunch and dinner wasn't in their DNA. There was too much money to make, drug territory to infiltrate, and bitches to conquer to worry about eating from the basic five food groups. It was either Blue's where they all ate for free, a Chinese restaurant, or Popeye's chicken.

Rehab and Lord were eating at an interior table. Seven of their men sat outside, low-key, trying to blend in with customers and not wanting to attract any heat from the police cruiser that had just circled the block.

"Fuck they came around twice for?" one L.E.S. gang member asked another.

"How the fuck I know?" he responded.

"You think we should go and tell Rehab?"

"Tell that nigga what? That five-oh was here but now they not? You's a paranoid muthafucka! Those pigs don't want it. They know what it is," he said confidently and made a few hand gestures repping his gang affiliation.

Rehab and Lord were enjoying their meal. Both men were smacking their lips and licking the gravy off of their fingertips, but Rehab felt the tension. Things weren't the same between the childhood friends once Lord was demoted. Rehab deduced that Lord felt threatened by his new status. Lord craved power; he needed to be the head nigga in charge, and being third in line to the throne had him vexed. Lately, if Rehab mowed down two enemies, Lord had to body six. He had to prove to everyone watching he was a heartless killer who gave no fucks. Lord wanted to be seen as the Shawn Carter of the group and he wanted Queenie to be viewed as Dame Dash, so if the Kanye Wests of the organization ever had to pick a side, they would unequivocally choose him.

Since he'd been with her crew, Lord knew Queenie was a ticking time bomb. Early on, he had tried to save her from herself. He wanted to avoid war so he would have time to fulfill his agenda, which was getting on a first-name basis with most of the cartel. He figured when it was his time to advance, he would have planted the seeds so he'd be able to step right in as head of the L.E.S. Crips.

Rehab drained a bottle of carrot juice and said, "Yo, our numbers are dwindling 'cause of that bloodsucking bitch Apple and her meddling. I'm lookin' in to doing something innovative and contacting Big Meech for an assist."

Lord eyed Rehab with a frown. Rehab was an airhead to him, and Lord hated dumb fucks with a passion. Big Meech was the head of the Uptown Bloods—their archenemies. Involving them wasn't innovative; it was reckless and would make them look weak. Lord knew that Rehab was trying to fill his shoes—use brains and not brute force to impress Queenie.

"Oh, word?" Lord said. He never looked up as he scraped the peas and rice from his plate.

"What? You don't think that's a good idea?"

Lord shrugged. "I didn't say shit. It's your call, homie."

Rehab hated his cavalier responses. "I mean, we sit back and let the Bloods do all our work while we continue to get this money. Apple won't see them comin'." Even as he explained it, Rehab couldn't understand why he needed Lord to cosign. It was like he was a kid again looking for his daddy's approval.

"A'ight," Lord said dismissively, hoping that Rehab would just drop it.

"You and me on the same team—"

"Rehab, I ain't your consigliere! Play ya position—" Before Lord could complete his sentence, the distinctive sound of a gunshot rang out.

Bak!

Outside, one of their goons was hit by a bullet. And then a hail of gunfire erupted.

Bak! Bak! Bak! Bak! Bak!

Pop! Pop! Pop!

"What the fuck!" Rehab screamed, going into battle mode.

Lord's head was on a quick swivel as he reached for the Glock 19 he had on him. The gunfire sounded like it was coming from everywhere as patrons, bystanders, and gang members all scattered. The high-pitched, deafening screams of those shot clashed with the succinct, loud noises from the automatic weapons. Absolute terror was coming from the staff and patrons, growing fears that were laden with worry and the uncertainty of impending death.

Apple, Hood, and IG charged forward, meticulously aiming for any live body patronizing the establishment. This ambush was calculated, all designed to bring the heat from local authorities to Queenie's front door. Apple needed Queenie distracted by trying to keep up the façade that Blue's was a legitimate establishment. L.E.S. Crips shot back, and the scene abruptly transitioned into an all-out gunfight.

Pop! Pop! Pop!

Boom! Boom! Boom!

Bak! Bak! Bak! Bak! Bak!

Tables were overturned, and chairs were broken in the melee. Apple thought she had Lord cornered in a losing position, crouched near a table reloading his clip. Apple's aim was center mass, but then he sprung forward and pushed a patron in front of his body to absorb bullets meant for him and then took off running. Lord dived between two parked cars for cover using a drop-and-roll technique. He was agile and hard to kill. Lord quickly recovered his bearings and shot back at Apple, bullets narrowly missing her vital organs.

IG and Hood tried gunning for Rehab. They wanted his murder to be payback for the attempted hit on Apple, but Rehab was protected. One of Rehab's triggermen became a barrier between his second-in-command and Apple's henchmen. He was fiercely firing their way, ready to die. Both running low on ammunition, Hood and IG had to retreat.

Apple wanted more death and destruction but knew that the window of opportunity had closed. Her bloody message would be like a postcard to Queenie that they were coming for her, and it would definitely make the news. Before retreating, Apple took one last look at Blue's. The restaurant now looked like Swiss cheese for a mousy looking bitch.

Blue's had turned into the Wild West. The shootout left four L.E.S. gang members dead, but the innocent bystanders and patrons weren't so blessed. At least nine were gunned down, and five were seriously injured in the senseless act of violence in and around the shabby eatery. Uniforms and detectives descended onto the scene, collecting evidence and questioning eyewitnesses. The assailants had gotten away. The city was going to hell in a hand basket with all of the recent gang stabbings and shootings. There was a rise in petty larceny and misdemeanor crimes committed by heroin and cocaine addicts, and the reemergence of The Huntsman wasn't helping the situation.

None of the recent crimes seemed connected. They happened in different jurisdictional areas of Manhattan and the Bronx, but the boroughs were suffering overall.

Lord and Rehab arrived at Queenie's posh building within seconds of each other. Both hoodlums were amped up off pure adrenaline, the type of high that only all-out warfare could produce. Blue's was Queenie's baby, and they were there to tell her that it was dead. Queenie was annoyed that they were at her front door unannounced, but she moved to the side to allow them entry.

"Who died?" Queenie asked.

"Lil' Roc, Lil' Mo, Rodney, and Manny," Lord said. "That Apple bitch came at us!"

"I figured she would," Queenie said with a giggle. "Rehab, make arrangements to pay for their funerals."

Lord was annoyed that she hadn't addressed him. "What's so funny?"

"We're even now. Mi came at Apple once, she came at me once." Queenie took her index finger and made invisible checkmarks in the air.

"The next time we go at her, she's dead. It's a mathematical equation. We are in favor with the gods."

"What are you talking about?" Lord barked. "Gods and numbers and shit. Our men are dead, Queenie. Dead! And speaking of numbers, you went after her twice, so that means she owes you one."

Queenie knew Lord's outburst was predicated upon her placing him lower in the pecking order. It was such a basic strategy that she thought someone as cerebral as he claimed to be would pick up on it, but each time he played right into her hands. Inside she was cracking up at his heavy scowl and shifty eyes, but disrespect was disrespect.

Queenie clicked her switch and turned dark. "Don't ever speak to mi like that again, puta!" At that moment, Stone came from out of the back bedroom, adjusting his jeans. Rehab and Lord looked sickened by the thought of them fucking. Stone gave them daps and then joined the conversation.

"Now what had happened?" Stone asked.

Rehab smirked. Just because Stone was fucking their boss didn't mean he had to answer to him. He addressed Queenie. "There's more. The shootout took place at Blue's. It's bad—a lot of causalities. Five-oh ain't gonna let this shit go."

Queenie became irate and transitioned into full Trinidadian patois. She stormed around her luxury apartment, screaming and throwing shit at walls. She screamed, "I want ah murda! Murda dem all! Badras bummboclaat kill 'em all tonight! Kill Hood and IG, 'em pussyclaaat's sweet like sugar!"

She screamed at everyone, including Stone, like she was a mad woman. She thundered, "This is your fault, Lord!"

"How you figure that?"

Queenie thought for a second. Visions of her beloved being violated in the horrific way that chaos, bullets, and shooters could accomplish had her sick. Blue's didn't look like much, but that was intentional. Some of the best dishes were made in dumps, and now she had nothing. Sure she could rebuild, remodel, and patch up the holes, but it would just be a replacement—the second child after your firstborn dies.

Queenie cleared her throat and spit phlegm on to Rehab's throwback Adidas sneaker. "This your fault! Mi left you in charge, niggah, and you couldn't hold Blue's down?"

"C'mon now, Queenie. Chill. I got this shit under control." Rehab felt disrespected, but it was better than what had happened to Killer Mike. "She not gonna get a second chance to get at us. We on it."

19

Apple stared at Hood resolutely and asked him, "What's the problem?"

Hood tossed her a few heroin packages stamped with the *Queen of New York* logo. There was one problem, though. The stamp was blue.

"Someone's been using our trademark and selling it on the streets, profiting from our name," Hood said.

The news was upsetting, and Apple immediately knew Queenie was behind the infringement. "That bitch got fuckin' balls."

"What you want us to do about it?" Hood asked.

Apple stared at the phony package in her hand and thought about it. They all were waiting for her reply.

"Is it any good?" she wanted to know.

"It's 90% pure for half the price. The fiends can't really tell the difference. Everyone is now asking for *Queen of New York* with the blue stamp, not the red."

Queenie was turning out to be a worthy adversary. The younger woman with the unique look, unconventional business habits, and questionable sanity actually knew how to problem solve. Apple was impressed if not shocked. She looked at Hood and IG, and their faces were frozen in scowls. Queenie was taking money out of their mouths. Both had signed on under Apple's tutelage, but she was taking a huge risk by not plugging a hole that was leaking. Apple had shared that Queenie had come after her twice, but now she was interfering in their business.

Hardheartedly, she locked eyes with her lieutenants and said to them, "Let her keep that stamp. If she wants to infringe on my brand and take our customers, then we'll make sure that she has fewer customers to steal."

IG asked, "How? You know fiends ain't loyal."

"Cut the heroin with fentanyl."

"The pure heroin mixed with fentanyl will be a lethal dose for most fiends. They won't be able to handle the product. Dead dope heads will put us out of business."

"It'll put *her* out of business. Use the blue stamp and flood the streets," she ordered. "Our *Queen of New York* is dead. Make a new stamp and call it, *Kiss the Ring*. That should get that bitch's attention."

"You already got her attention, and it's bad for business," IG assessed. "If no one else is gonna speak up, then I will. Innocent people shouldn't be the casualties of you and Queenie's war. Fiends or not, they're still human beings."

IG was taking it personally because his mother was addicted to drugs, and he watched it wreak havoc on her mind and body. She was addicted to crack not heroin, but he still felt some kind of way. What if the dope boys sold his mother contaminated crack vials just to settle some silly presumed disrespect between two females going to war over a sideways look?

"Do I look like I give a fuck!" Apple shouted.

"That's crazy—you gonna have bodies dropping all over the city," IG continued to counsel her.

"IG, I'm not gonna repeat myself. What you won't do another will. Choose, nigga!"

IG looked at Hood and realized he didn't have his back. Hood stood stonefaced and erect like a yes-nigga.

Apple glared at her crew and coldheartedly uttered the words, "Get it fuckin' done."

What they purchased from the young dealer was worth more than platinum and gold to the two young fiends in the Bronx project. With *Queen of New York* in their grasp, they would shoot up somewhere private and find themselves in paradise. Yes, paradise. They were ready to fly a mile high and have out-of-body experiences. Heroin made them feel like they were on top of the world. For several years it'd become their escape. It made their pain go away—an injection into their bloodstream that made their minds go numb and a euphoria that cost ten dollars a bag. The rush of dopamine flooding the brain instantly gave the user an intense amount of pleasure. Heroin was better than sex for many, and *Queen of New York* was the Ferrari of heroin.

The two fiends, one female and one male, hurriedly walked away from the street dealer and headed for the Soundview projects. The two fiends hastily found isolation and seclusion inside the project stairway, between the third and fourth floors. Huddled against each other on the concrete stairs, they started their process. The heroin was placed into a spoon and heated up with a cigarette lighter. The powder form soon transitioned into liquid and bubbled under the flame. The female was the first to tie a shoelace around her upper arm to cause her vein to bulge. She then took the syringe and drew the liquid heroin from the spoon and injected the poison into her arm. With the product now flowing through her system, she needed only to sit back and allow its effect to work on her like it always did. She untied the shoelace from around her arm and handed it to her male partner. He was next. He mirrored her same actions, injecting the poison into his bloodstream.

For a moment, they felt peace, and they felt near ecstasy. And then it happened. Something was wrong. The female reacted first. Her skin got very pale right before her breathing became shallow. Soon she was struggling to pull air through her nose. Her pulse grew weak as her blood pressure dropped. She was disoriented and drowsy as she sat on the concrete stairs.

"This shit got me . . ." She couldn't finish her sentence. Her eyelids slowly lowered and she went into a full-on dope-fiend-lean that was interrupted when her body thrust into a violent seizure. Her body jerked uncontrollably, each limb moving in different directions, slamming against the concrete with hard thrusts. Her mouth foamed as her eyes rolled back in her head. The pain she felt was incomprehensible as her insides felt like they had been doused in gasoline and ignited. The female wanted it to stop; she took heroin to take away her pain, not induce it.

The male user was horrified by the scene. Her movements were blowing his high. He tried to scurry away so he could enjoy his dope in peace, but then he, too, fell ill. His violent seizure was only moments away. His body slammed against the wall before jerking a few times. He went tumbling down the concrete stairs, hitting his head several times on his way down. His skull split open down to the white meat, but that wouldn't be his cause of death. Unknown John and Jane Doe died on the scene from lethal doses of a street drug called *Queen of New York*.

A week later, three fiends died from hot doses on the lower east side of Manhattan, and a few days after their deaths, two more overdosed on a bad batch near 125th Street. Within weeks, bodies dropped all around Manhattan and the Bronx. The news called it a drug epidemic. Drug users were dropping like flies, from the Lower East Side through Castle Hill. The sudden overdoses of dozens of fiends were setting the culture and the community back three decades.

New York was a state in crisis, and something had to be done. In response to public outcry from Manhattan and Bronx residents, the mayor put together a task force to combat the war on drugs.

20

Touch had texted Apple several times since the night they hooked up, and she never texted him back. He wasn't used to pursuing a woman and had to admit she had him fucked up. The sex was good, real good, and he had a hard time believing that she was getting fucked by someone better than him in bed. So what was it? He wasn't an average looking dude and could pull any woman he pushed up on. Touch had to admit that Apple's platinum pussy had him bugging. He sent one more text, hoping he could get her to respond.

I WANT 2 SEE U IN THE DAYLIGHT. TEXT ME UR ADDRESS. BE READY AT 11. DRESS COMFORTABLE. IF U DON'T REPLY THEN A NIGGA GONNA MOVE ON.

To his delight and surprise, she hit him right back with her address.

Touch didn't want to be too forward by going up to Apple's apartment door. He wasn't ready to see how she lived—if she was nice and nasty, junky, disorganized, or if she had OCD. All those intimate details are best unfolded as feelings grow. He wanted to do things differently with her; take things slow now that they had gotten the sex out of the way. He stood in front of her building and texted her to come downstairs. Ten minutes later she stood before him sexy as ever in a one-piece jumper that hugged her curves and six-inch stilettos. Her hair hung seductively down her back in loose curls, and her face was natural with red lipstick and mascara from Fenty beauty.

"You look gorgeous," he said. "But we're going to have to tweak a few things."

"Excuse me?" Apple said. She looked down at her outfit, which took her hours to settle on after trying on almost half her closet.

He grabbed Apple's hand and walked toward the corner. "Don't worry. I got you."

His hand clasped into hers was different—unfamiliar—but she liked it. Apple allowed herself to be led to what she thought was his vehicle. When they kept walking and turned the corner, she asked, "Where are we going? Where's your car?"

"Do you trust me?"

"I don't trust anyone."

"Fair enough," he replied as they kept walking. "We're going in here." Touch pointed to the sneaker store now just a few feet in front of them.

"What? Why?"

Touch held the door open, and Apple slid into the air-conditioned space that was virtually empty this time of day. The air conditioning was a bit cold for September, but they wouldn't be inside for long. She sat down and looked at Touch's Jordans and figured that he was showing off. He was about to buy himself a pair of kicks; maybe pull out a wad of cash to impress her. She was losing interest fast. Impatiently she asked, "How long is this going to take?" as he perused each aisle.

"Not long at all," he called back. "Have patience, Queen."

That last line put a smile on her face. That nigga recognized her excellence. Apple watched as he chitchatted with a salesperson and then strolled back over to where she was seated. He sat next to her, and she inhaled his cologne. It was a new scent and she liked it.

The female walked over to them with a sneaker box and a pair of white socks in her hands. When she kneeled down, Touch said, "I'll do it."

He took the box and leaned down next to the puzzled Apple.

"What's this?"

Touch was already unbuckling her heel as he explained. "I asked you to dress comfortably because what I have planned is a full day of activities, and I don't want to give you an excuse to leave me—I mean, leave the date—early complaining that your feet hurt."

As he spoke, he admired her beautiful pedicure as he rolled the sock onto her dainty feet. Next, he put on and laced up the old school Pumas. Apple didn't mention this, but she had the same pair. And how was he able to correctly guess her shoe size? Apple wore a woman's size six and a boy's four.

"I could have gone upstairs to change. I do own sneakers . . . You didn't have to do this."

"But I wanted to."

As he placed the second Puma on her foot, she had to admit to herself that this was turning her on. He had captured her interest, and now it seemed as though he would keep it.

Touch placed her heels in the sneaker box and pulled out a C-note to tip the saleswoman. "Hold these for her? She'll pick them up in the morning."

The moment they exited the store, Touch slid his hand into hers, and they were back to strolling the block, hand in hand. Once again, Apple looked for his vehicle and wondered where he would take her. As the subway station grew near she voiced her thoughts.

"Are we taking the train?" She didn't know she came off bougie, but she did.

"We are."

"C'mon, now. My car is literally across the street."

"I'm a man, Apple. Let me do this my way, and if you have a miserable time, then you'll just have to give me a second date to make up for the first one."

He smiled and she did too. *Fuck it*, she thought. There were worse things than New York transit.

Turns out they only rode the train a few stops from SoHo to Midtown. When they got above ground Touch led her to a group of people waiting in a small crowd. Apple was going to ask more questions but allowed things to unfold in real time as opposed to getting ahead of his plans.

"I guess now is a good as time as any to ask if you have a girlfriend." Apple didn't know where that came from. This wasn't her. Even if he did have a special someone, that didn't have anything to do with her. She wondered if she sounded insecure.

"I wouldn't be here if I did."

She nodded.

"Are you spontaneous, Apple? I hope so, 'cause that's me all day."

"It depends. I mean . . . I'm not down for whatever, but I do like to have fun."

Just then, the double-decker bus pulled up, and Apple realized that they were about to go sightseeing around the city. She hated to admit it, but her interest was piqued. Still, she said, "This us?"

"First class everything," he joked.

"Then we better get the best seats!" Apple said and pushed her way through the crowd to ensure they got seats on the top level. Once there, she couldn't describe the excitement she felt. She was a native New Yorker, but the idea of sightseeing was awesome. And, most importantly, it was a first. Usually, a date with a new dude was dinner and maybe a movie and then eventually you fucked.

Once seated, Apple looked over at Touch and just grinned. "I like this," she said.

"The tour hasn't begun yet."

"I know, but I wanna say right now that I'm having an amazing time."

Just as Apple and Touch were connecting, Kola called. Apple promptly sent her to voicemail, and Kola responded by sending her a barrage of angry texts. Kola threatened to beat the shit out of Apple if she didn't come and pick up the kids. Apple shut off her phone, but not before noticing that Touch's jaw tightened. He assumed that the exchange concerned another man.

The sightseeing tour bus was only the first on his list of activities. The second stop was the Empire State Building's observatory, and the last was the Statue of Liberty. Apple couldn't believe that she was born and raised in New York and had never gone to those sights. While on the ferry boat heading toward Ellis Island, Apple got cold. Touch watched as she ran her hands up and down her arms.

"You cold?" he asked.

She nodded.

Without a second thought, Touch pulled his hoodie over his head, leaving only his white t-shirt underneath.

"I can't. Then you'll be cold."

"I'm good. Don't worry about me."

"You sure?"

He was already helping pull the sweatshirt over her head. It nearly swallowed up her petite body, but she instantly felt better. The warmth from the shirt made her feel cozy and safe. Without warning, Touch leaned in and gave her candy apple red lips a quick kiss. Her lips were soft. He pulled Apple in under his strong arm, and she snuggled up close.

When they arrived back at Apple's apartment, she invited him upstairs. She was ready for another sex session, but he declined. He wanted more.

"I'll call you," he said. "Pick up when I do."

21

T ouch was inside his father's rent-controlled apartment in Spanish
   Harlem eating a vegan meal prepared by his father's longtime
partner, Gabriel. Gabriel was tall and lean, and his blond hair with hints
of gray was cropped short. Touch assessed that Gabriel was the feminine
one in the relationship, a replacement for his mother, as Gabriel walked
around the apartment in long, flowing robes and furry slippers and had
effeminate gestures. He was a pretty man by anyone's beauty standards
and had an equally pure heart. Touch was eavesdropping on his father and
Gabriel's conversation from the kitchen.

"I'm disgusted by this. My god, so many people," Gabriel cried out as
he read the daily newspaper. The headline on the front page read: Drug
Overdose Death Toll Continues to Soar.

Gabriel and Jorge were in the living room of their cluttered apartment,
and they were seated in their favorite wingback recliners. Gabriel was glued
to the paper while his partner Jorge was reading *The Walking Dead* comic
book. For both men, it was a nice and quiet Sunday evening. They had a
routine. Earlier, they'd gone to church and then went food shopping for
the week. Gabriel would come home and prepare a vegan meal, and then
Touch would come over for dinner. It was usually peaceful, with some jazz
music playing in the background.

"What are you disgusted by, Gabriel?" Jorge asked. "What are you reading about?"

"There's a new drug in Harlem that's killing people, even in our own neighborhood. They're calling it '*Queen of New York.*' Did you read this?"

"No, I haven't."

Gabriel passed Jorge the article. It read that in the past month, at least three dozen people had died of drug overdoses. The city's drug problem was spiraling out of control. Uncut heroin laced with fentanyl continued to drive the death toll higher.

"It's terrible news," Gabriel added.

Jorge scanned through the article. Like Gabriel, he became upset. "How can our city—our law enforcement—allow this to happen? This feels like the eighties!"

"We have to do something about this," Gabriel said.

"Us? Are you crazy, Gabriel? What can we do besides get ourselves killed too?" Jorge cautioned. "I don't want anything to happen to you. I'd lose it."

"We can't just sit here on our comfortable asses while there's a problem out there, Jorge. I mean, this is happening right outside our front door."

"Trust me, this will be dealt with," Jorge replied.

"By who? The police? The vigilante? People are dying out there from this drug while dealers are getting rich. This isn't right," he fussed.

"I understand your anger, but who are we? It's just you and I, Gabriel, and it's not like we have some kind of superpower to fight what's going on out there. You know my health is failing me, and you're no spring chicken. We're not The Huntsman. We're not vigilantes, so how can we help? It's a problem for the authorities."

"We can go out during the day and start our own investigation. We can ask around about the dealers and talk to the drug addicts and ask the names of their suppliers. We can keep our eyes and ears open and search for drug dens. We can gather information for the authorities, and hopefully, they can start making arrests from there."

Jorge thought about it for a minute. "Maybe, Gabriel . . . maybe."

At that very moment, Touch walked into the living room. "That's what y'all *not* gonna do. This drug epidemic ain't your business. Let it go."

"Why should we?" Gabriel challenged.

"Yeah, why should we?" Jorge now cosigned.

Touch stared at his father. The man was in his mid-fifties and still looked physically fit although he had been complaining lately that his health was failing him. Jorge stood six-two and was a powerhouse fighter back in his day. He would often brag to his son how he could knock a nigga out with one punch. He was balding yet still handsome, sporting a dark, black beard with one polka-dot-shaped patch of gray hair, which gave him a unique look.

"I don't want to see anyone get hurt." Touch weighed his words. "There are some situations that I won't be able to help you—y'all—with if shit got too crazy."

Jorge snorted. "You help us?" He looked at Gabriel. "Did you hear this? My son helps us."

"I've offered to help you financially, but you won't take my money!"

Jorge pursed his lips together, an action he knew sent his son over the edge. "I don't know where your money comes from."

"What's that supposed to mean? *I'm* dope, Pops. I don't sell it."

Jorge's eyes rolled. "There are other unscrupulous ways to make money."

"You know I play professional poker!"

Touch's voice elevated, and he hated that his father could always bring him to the brink of pure rage.

Gabriel needed to intervene as usual and play the referee. "Malcolm, you know your father is a proud man and doesn't like handouts. Please don't be upset with him. He's been feeling under the weather lately, and his insomnia is back."

"Don't talk as if I'm not here, Gabriel. I told you about that."

Touch smirked. "Insomnia, huh? Is that what we're calling it?"

Gabriel looked at Jorge, looking at Touch. Father and son exchanged silent words before Touch grabbed his jacket and left.

"What did he mean?" Gabriel demanded to know. "Are you having an affair?"

"Affair?" Jorge roared. "With what energy!"

Gabriel watched as Jorge stormed into their bedroom and slammed the door shut. It was another ruined Sunday dinner. He didn't understand why Touch continued to come around each Sunday to see his father. It was a contentious relationship—clash of the Titans—yet there was codependency that couldn't be broken.

Gabriel looked out their second-story apartment window at all the shady activity below. He would not let the drug dealers get away with bringing down his community.

He vowed to do something. It was time to react, and Gabriel felt that with Jorge by his side, they could help fight the war on drugs.

It was a beautiful day for a rally and a public protest. Jorge and Gabriel were dressed for the event in comfortable sneakers, jeans, and windbreakers. They were a cute couple, both handsome men; distinguished most would say. They held hands as they joined in with the crowds of people gathered in front of Soundview projects in the Bronx. The march would start from the Bronx and end in Spanish Harlem. Hundreds of people carried signs opposing drug use, gang violence, and the decay of their neighborhood. They were sick and tired of the overdoses and the gang shootings plaguing the communities, and most were angered by the teen boy violently stabbed to death in the local bodega by a Latin gang. The local businesses had helped organize the march to protest dealers flooding their rebuilt neighborhood with narcotics.

The people chanted, "We're sick and tired, and the drugs must go! We're sick and tired, and the gangs must go!"

Their mantra could be heard for blocks. Castle Hill was swollen thick with people marching and chanting. Gabriel and Jorge soon blended in with the moving crowd, and they, too, chanted and became a blended voice. They continued to hold hands as they moved with the group, expressing their outrage and anger.

The march throughout Castle Hill had attracted the local media, and bits and pieces of it were being televised. The community wanted to emphatically state to every drug dealer and drug fiend that they would not tolerate the demise of their area. They were ready to fight back and take back what they had built.

"We're sick and tired, and the drugs must go! We're sick and tired, and the gangs must go!"

Gentrification was palpable. Throughout the march, there was a sea of multi-colored and multi-cultural faces. Every race, gender, creed, and sexuality was out in full force, trying to keep the new integrity of their neighborhood.

"We're sick and tired, and the drugs must go," was chanted loudly out from block to block. "We're sick and tired, and the gangs must go!"

The police were in attendance. They silently monitored the protest. The people had their permit to march, and it was a peaceful demonstration. While marching, the people conversed and threw up their signs for the cameramen; their slogans against drug use and drug dealers needed to be read.

"We're sick and tired, and the drugs must go!" Gabriel and Jorge shouted together. "We're sick and tired, and the gangs must go!"

They were happy to see they weren't the only ones who felt the same way about what was going on in their neighborhood. Everyone thought they could no longer be complacent to the danger happening right next door, in the parks, on the streets, and directly in front of their children.

"We're sick and tired, and the drugs must go!" she shouted. She was in the mix of things with the people—Queenie. She held her fist high in the air and shouted passionately about the cause. "We're sick and tired, and the gangs must go!"

She was marching with her peoples. The Hispanic Women Against Crime was a small organization headquartered in the South Bronx area and one of many non-profits Queenie donated to. Her gang affiliation teardrop was covered with makeup, her cartel connections masked through charitable donations.

"We're sick and tired, and the drugs must go! We're sick and tired, and the gangs must go!" she shouted again.

At some point, those rallying locked arms to show solidarity to the parasites trying to break down the neighborhood barriers. A hippie-looking chic with multi-colored hair gazed at Queenie. She couldn't stop herself from blurting out, "You're beautiful."

Queenie smiled and replied, "Thank you."

And together, they shouted, "We're sick and tired, and the drugs must go! We're sick and tired, and the gangs must go!"

22

Apple was sound asleep in her plush king-size bed when her cell phone vibrated on her nightstand. Lazily, her eyes stretched open as the dim blue light lit up her dark room. The noise alone crackling through the quiet of her apartment was enough to irritate her. Reluctantly she clumsily reached for her iPhone and it slipped through her fingers and landed on her carpeted floor.

"Fuck!" she cursed and wondered what time it was. It felt late, or early, depending on one's perception. Apple was still lying on her stomach when her manicured hand fumbled below to retrieve her phone. It couldn't have fallen far, yet it was eluding her as she could not pick it up with the least effort. If she wanted her phone, she would have to cut on the light and get up, none of which she planned on doing until her gut told her it could be serious. It had to be business related, she figured. Maybe Hood or IG. When she heard the *ting!* alert telling her she had received a voice message, she jumped up.

Apple clicked on her light, and it was 4:45 a.m.—hustling hours. Something had happened. She grabbed her cell phone and saw the missed call was from Touch. *Touch?* She didn't know whether she should feel flattered or furious. She hit the play button.

A deep, baritone voice sang, "If only for one night."

Apple knew the song well. Her mother Denise would play it throughout their project apartment when she and Kola were young. It was a Luther Vandross song, only this wasn't him. Was Touch singing to her? She hit play again, and his sultry voice filled her room and connected to her in ways she didn't know existed. Apple was now snuggled under her covers fully awake. She hit play again, and again, and again. She realized that she had things to say too. With one hand and her thumb, she operated her iPhone with ease, moving from music to download within seconds. When she had the song she wanted, she dialed Touch's number and hoped he wouldn't pick up. But he did.

"Hey, gorgeous," he said.

Apple didn't speak. She hit play, and he heard the chorus to "Delicate." It was a Taylor Swift song. Taylor sang about keeping a relationship casual because she feels it won't work out due to her terrible reputation. The song was a downer to Touch—not at all what he wanted to hear.

Apple then hung up, wondering what they were doing. What was she doing? She hadn't felt this excitement—this heightened stimulation—since she was crushing on Cross at seventeen. Apple sat in bed and waited. She didn't know what she was waiting for, but she felt she had put herself out there and didn't want to be left hanging. Her breathing was fast. She could see her chest heaving up and down as she gripped her phone. Just when her anticipation was about to turn to agitation, he called back. She grinned and allowed the call to go to voicemail. It felt like minutes passed before she got the message notification. Apple hit play and listened as Touch sang the words to 112's hit song, "Cupid." He needed Apple to know that he was all in; he was just waiting on her.

Damn, he's good, she thought.

Apple panicked as she racked her brain for a rebuttal. As the minutes ticked away, she felt the pressure mounting, swelling her chest and swirling around inside her head. She closed her eyes and thought about what her mind wanted to say because her heart was yelling at her to play Ella Mai's, "Boo'd Up."

Finally, she settled on this: She called his phone, and he played along and allowed his phone to go to voicemail. The wise voice of Erykah Badu filled the air when he played the message.

Touch heard Erykah's voice explain to him that he had no chance whatsoever with Apple. The lyrics to "Next Lifetime" unequivocally outlined this. Touch would have to die first before he could get with her if he were to take this song literally.

Apple hoped this summed up her current situation. Her body still felt like it belonged to Nicholas. She felt guilty even entertaining another man in her bed, fantasizing about someone else's touch, someone else's lips, tongue, thighs, dick. Nick was the only man to put his dreams on hold for her. He gave up something he couldn't get back, and she felt she needed to honor his memory longer. But damn, Touch was persistent. He was different. His eyes had depth, like an explorer. Touch had that masculinity she was drawn to, but he also had a side to him that was guarded and childlike—an uncharted place that hadn't been corrupted.

Apple realized that nearly fifteen minutes had passed and he hadn't hit her back. He went radio silent and left her to second guess her last song selection. *Did I push him away?* she wondered. She tried to shake the voice in her head because she was bugging. Wasn't the whole point to the song to push him away? To make him see she wasn't ready to give her heart away to anyone?

It was now half past five in the morning, and she couldn't go back to sleep. Apple clicked on NY1 news, and within minutes, a new report about The Huntsman was breaking. Police vehicles, yellow tape, and detectives in suits were videoed at a Bronx location. What caught Apple's ear was that two drug dealers were massacred in the Castle Hill area for allegedly selling the drug *Queen of New York*.

"Shit," Apple said. She refused to believe this guy couldn't be caught in nearly thirty years. No one had a run like that. Either this was the work of copycats, or he was law enforcement. Now this psycho was zeroing in on her territory with his vigilante bullshit. What the police couldn't do she would try, which was put this piece of shit six feet deep. He was fucking with her takeover.

Apple stared at the blue and gray suits and said, "Y'all probably investigating y'all own, crooked fucks!" She shut off the television.

Her mood had declined since Touch hadn't called her back. She felt dumb. Apple had a few hours before Tokyo was coming to pick her up, so she cleaned. Apple had finally found a three-bedroom in Tribeca and wanted Tokyo to drive her to order bedroom sets for the children. Ever since her run-ins with Queenie, her block was hot. A patrol car would randomly circle to ensure the safety of the residents of this privileged community. Tokyo was ordered to come through to do errands with Apple; that extra set of eyes was necessary when she was at war.

Touch felt a surge of energy he hadn't ever felt with any woman. Ever since his mother broke his young heart, he vowed to allow no girl to get close again. The younger Touch thought he would never fall for anybody. He wanted to tell himself that the feelings weren't true, that he was just lusting after someone he couldn't have. How could a stranger have such a pull on him, someone he didn't even really know? But she did. He wanted Apple to know the best parts of him. He wanted her to see his potential and not his pitfalls, but she wouldn't let him in. Her song choices were clear; her heart was filled to the brim with another man's love, and since he had run into her twice without a nigga hovering and they had fucked, it could only mean one thing. Apple's man must be incarcerated. Touch had no issues pushing up on another man's girl while that man was locked up. *You snooze you lose, nigga.*

Touch said his morning prayer and then got into a hot, steamy shower and thought about all the things he wanted to ask her. He lathered up with his pricey shower gel, and as the water cascaded down his back, her face kept flashing before him. She smiled little, but when she did, it was broad, authentic, and carried all the way to her eyes. Touch wanted to know what her interests were, what her favorite foods were, and, more specifically, who had her heart. Who was he?

Touch changed his clothes three times before settling on a pair of velour sweats, Balenciaga sneakers, and a pullover. His haircut was fresh, so he didn't need his fitted. Touch grabbed Girlie's leash and his vintage radio and was out.

It was an old school move, but Touch would try anything to hold her attention. He knew that standing outside Apple's apartment uninvited and so early in the morning was a sucker move—also borderline stalking. Their flirtatious banter this morning was unresolved. He had so much he wanted to say, and even though he had started their musical conversation, what he had to say needed to be said with his own words, looking into her eyes. Touch parked his black Audi near the curb and climbed out. It was shortly before ten a.m. He had made several stops early this morning, but the most important was to a florist to get a dozen red long-stemmed roses. He figured her favorite color was red, because her nickname was Apple, it not occurring to him that it could just as easily been green. He quickly walked Girlie up and down the block while keeping his eyes peeled on the entrance of Apple's building. He hoped that she hadn't left already because he wasn't prepared to wait there all day, but he would. She was worth it. Touch pulled out his old school boom box and placed it on the sidewalk near the curb. The roses sat perched on the hood of his car, and he leaned back on his pricey vehicle with his arms flanking his sides and waited. Girlie sat obediently on the curb as if she knew what was up. She and Touch stared at the building's entrance with hope.

Each minute felt like an eternity to him. He knew he could easily call Apple and tell her to come down, but he also knew that the spontaneity was the money move. The look on her face when she saw him would determine whether he had a chance of getting into her life. Although Touch was on his Romeo, he was still a street dude. So when the Lexus circled Apple's block twice, he instantly switched to protective mode.

A few minutes later the Lexus pulled into an open spot directly in front of Touch, and a young female hopped out. She glared at him aggressively, looked at his dog and the flowers, and then nodded. He wasn't a threat, she felt.

Apple came downstairs a few minutes after she had received the text from Tokyo. She almost wanted to cancel because Touch had fucked her whole mood up. Apple felt played that he initiated something and just went MIA, despite the message she was sending with the Badu song. Apple reasoned that if she stayed home today, she would just wallow in her negative thoughts and continue to overthink their exchange, so the best thing was to distract her mind with shopping.

Apple had washed her hair in the shower and added a patchouli-scented leave-in conditioner. Her hair was in a loose bun on top of her head, and she kept it simple with hoop earrings and pink lip gloss. Her hoodie and sweats were the least sexy thing she could put on, but it matched the way she felt. Apple figured she was only running out for a quick minute so there was no need to get dolled up. The automatic doors to her building opened, and Apple did the usual and scanned the block, only her eyes didn't get far. They lingered on Touch, freshly dressed in sportswear. He grabbed a fist full of long-stemmed roses and just grinned. She grinned back. Near him, a chocolate colored French bulldog was dressed in a pink doggie dress with matching pink doggie socks. The dog sat obediently with her tongue hanging to the side, panting. And then Apple heard it, the music, and looked and saw a boom box. Touch was posted up against his whip and had hit play. Al Green's distinctive voice switched from tenor to alto as he sang his megahit, "Simply Beautiful."

The song was laced with promises and expectations—sensual and sultry. This was a baby-making song, meant for all-night fucking to melodies and rhythms, bodies moving over bass and beats. Apple froze as they locked eyes, and everyone around them dropped away as Al sang.

Their connection was broken when Tokyo stormed out of her vehicle, thinking her boss had encountered a threat. Maybe the guy wasn't as harmless as she had initially thought. She was ready to react with violence. She looked at the man with the dog, the music, and the flowers and asked, "Who this fool?"

Apple shot her a dirty look. "Chill."

Tokyo acquiesced. She had no idea what in the nineteen eighties was going on, but this shit was corny. She watched as her boss walked closer to dude and decided to sit this one out. Tokyo got back in the car and waited for further instructions.

"These for me?" Apple asked.

Touch handed her the roses, and she graciously bundled them in her arms like they were a newborn baby.

"Ruff! Rufffff!" Girlie barked, tired of being ignored. She wanted to meet Apple too. Touch and Apple both laughed as she kneeled in front of Girlie and got a face full of licks.

"Who is this sweet thing?" Apple asked, rarely showing this much niceness around anyone other than her daughter.

"This Girlie. And she likes you for sure; she usually doesn't allow anyone to get close to me."

Apple spoke directly to Girlie. "I'm honored, pretty girl. You're so pretty," Apple repeated as she stroked her beautiful coat. Finally, she stood back up.

"What are you doing here?"

"Isn't it obvious? I missed you. I wanted—no, I needed to see you. You placed me on timeout, and I wanted to come up off the bench."

"I've just been bus—"

"Nah, don't give me that busy shit. Keep it one-hundred with me. I'm a grown man. I can handle the truth."

Apple nodded. She was about to kick game and was relieved he had stopped her. Apple didn't know what the future held, but she knew she didn't want to start off by lying to him. "It's complicated."

"I like complicated women and makeup sex," he joked, and Apple's eyes widened. "Too soon?"

She smirked and said, "Absolutely." Then she grinned. Touch was silly and had levity to him that was nice.

"You want to go to breakfast with us so we could talk about it?"

Apple looked at Girlie and said, "Us?"

"I know a place."

Apple walked back to Tokyo's passenger's window and leaned in. "I'll need to reschedule," she whispered. "This afternoon, I want you to go with Hood and IG to pick up the shipment from the Mingo cartel and oversee the transport to the Westside trap house."

It was a huge responsibility, a task that made Tokyo somewhat nervous. "You sure?"

"Tokyo, when I give an order, don't ever question me. It undermines my authority. It's time you start earning your money. I'll call Hood and let him know to expect you. Hit me if there are any issues. Otherwise, I don't want to be disturbed."

Tokyo nodded, placed the car in drive, and peeled out.

23

Touch walked over to his passenger's side door and opened it. The vehicle was recently cleaned and waxed, and the new car freshener was subtle and welcoming. His doors looked like mirrors as his exterior glistened under the sun. Apple hopped in the passenger seat of Touch's car, and when she peered over at him, he had a look on his face that said he was a happy man. *He's so corny*, Apple thought. He looked like he was taking her to prom. Girlie, who had started in the backseat, had no reservations about jumping her substantial body into Apple's lap.

"I told you she likes you," Touch said. Apple felt that Girlie's approval was validation to him. She rolled down the window so Girlie could feel the wind on her face as Touch steered his car to one of his favorite dog-friendly cafés in Little Italy. He parked and they walked two blocks. The quaint café was huddled among the huge city buildings on the wide city block. They were seated outside, and Girlie sat at their feet.

When the waitress walked up to take their orders, Girlie growled. It was a low warning shot that she liked no one getting close to her dad.

Apple's eyes widened.

"See?" Touch said. "What I tell you? She likes you."

Apple looked under the table and rubbed her head.

They ordered breakfast, and then Touch had his opportunity to get to know her. He wanted to ask more profound questions that weren't broached on their first date. He started off slow but was ready to build.

"What's your real name?"

"It's Apple Evans."

"Apple? That's your legal name?"

She nodded. "And yours?"

"Malcolm Xavier Nuñez."

"Malcolm X Nuñez is unexpected," she responded after allowing her eyes to sweep over his smooth milk-chocolate skin with just a hint of hazelnut. Touch had shiny, thick eyebrows with long lashes and bright white teeth. His hair was soft, curly, and low, and he had a full mustache and beard. "Nuñez? Is your father Spanish?"

"My mother was a member of the Black Panther party, so she named me after Malcolm X, and my father is where Nuñez comes from. He's Puerto Rican." Touch couldn't believe he had just mentioned his mother, even in the most inconsequential of ways. Her question was specifically about his father, but without provocation, he let her in. Apple's eyes told him that he could trust her.

"That's impressive. Your mother seems solid, like she raised you to be a strong man."

Touch quickly shook his head. "She didn't raise me." He was ready to take the conversation to places he vowed he never would. Instead, he stopped short.

"I feel you. In theory, my mom didn't raise me either. The streets did, but you don't feel like a street dude. You seem different, in a corny kind of way. I get the feeling you graduated from high school."

The waitress came with their Belgian waffles, caramel lattes, and a bowl of water for Girlie. Touch sipped on his hot beverage with its sweet froth and felt indifferent. He was mercurial, a man with two sides. He was college educated, had a few talents—he could play poker, sing, few people could beat him in pool, and he loved to cook. He was someone a girl would like to bring home to meet her parents. Still, he had a dark side, the side of him he kept suppressed that only came out for business. Touch took no pleasure in murdering people, had no grudge or animosity toward each victim. This side of him couldn't be shared, couldn't be placed at someone's feet. But he wanted to share things with her on an intimate level that he couldn't communicate with others. Now just wasn't the time.

"I did go to college. I have my bachelors in science. You? What's your highest level of education?"

"I dropped out long ago. School wasn't my thing, but I want my daughter to go all the way and finish college like you."

"What's her name?"

"Peaches." Before he could ask, Apple had pulled out her iPhone and showed him her screensaver of her beautiful little girl. Touch stared intently, picking out the features that were the same as her mothers.

"And she makes beautiful babies . . ." he said and allowed his statement to linger in the air.

Apple blushed and pulled her bottom lip between her teeth. This small gesture did not go unnoticed by him.

"You know that's sexy, right?"

"What?"

"Everything." Touch sat back in his chair and drank her in. She didn't have sexy moves; Apple *was* sexy. She was the personification of the word; she embodied it. Dressed down in sweats she was turning him on. He could smell her hair from across the table. She was freshly showered, and her hair was still wet. He wanted to run his hands through it and inhale her scent—all her scents.

Apple had heard compliments before. When niggas wanted to fuck you, they usually laid them on thick. You were the prettiest bitch, sexiest bitch, there was no other bitch until you caught them with the next bitch.

When fucking you had the bomb pussy and could suck dick like no other until you got into an argument with the next female and realized that the things he said to you, he said to her. So at breakfast, Apple wanted to focus on more than sex and lies. Touch had made her cancel her plans, so now he had to earn her time. It would not be easy.

She got to the point. "How do you support yourself?"

It didn't elude him she had changed the subject. He liked that. She steered him back on track to what mattered: substance.

"When my mother left, it was just my dad and me alone. We'd spend weekends and evenings playing poker. He taught me the game as a way to keep my mind sharp and focused on something other than why I was a seven-year-old boy without his mother around. In college, I started playing in tournaments, and then that parlayed into a career." There it was again. He'd mentioned his mother.

He was smooth, Apple thought. The way he corrected her assumption that his experience with his mother was similar to hers was effortless. She could see and also feel it was painful for him. His bright eyes somewhat dulled as he mentioned her. Apple wanted to ask her name but fell back. Fuck her. Whatever reason she had to leave wasn't good enough seeing how torn he still was.

"I hope poker pays enough for the eggs that I'm going to order after I finish these waffles." She grinned. "And I'd like the fresh squeezed orange juice too."

"I got you," he replied. "What about you? How can you afford to live this way and also support your child?"

Touch already knew what it was. Well, he knew the outline. He wondered if she would fill in the details. Whether she had a diplomatic answer or told him a fantastic lie would determine how she saw him. It almost wasn't fair putting her in that position knowing his side hustle wasn't exactly something you divulged either.

Apple allowed the outwardly innocent question to ground her. To strip away all romantic feelings for a moment, she needed to filter logic through not only her mind, but it needed to pierce her heart. No one had ever asked what she did for a living. All of her men had been street dudes, men who busted their guns and stacked their ones. There wasn't a need for full-fledged confessionals because there was transparency from day one. Who was this poker-playing, rhythm-and-blues-singing, Malcolm-X-namesake, half Puerto Rican? A cop? Apple needed to tread carefully, and yet she didn't want to outright lie.

"The first few years of my daughter's life, I didn't take care of her. At some point, my sister became her guardian until I was able to get her back. That part of my life is off limits. I don't want to talk about it. It's my past, and it's buried. Right now, I'm in the process of looking for a new apartment, so she could live with me full time. The fact that I'm sitting here with you at eleven in the morning on a work day is a testament that I don't work." Apple felt good about how she had addressed his question, but his eyes told her she hadn't answered his inquiry. "For you to pull up knowing I would be home tells me that you already know what I do."

"There are two different types of men—the ones that ask direct questions, and the ones that listen to rumor and innuendo. I did ask around, only wanting to know if you had a man. I was told that you were trouble, and that you were a stick-up chick. You set niggas up to get robbed. Now if I believed any of that, we wouldn't be sitting here. So again, what do you do for money?"

Apple was stuck on a stick-up chick. It sounded so petty. The streets had no chill button. "My ex left me some money." Her answer was short, honest, and succinct.

"How long has it been since you two separated?"

"I don't want to talk about him either," she admitted.

Touch wanted to let that response ride, but he couldn't. He was becoming territorial over her time and wanted to know more about his competition. "Try, please . . . for me."

Why was he making her so weak right now? It was like she would do whatever he said. Apple took a deep breath and blew out a lot of negative feelings. She said, "He was murdered last year."

Touch slowly nodded. It was like the fuzzy picture on his television screen had just cleared up. He now had an HD 4K ultra view into her life.

"You still love him?"

"I do," Apple said without hesitation.

"Is that why you didn't call me or return any of my calls?"

"You don't give up, do you?"

"Nah. I'm stubborn like that."

"Maybe," she said coyly. "But then you came with all this—which, by the way, is so fuckin' extra." She laughed.

"Which part? Girlie? The roses? The stalking? The singing? The boom box?" he countered.

"The pursuit," she answered honestly. "You're coming on strong as if you're going to run out of time or be exposed as a liar. You feel too perfect, like I'm going to find out something about you that won't sit well with me and you'll become an enemy . . . You don't want me as an enemy." Apple stared fiercely into his eyes, and he didn't flinch.

"If you give me a chance, I promise I won't ever break your heart."

"It's your heart that I'm worried about."

Touch's breath hitched as he came to terms with her words. She was his challenge. He wanted her because she made known that he couldn't have her. Her heart belonged to another man, her body was on loan, and her time was monopolized by the streets.

"Let me worry about me," Touch said.

"So what now?" she asked.

"What now? Let's make the best of the morning," he said. "And so it begins."

"Begin what?" she asked him.

"Our second date."

24

Y ou're late," she griped. "In fact, beyond late. This is downright
disrespectful. Only whores keep these hours, and I'm no whore!"

"It ain't that easy for me like it used to be," he explained. "She was out
of town, but now she's back."

Melinda stepped to the side to allow Kamel to come in. He coolly
entered the apartment, simultaneously removing his jacket. She closed the
door behind him and tightened her silk robe. Underneath she had on a
two-hundred dollar pair of La Perla thongs, and pasties covered her perky,
toffee colored nipples. Her breasts were firm, voluptuous, and real, as was
her ass—solid facts she took great pride in. Her body was a perfect ten,
her mind was filled with knowledge, and her life was full of family and
friends. Melinda was loved beyond measure, and on the outside looking
in, she had it all.

His lateness had her in a foul mood. It was nearly one o' clock in the
morning, and she had to be to work by eight. Melinda was an investment
banker at J.P. Morgan & Chase, and she took her job seriously. This affair
she was having was a first for her. It was against everything she thought
she believed. Married men were off limits. It was an unspoken rule in her
life, a commandment just as crucial as Thou Shall Not Kill. Right now,
she was coveting another woman's husband, and the guilt was eating her

up inside. However, the shame of it all wasn't enough for her to end it. She loved him, and he promised her it was over with his wife. He swore that he had asked for a divorce. Melinda had Sza's "The Weekend" playing softly in the background, the song an in-your-face reminder of what was going down inside her four walls. Was the weekend enough for her? And she wasn't even getting that. He broke her off a few evening hours a couple times a week, never allowing the sun to beat him home.

"I like this song." He said as he kicked off his Ferragamo shoes.

"I bet you do."

"C'mon, not like that. That's not us. We're more than sex."

"Are we?"

"Melinda, please don't start. I've had a long day, and I just want to chill wit' you."

Kamel looked around at the dinner that sat untouched on her dining room table and the champagne now soaking in a bucket of warm water. Melinda always put in the extra effort to make him feel wanted and needed. Her eyes spoke to him each time he walked through the door, begging him to make a home with her.

"You hungry?" she asked.

He nodded, even though he wasn't. He had cooked a massive meal for Kola and the children, but he couldn't allow Melinda to feel neglected and her time to feel wasted. She had gone through a lot of trouble for him.

Melinda got right to work placing his steak and potato in the microwave. Her lips were poked out, allowing him to absorb her attitude. Kamel took a seat at her table and leaned back in the chair. How had he made such a mess of this woman's life? He could tell she was hurting, and he didn't want to cause her more pain, but he didn't know how to unravel his lies so they both could walk away without regrets.

Melinda was only supposed to be someone with a warm bed when he needed a companion. From day one, he told her he was married. Kola had left him and the kids and gone to Apple's rescue in South Beach without an ounce of understanding that he was a man. And when she came back, she was even more fucked up in the head and distant. He begged her to see a therapist, and she did, but they placed her on a cocktail of meds, which numbed her mind and dried up her sex drive. Kola kept pushing him away, and Melinda kept begging him to stay. What was a man to do?

The microwave sounded and Melinda pulled out his hot plate and dropped it in front of him. Her energy was so dark that Kamel thought about turning around and going back home.

"You not going to eat too?" he asked.

"I'm not hungry," she scoffed.

Kamel grabbed his steak knife and fork and cut a small piece of the meat. He chewed a forkful and told Melinda how good her food tasted. "You can burn," he flattered, and he could see a small smile take root.

"You should have tasted it without the million volts of artificial rays. Your mouth would be watering right now."

"Nah, it's good. No complaints."

Melinda relaxed. She looked at his chiseled jawbone and broad shoulders, with all of his gangsta swag and couldn't stay angry. She yawned and wished he would eat faster.

"You tired?"

"No, I'm good." Melinda lifted her eyes open wider, not wanting to give him any reason to leave. "You want some steak sauce?"

Kamel shook his head and reached out for her. She got up and came willingly. He hadn't been fussed over and catered to in a long time. He knew he was using her; he would never leave his wife. Kola, he loved. She was a woman he would die for and shamefully, Melinda's good loving allowed him to stay with his wife. She was the bridge he walked over to get to the other side of his loneliness and feelings of rejection. He and Kola were going through a rough patch right now, but he did see things leveling out and getting back to normal one day. Melinda undid her robe to reveal her temple. Her body was something special—curvy and thick in the right places, dark-chocolate, smooth, and supple. She was insatiable, but Kamel knew how to tame her. Melinda sauntered to her bedroom, her ass jiggling with each step. Kamel followed her while undressing himself. His pullover hit the floor and he stepped out of his jeans, hopping one leg at a time until he was free. His designer boxers came off last. Kamel stood before her, muscles flexing and dick fully erect with a condom in his hand.

Melinda crawled onto her bed, positioned herself on her back, and spread her thighs for him. She slid her panties off, tapped her pussy, and moaned, "C'mon baby, eat."

"Could we not do this tonight?" he asked as he rolled the condom back on his penis. That level of intimacy was reserved for Kola. "I told you from the gate that I don't go down." And then he added, "I'm married."

That last line nearly ended her. *Married!* The small word with the tremendous meaning had eluded her throughout her twenties. Melinda was now thirty-one and no closer to walking down the aisle than her twelve-year-old niece. It took all her power to not burst into tears; his remark was a dagger to her heart. What was she doing? Why had she reduced herself to being a mistress? Her parents had taught her better. Growing up she vowed to never be someone's baby momma, jump-off, or sneak fuck. She frowned upon such women and their woes and had less than kind words to sistas who found themselves in those compromising positions. Now she was the pot and the kettle, blackening her days with a street thug with good dick. Why couldn't Kamel see she could be so much more to him? What did his wife have that she didn't?

Melinda was what most would consider a freak. She had sucked Kamel's dick without provocation and loved it. She enjoyed giving head, seeing pleasure written on his face when she glanced up from his nether regions. Melinda loved the control she felt when she deep-throated her man. And yet, it wasn't reciprocated. He was a selfish lover with her. The more he refused to eat her out, the more she wanted it. Melinda had wet dreams of Kamel going down on her and waited for the day when his wife discovered the affair and called so she could brag about how good Kamel ate her pussy. Wasn't that the *coup de grâce* of all clapbacks?

Kamel could fuck for hours and would give her multiple orgasms, but tonight she could no longer place her pride on pause while all of Kamel's needs were met. Each time his cell phone rang and it read *Mrs.,* it chipped away at her self esteem. If she stayed in this relationship a day longer, she would have none left. It would have dissipated with her lifelong search for satisfaction. Melinda needed this to end. She closed her legs and got dressed.

"I can't do this tonight," she began. "I have to be to work early."

"Because I won't go down on you?" he asked, incredulous.

"Because you won't be honest."

Kamel was irritated as he stood butt-naked literally with his swollen dick in his hand. And then he saw her tears. Kamel was gutted, but he couldn't do what she wanted him to do or say what he knew she needed to hear. He quickly got dressed as she stood impatiently waiting for him to leave. Melinda wanted Kamel to beg her, to say he loved her and would leave his wife. She wanted him to make love to her and hold her throughout the night and not creep out before dawn. In those awkward, uncomfortable moments she wanted him to lie to her.

"You wasted my time, Kamel. You were never going to leave her!"

"It's not like that. She needs me; she's sick."

"Stop," she yelled. "Stop with your lies, Kamel. One moment you've filed divorce papers and the next second you're repping your ring finger. If you're truly leaving her, if you want to be with me, then stay with me tonight. We can work out the details in the morning."

Kamel knew Melinda was a good woman when he had met her. He didn't want to corrupt her or force her into a box where she didn't belong, but she was so smart, so sexy, so irresistible with just a hint of gangster. He was only looking for sex and could have easily found comfort between the thighs of a stripper. However, he was getting older, and the likelihood of having enough patience for random, vivacious strippers was slim. Kamel went looking for a grown woman and found everything he needed in Melinda.

The silence felt like an airborne toxin had been released. Melinda was self-destructing right before his eyes. She crumbled to the floor because she knew she didn't have to tell him to not come back. She saw in his eyes that this would be their last rendezvous.

25

Jorge and Gabriel were lying naked in their comfortable bed together after just having some great sex. Jorge had to prove to his partner that he wasn't cheating thanks to his son and his big mouth. Gabriel wanted to cuddle with his partner and have some pillow talk when someone knocked on their door. They had company.

"Are you expecting someone?" Gabriel asked Jorge.

"No."

"It's ten o' clock at night. Who would be dropping by at this hour?"

Jorge shrugged.

Gabriel donned a long robe and Jorge removed himself from the bed, put on something decent, and followed Gabriel into the living room toward the apartment door.

Gabriel glanced through the peephole and smiled out of the blue. "Jorge, it's Malcolm."

Jorge's face carried a look of surprise. "Malcolm? On a Wednesday?"

Gabriel couldn't open the door fast enough to let his favorite person inside the apartment. He made sure that he was decent first, tying his robe together. The last thing he needed was to greet Malcolm with a swinging dick.

Touch walked in and both men smiled.

"Malcolm, what brings you here at this hour?" Gabriel asked.

"I was in the neighborhood and thought I'd stop by," he replied.

Touch walked farther in to the apartment and took a seat inside the living room without being invited. He sat back and stretched his arms out on the couch's headrest and got comfortable. Both Jorge and Gabriel didn't know what to expect.

"You're spying on us?" Jorge asked him.

"Nah, not at all."

Gabriel sucked his teeth. "Of course he's not. He's just coming around to see us because he's lonely. Malcolm, when you going to get yourself a nice girl and settle down?"

Jorge snorted. "Settle down? My son? Never gonna happen. He too fucked up in the head."

"Courtesy of you and my mother."

"You can't blame me for what your mother did to you."

"That's what happens when a gay man marries a straight woman. She cheats," Touch said.

Jorge placed the palm of his hand to his forehead and counted to ten. It was his learned way of quieting the storm that was brewing. Was his son condoning his ex-wife's behavior? After all these years the one thing both father and son could agree on was that she was the culprit in that situation. Jorge swallowed his temperament and with a calm, level voice he said, "I guess you're right about that."

Touch didn't come to argue; he came to spend time with his family. "Y'all hungry? I can order some Thai food."

"This time of night?" Gabriel asked.

"Yeah, why not? No one has work in the morning."

Jorge and Gabriel were out on full disability benefits from their former jobs, both complaining of some ailment or another. It was an old school hustle. If you were born in the fifties or early sixties then either you or someone in your immediate circle would pull this.

The trio ate the Thai food in harmony before Touch surprised the couple by saying he was spending the night. Gabriel was thrilled, but Jorge, not so much. Touch made himself comfortable on the couch with a blanket and pillow and drifted off to sleep. Three hours later he was wide awake.

Jorge snaked through the living room, trying to not wake his son, when he heard, "Where are you going?"

The sound crashing through the silence of the night nearly caused him to have a heart attack. Jorge placed his hand over his heart and said, "You scared me."

Touch repeated, "Where are you going?"

"You know I'm an insomniac." He then looked at his son, who was fully dressed, and asked with a raised eyebrow, "Where are *you* going?"

"Nowhere," Touch replied. "I couldn't sleep."

"Neither could I."

Touch grabbed his jacket and said to his father, "Wait up. I'll walk with you."

26

Peaches stood at the front door with her overnight bag and backpack with a huge smile. Apple had just pulled up into the circular driveway and tapped on the horn. It was late, nearly ten in the evening, and Kola had so many issues with this exchange. Her sister had all day to come and pick up her daughter. She'd had months to arrange to have the children full time. Apple was still making excuses, so much so, that Kola just stopped asking.

Kola walked Peaches to the passenger's side door and peered in. "Junior and Sophia are mad with you," she said.

"I know, but tell them next time. I want Peaches one-on-one. Maybe I'll pick them up next week." Peaches was spending a few nights with her mother, and the young girl was so excited.

Kola nodded and gave Peaches a quick hug before helping her into the passenger's backseat. Apple watched her sister like a hawk. She seemed withdrawn and sluggish. "Hey, you good?"

"I'm getting by."

Apple said what she always said, "Let me know if you need me."

Kola went back inside and watched as Kamel came out of the shower. His monogrammed towel hung low around his waist, his deep V on full display. He reached for the whipped shea butter and coconut oil blend that

Kola had mixed and massaged in the moisturizing lotion. The thin layer of balm gave his skin a glow. With little thought, he grabbed his favorite cologne, Tom Ford's Black Orchid, and squirted the expensive liquid to all his pulse points—wrists, neck, and chest. Kamel walked around their bedroom readying himself for an outing almost oblivious that Kola was watching him like a hawk. She gawked as he popped a few tags off some clothing. Whoever he was going to see, he wanted to look like money. Kamel put on his most expensive drip—platinum Rolex watch, diamond cross and Jesus chains, and a two-carat diamond pinky ring.

Kola sat on the edge of their marriage bed and studied her husband. His concentrated focus was almost something she envied. For some time now she had felt scattered, like she was broken into a million tiny pieces—a shell of her former self. She was forewarned of the side effects drugs can have when treating a mental health disorder. Kola was dealing with depression, post-traumatic stress, and social anxiety disorder, all triggered by the loss of her son.

Her therapist had prescribed Prozac and then monitored her for success. When Kola kept exhibiting unhealthy signs of depression, feeling withdrawn, and mood swings, the medication was switched to a cocktail of Zoloft, Ambien to help her sleep at night, and Xanax. With mental health, it takes time to find what works for each person, and her therapist counseled her to alert him if she experienced personality changes.

Kola cared less about the present as her mind kept traveling back to the past. This new drug mixture had her fucked up too. During the day she was drowsy and found it hard to concentrate on menial tasks. Her head was always buried under her covers and she pleaded with the children and her husband to not disturb her while she was resting. Kola had lost her appetite and had dropped a substantial amount of weight. Kamel would complain that she wasn't eating enough, just picking at her food until ultimately throwing her food into the trash.

Some days she was irritable, other days she was overly gleeful. At night she turned into a zombie—wide awake, roaming the house doing shit. Kola would start her nights cleaning while chain-smoking nearly an entire pack of Newports. And then when the house was quiet, she would sneak out and go to the cemetery to visit with Koke. Kola wrestled with her son lying alone in the ground without his mama.

Finally, she noticed that she was spending long hours out, and when she came home, Kamel would outstay her. His business meetings went from five hours to six, and now he was maxing out at seven hours gone.

Right in front of her were clues that her husband was having an affair, but all she felt at that very moment was relief more than anger. Kola had no desire to make love to him. Her sexual appetite had been suppressed, and she couldn't remember when he had made a real effort to touch her. She asked, "When was the last time we fucked?"

The random question halted his movements. Kamel turned around to face her, and their eyes clashed. His fury simmered, like a slow burn in the pit of his stomach, growing with each silent second. Kamel's guilt had manifested into anger; it was self-preservation. He'd rather be angry with Kola for suspecting he was cheating than allow his guilt to consume him. It was a defense mechanism, and he would use it.

"Fuck you trying to say?"

"Watch your mouth, Kamel. I may be flying with a broken wing, but I'm not broken. I will still fuck shit up if I have to."

Kamel knew how he could end this real quick. "Do you want to make love?" he asked her, dropping his towel and allowing his large dick to swing low.

Kola released a long sigh; it was an exhausted moan that personified her ambivalence toward the situation. She only wanted to know so she could discuss this with her therapist. Kola wasn't so doped up that she wasn't aware that had her mind not taken a sharp left turn, then she would have murder on it.

She asked him straight up. "Are you having an affair?"

Kamel chuckled nervously. "This is business, Kola. You know how important building my construction company is to me. These politicking hours I'm keeping so I can build. You know all day I'm here wit' you and the kids. How I got time to be smashing someone?"

She warned. "I won't be like this forever."

"What that's supposed to mean?"

"It means cancel that bitch before I do."

"Here we go," was his dismissive response.

Eduardo Jr. and Sophia could still be heard playing games in their rooms. "Are you going to put them to bed?" he asked, as he began ironing his clothes.

"You do it."

"Kola, you see I'm on my way out." Kamel was tight.

"Put them to bed . . . or not," she said and shrugged.

Kola stood in the doorway of Junior's room and watched her little king count sheep. He was the spitting image of his father. Next, she walked to check on Sophia, who also was sleeping peacefully. Kola wasn't so lucky. She had taken two Ambiens but had only managed to clean the house from top to bottom. She needed her son.

Kola arrived at the cemetery and parked on a side block. It was closed this time of the morning, so she had to scale a small wall. This was routine, so she was dressed accordingly in jeans, sneakers, and a hoodie. She kneeled down and placed her lips on his cold headstone before lying on her back, staring at the stars. She rarely said much during her visits. She would just sob for hours before eventually heading back home.

Oddly enough, the cemetery was where she felt safest.

27

The fire department, police department, and a coroner's van were all camped on Kola's property. She had pulled up to her residence and walked directly into chaos.

A uniformed cop stood protectively at her front door that had the yellow tape that read, "Biohazard." He placed a firm hand up and said, "You can't go in there."

"What do you mean? What's happened? Where is everyone?" Kola's voice was low and shaky.

"Who are you?"

"This is my home. Where's my husband? Where are my children?" Her voice was now more assertive. Kola was Mama Bear looking for her cubs.

"There's been an accident—"

"Yo, Ko-laaaa!" Kamel yelled. She spun around toward his voice and was confused as to why he was sitting handcuffed in the back of an unmarked police car. Kola ran to him at once. She reached to open the door, but it was locked. The windows were cracked a couple inches, and that's how they were able to communicate. Kamel had been sitting in the back of the police car since nine that morning, and it was slowly approaching three in the afternoon. With two dead children, the detectives treated him like shit. His legs were cramped, his wrists were swollen, and he was sweating profusely from the lack of air circulation. "Baby girl, I got some bad news."

"Why are you arrested?"

"Look, ma, we don't have a lot of time. There was an accident, and Junior and Sophia," Kamel's voice cracked as he tried to hold back his emotions. He needed to be strong for his wife. "The basement—I fucked up. Carbon monoxide leaked, and Junior and Sophia didn't make it."

"What? What are you saying?"

"They're gone, Kola."

Kola smirked. "Gone?" She didn't understand what that meant. "Where's Junior and Sophia?" she repeated.

"Kola, listen. Wake up! I need you to focus. I already gave a statement that you spent the night at your sister's and that it was me who left the kids alone. I told them I had only stepped out for a moment—"

"Why are you making statements?"

"So my wife doesn't get locked up for child abuse or neglect or some other shit. I told you 'bout leaving them alone, Kola. This was an accident, but those pigs gonna try to spin this as something more. If I don't beat this shit then it's my third strike," he explained. "I'm done."

Two detectives came from out their home with hazard masks on. They saw a female talking to their suspect and immediately closed in.

"Here they come," Kamel warned. "Remember, you weren't here."

Detectives Rothman and Brown were determined to make someone pay for what they had witnessed. It wasn't an exceptionally gruesome crime scene, but they felt that a crime had been committed. It appeared Sophia had died in her sleep, but Eduardo Jr. had apparently woken up when he heard the alarms sounding. For the child to experience the exposure while awake would have made for a cruel and prolonged death. Common symptoms are nausea, dizziness, headache, abdominal pain, and impaired judgment. He was found in the master bedroom lying in a pool of his own vomit. Eduardo, Jr. had suffered. These children were murdered by the silent killer, and their guardians apparently had more important shit to attend to.

Rothman didn't like this couple. They were too young, and their home was too opulent. Both he and Brown could work three jobs and not afford to live this way. He had already run their names, and both had criminal records spanning back years for assault, guns, and drugs. Rothman deduced that they were drug dealers, hidden in plain sight of the community he vowed to protect and serve. The only way you could live like this and be young and African American is if you played sports or rapped. And they did none of the above. Detective Rothman had summed up the occupants of the home within minutes of arriving. His blood boiled when he saw Kamel's Range in the driveway. His blinding diamonds and arrogance were like nails against a chalkboard for the seasoned detective. As he had walked through their home he wanted to fuck shit up—just take a baseball bat to all their nice shit—chandeliers, custom tables, and antique mirrors. He tried to charge them both, but the husband had readily absorbed all the blame.

As they walked toward the female, Rothman eyed her vehicle. The sleek Benz was top of the line, at least six figures. He whispered to Brown, "I want her too."

Detective Brown pulled out his pad and asked, "Your name is?"

"Why is my husband being detained?"

Brown looked down at his notepad. "Are you his wife, Kola?"

She nodded.

"I'm sorry for your loss." Detective Brown was sorry, but not for Kamel and Kola. His condolences were part of his shtick. Today his role was the good cop.

Kola nodded again. Detectives Rothman and Brown gave it a few seconds, expecting her to have a full meltdown. They both stared at the attractive female and assumed she was in shock when they didn't witness a waterfall of emotion. Everyone processed death differently.

"Where were you last night?" Rothman asked aggressively.

"I already told you where she was," Kamel shouted.

Rothman gave him a stern look and then whistled. He caught the attention of a uniformed officer. "Gates, take him down to the station. Now!"

The officer nodded and got into the driver's seat of his patrol car. Kamel scowled at the detectives and snickered. "I'll be out in a day!"

When the police cruiser left the scene, Kola repeated what she was told to say.

"And what's Apple's telephone number so we could verify?" Rothman pressed.

"Am I being arrested?"

"Not if your alibi checks out."

"I don't need a fuckin' alibi. My husband told you he left the kids."

"Ma'am, you do understand that two children are dead. I know they're not your biological kids, but they're human beings and deserved better than what they got," Brown said.

"It was an accident," Kola said. Her voice was monotone and not an accurate representation of how she felt. "Accidents do happen."

Neither of the detectives couldn't believe this woman. She sounded cavalier, unaffected, and unmoved by today's events. They didn't know that she was on medication and sleep deprived. "Accident? Our preliminary investigation concludes that all the carbon monoxide detectors were working and went off inside your home. There wasn't any adult supervision to get both children to safety. Sophia was found dead in her bed, and Eduardo Jr. was found dead in the master bedroom. Apparently, he got up when he heard the alarm and went looking for someone—anyone—to help him. That young boy suffered!" Rothman shouted. "And you fucking say accidents do happen? You're some piece of work with your fancy house and fancy car!"

"Are you done?"

"Oh, I'm just getting started," Rothman threatened.

"Your time to waste."

If this weren't an affluent neighborhood, Rothman would have body slammed the slick talking bitch on the hard concrete. He wanted to smash his fist into her face and make her choke on her own blood. The rage he felt was palpable and beyond measure. Rothman didn't like strong women, and he hated strong *black* women even more. When he was in college, his mother told him he was a misogynist. He countered and explained that he liked his women subservient.

By now, Rothman was breathing heavily through his nostrils, angered and annoyed. He said, "Your husband will be arraigned tomorrow on two counts of negligent homicide and child abuse."

"Homicide?"

The gravity was finally sinking in. Kola watched as two tiny bodies were carried out in black body bags. She wanted to run over and let them know that she was sorry, that she had failed them. Those were her babies. But her legs felt like slabs of steel, and although she willed them to move toward the van, her body was being less than cooperative. A round, plump tear slowly slid down her cheek as her bottom lip quivered. She had fucked up. Their deaths were on her sullied hands. She'd repeatedly left them home alone even though Kamel kept begging her not to. God had taken three children from her. This was more evidence that she wasn't put on this earth to be a mother. Her mind crawled deeper into her dark pit and she lost herself in despair.

"I wonder, Mrs. Carmichael, are your tears for the two dead children or your husband?" Rothman quipped.

Kola didn't respond. Eventually, she walked back to her car and got into her driver's seat. Her eyes drank in the scene. House. Dead. Kids. Kola stared her ignition and slowly drove away. Where she was going? She didn't have a clue. Suddenly, as if she had been struck by lightning, she slammed on her brakes as one word sent chills coursing through her veins. Eduardo!

Hood steered his truck down the residential block just in time to see Nerd's denim blue Volkswagen Beetle turn into a long driveway and pull around to the back of the house. Hood killed the ignition, glanced at Apple and IG, and chanted, "Let's go get that nigga!"

The three geared up with latex gloves and pistols. Apple surveyed the block crowded with tenement buildings and single-family homes and knew this was risky. Various interior lights were on, some shades were drawn, some weren't, and at any second there could be movement on this street. But if done correctly, a home invasion could take place at any time, in any neighborhood, on any day of the week.

Every movement they made to advance toward the house was calculated. Ski masks were pulled down because this wasn't just an ambush. This would be a home invasion, and Apple wanted no casualties. They crouched low in the shadows under the cover of darkness doing a slow jog around back where Nerd was about to pull his trashcans to the curb for morning pickup.

He saw the shadows from his peripheral vision and got spooked. There wasn't anything he could do but put his arms up in surrender. Nerd wasn't built like them. He wasn't a killer. He didn't carry a weapon. IG shoved the gun in his ribcage and commanded, "Open the door, tough guy, 'fore I open you up!"

Nerd didn't even realize he was crying until he felt a cool breeze on his face as his tears rolled down his cheeks. His body involuntarily shook, and he searched for the words to make it out of this alive, but none came.

"Open the fuckin' door!" IG barked again and bashed him on the side of his temple, causing Nerd to see spots of white lights that temporarily blinded his vision. The deep gash caused him excruciating pain as blood oozed through the open wound.

It wasn't that he was defying the orders; he just was slow to move and quick to process that this was it. He was a dead man. Nerd was being shoved by IG, and then he heard her voice. She was ski masked up, but he knew who she was.

Apple spoke, "You gonna die tonight, nigga, if you don't do what he said! Now open the door, and we'll let you live."

Nerd then remembered that he had something to protect besides stalling to save his own life. His family—his mom, Gloria, dad, Henry, and little sister, Alexis—was upstairs, and he would not be the one responsible for literally bringing death to their front door.

"I can't. My mother—" Nerd's airwave was cut off when Hood grabbed him in a chokehold and pulled. His strength lifted Nerd off his feet. Hood's muscles bulged on his forearm as he applied direct pressure. Nerd was balancing on his tippy toes as he struggled to stay conscious. IG walked up and hit him with a two-piece, one quick jab to his ribs and an uppercut to his stomach. Nerd felt like he was about to go into cardiac arrest, trying to suck in air and slow his heart rate. Instantly his body went limp in Hood's arms.

Apple searched his pockets and found his house keys. They already knew that he rented the main floor apartment from his parents and anticipated that they would have his whole home to themselves.

"Money," Apple uttered and dangled the keys. The back security gate was unlocked, and then she placed the key inside the back door. Before she turned it, she said, "Do you have an alarm system? And before you give me the duress code, think about who lives upstairs. It'll take less than a couple minutes to go from murder to quadruple homicide!"

Nerd was still dazed and confused, but he had understood the word *murder*. "I-I-I," he stuttered, "thought you said you wouldn't hurt me?"

"I won't if you give me the correct code."

"2-4-7-8."

Apple entered first and disengaged the alarm. She placed a police scanner on the coffee table and turned it on. It crackled first before a dispatcher was heard running down reported crimes in the nearby neighborhood.

Hood dragged Nerd inside by his collar and threw him on his couch in his living room. "Watch him," he ordered to IG, who nodded while Hood searched the small one-bedroom apartment for any signs of life.

Nerd was baffled. They weren't supposed to be there. He did not protect trap houses, and he wasn't cutting up coke or bagging up the dope. This was his parents' two-family home that should have been off limits. He understood the obvious was that he assisted a drug organization in obtaining information, but he wasn't dealing drugs. He was a geek, a hacker, a twenty-year-old virgin—but nonetheless, he was preyed upon. Naively, Nerd thought a home invasion's sole purpose was to steal the ill-gotten gains acquired from distributing drugs usually hidden in someone's home. He said, "I don't have any money."

Apple looked around and snorted. "Obviously. How much that bitch paying you?" It was a rhetorical question. "Had you worked for me, you would have seen better days."

There it was again, the threat of his impending death hovering in the air, strangling any morsel of courage to face his consequences like a man.

He couldn't accept that Apple used past tense verbiage when summing up his life. Like a fiction novel, she could turn the page, and what was written next was solely in her hands.

Apple knew Nerd was important to Queenie's organization. His spying skills gave the L.E.S. Crips an edge over rival gangs. Nerd's hacking and cyber-stalking were what placed this voyeur on Apple's kill list.

Nerd had one job to do. And from the first day Queenie showed up at Apple's front door, she knew that he did it well.

"Where's the DVR?"

Nerd's eyes widened. "What?"

"This nigga wanna lose limbs? Or maybe he wants me to send y'all upstairs?" Apple glanced at his interior cameras, which was expected from someone of his caliber. "The DVR that records all of it. Where is it? And if I have to ask you again you're gonna have a problem."

Nerd gave up the hidden location of his DVR and now wished that he had a live stream to his security company. But the voyeur who took great pride and pleasure snooping into people's lives wanted something that he never afforded his victims: privacy.

He whined, "Please don't kill me. I can be of value to your organization. Just let me live, and I'll do whatever you want."

"You're gonna tell us what we want regardless," Apple said. "You have no leverage, so stop fuckin' talking until I ask you a specific question."

Hood retrieved the DVR and dismantled all the interior cameras before walking back into the living room and giving Apple a head nod. Now, everyone relaxed. The trio pulled their ski masks back just above their eyes so they could continue with a conversation where Nerd either dispensed intel or be tortured first. The choice was his to make on how he wanted his life to end. The fact that they were now unmasked was the last act of confirmation needed to snuff out that 1% of hope to live to see another day lingering for Nerd.

Apple kneeled in front of the wounded victim and asked, "What's Queenie's address, the addresses to all her stash houses, and what's numero uno? What that bitch got planned?"

Nerd thought about lying, he did. Why give them what they wanted? They wouldn't know if his information would be legit or not until they tested it, and he would be dead so there would be no additional way they could retaliate against him. They would just have to trust him. But Nerd was cerebral. He was thinking a couple steps ahead to his death and his burial. He was about to be murdered, a casualty of war, and his family would grieve. His parents and his sister would deeply mourn him, and yet he knew that his boss would give no fucks. Queenie was protected by her goons—her armed henchmen who had a shot at winning this war between the two factions. If he gave up his boss, then maybe he would see her on the other side. He couldn't stand to be the only one going in the ground for beef that wasn't his to begin with.

"And if you're thinking about giving me false information, I can promise you this: We will come back and park a bullet in your little sister's head and make your parents watch. And then my guy over here," Apple pointed toward IG, "he'll get his hands dirty torturing your moms while your father watches, and you know how the rest will play out."

Oh wow. He hadn't thought of that. But the threat was no longer needed. Nerd gave it all up. Any information he knew about Queenie and the L.E.S. Crips was dispensed to the stone-cold killer, the Baddest Apple.

The click-clacking of a lock turning and the sudden entrance of Nerd's mom startled everyone, including Nerd. He had told his mother on a million occasions to stop using her spare key to invade his space. He was a grown man.

But there she was, holding a plate of food she had made for him at her office party earlier that evening. Her eyes looked at all the intruders, her son's bruised and bloody face, and she still had the wherewithal and wits to run. Nerd's mother took flight toward her upstairs apartment with Hood and IG right on her heels.

"Ma, run!" Nerd yelled, and the butt of Apple's gun swiped him across his mouth, knocking out both of his front teeth. A surge of adrenaline coursed through his veins and Nerd lunged forward and tackled her to the ground. Apple fell backward and hit her head on his tiled floor with a hard thud. There wasn't any time for her to process the pain because Nerd's lean body was lying on top of hers. His bodyweight made it difficult for her to regain control of her pistol. The struggle was intense as the barrel of the gun turned into a compass, pointing north and then back south. If the bullet landed true north, then Apple would be dead. This was a battle of strength, survival, and sheer willpower. Who wanted to live more? Blood from his wound was spilling into Nerd's blurry eye, but he fought through his pain. With his vision impaired, he squeezed the trigger.

Bak! Bak!

The bullets landed just inches from Apple's ear, nearly rupturing her eardrum. This close encounter was the most fear she had felt in a long time. The sound startled Nerd, and for one split second his grip on the pistol eased up just enough for Apple to get the upper hand. She twisted Nerd's wrist back and fired her cannon into his chest.

Bak! Bak! Bak!

Nerd stopped struggling and collapsed his head on Apple's face. She forcefully pushed his dead weight off of her and climbed to her feet. This was messy. It wasn't supposed to go down like this, especially when she saw Hood and IG march Nerd's parents and his seven-year-old sister into the living room that was now a crime scene.

Everyone was crying and screaming hysterically, and Apple didn't know if the gunshots had alerted the neighbors. Police could be on their way. Time was of the essence, and she had a crucial decision to make.

Apple held up two fingers on her hand. Both Hood and IG looked at the little girl, and Apple shook her head.

"But she's seen our faces!"

"You heard what the fuck I said. Now let's go!"

Without hesitation, Gloria and Henry were shot point-blank in the back of their heads. Their bodies keeled over and slumped to the ground. Alexis threw her body over her mother's and just sobbed. She was young and understood little, but she knew murder. She realized that everyone had been shot and she needed to get help. Alexis looked up, and the bad guys were gone. She did as she had been taught to do and went searching for a cell phone to call for help. Her small hands were saturated in her mother's blood as she dialed 9-1-1.

"This is nine-one-one dispatch. What's the emergency?"

Her tiny voice was barely a whisper as she reported, "My parents have been shot."

The ride back to Apple's apartment was ridden in silence. Hood and IG felt uneasy about leaving a witness alive. This was a triple homicide, and adding another body to the count wouldn't change a thing in the eyes of New York State's judicial system. If found guilty, it was still the same sentence: life without the possibility of parole.

Apple sat in the backseat unaffected by her team's ambivalence toward her. There was no connection between them and Nerd, so any description a child gave to police would be fruitless. They would go looking into his past, and Apple wouldn't come up on the police's radar. Nine million people were living in New York City. Looking for a black female with light skin and no history with the victims was a needle in an enormous haystack. Besides, she was a murderer, not a monster, and there wasn't any way she was killing a kid. The little girl was a child with her whole life ahead of her, and Apple didn't want to push fate. Karma had a way of coming back around, and sins of the mother were real to her. For all she knew, had she killed that kid it could trickle down to her own daughter. Despite the messy outcome, she still felt they scored a win. Nerd had dropped a dime on Queenie, and it was finally time to bring down the L.E.S. Crips and the woman masquerading as the Queen of New York.

28

Rehab lectured their men, "Yo, y'all niggas watch your six out there. We gettin' heat from that twin bitch. She trying to take Queenie's crown! Each move she successfully makes against us takes food out all our mouths. Y'all feel me? Keep ya eyes peeled on your product and your blocks 'cause we ain't paying for any more funerals."

Queenie's soldiers were ready. She had handpicked them all. Her henchmen had survived gang initiations, turf and drug wars, and police raids. Most had been shot or stabbed up for a cut of that drug money. Rehab looked into the faces of the meanest muthafuckas the streets had raised up—angry goons marginalized all their lives with boulder-size chips on their shoulders. Each night they made it home alive gave them another day to flood the streets with their product, terrorize neighborhoods with their presence, and take rivals away from their loved ones. These men would kill your grandma over an ounce of weed, your child for a ki of cocaine. Some had battle scars etched in their faces that resembled a closed zipper, and others had keloids that now replaced wounds where bullets had entered and exited. These men had waged wars against the most thorough triggermen the boroughs had produced and lived to brag about it.

Rehab was paranoid because they were taking too many losses and also because Queenie had put him in charge over Lord. His new position as her right hand came with a lot of responsibilities, and one false move could cost him his life. Rehab wasn't fucking around with this Apple bitch. The beef had him carrying three pistols. He had a 9mm tucked in his waistband, a .45 in his shoulder holster, and a snub-nosed .380 attached to his ankle.

The latest trap house was in a densely populated section of Spanish Harlem, a location where high activity was regular. Tonight, everyone had a part to play. They had just received a large shipment of 35 kilos of heroin from Queenie's connect Diego Guzmàn and a cargo van full of immigrant women who would be sold over the border in Canada as slave labor. The murder of Pastor Foster and the tainted heroin had set them back, so these new shipments were needed to build them up again.

Lord spoke up next. There was no way he would allow only Rehab to address who he still considered his men. To Lord, it was just a matter of time before Queenie was snuffed out and he could take his rightful position over her organization.

"I would trust any of y'all soldiers with my life. We all came up L.E.S. Crips for life, and we gonna die that way!"

Lord threw up a few gang signs, stiff finger and hand movements that got the crowd hyped. A few goons began to Crip Walk, showing off their footwork.

He continued. "I've bus'ed my gun beside most you niggas, fucked the same bitches, and we all rep the same L.E.S. Crips tattoo. We have a brotherhood—that means something. None of us take handouts; we earn ours. This here product is how we feed our families, take care of our women, and support ourselves, so if any muthafuckas come between us and our livelihood, make it bloody."

The men nodded their agreement.

Stone wondered if he should make a speech next, but Rehab apparently wasn't done holding court. He addressed his top enforcers. "Gee, Mitch,

Bliss, and Pop, y'all on the women. Stop and get them something to eat before y'all hit the road. And Peanut, Tank, Kidd, Spanky, and Lil' Whop, y'all niggas on the dope. Make y'all drops and hit me up later."

Gee nodded. "We on it, Rehab."

"One more thing. Any time, any place y'all see Apple, Hood, or IG, shoot on sight."

"They better hope they don't cross my fuckin' path. I will blow their heads off," said Peanut as he brandished his Desert Eagle to punctuate his point.

Rehab took a pull from the blunt he had just sparked up and then passed it to Lord. "Y'all hold it down out there."

"A'ight, y'all go feed the streets," said Stone, adding his two cents as everyone dispersed.

Apple, IG, and Hood patiently watched the trap house like hawks. They knew Queenie's men were inside. Lord, Stone, and Rehab were their primary targets tonight.

"This shit gonna be like shooting crabs in a barrel." Apple inhaled her cancer stick and exhaled the carcinogen into the air, which mixed with the weed haze. She looked at Hood in the driver's seat—his eyes were low— and then glanced over her shoulder at IG and Tokyo in the backseat. "Y'all better not get too faded. We got some murders up next."

Hood was already faded, but he felt this was lightweight. He'd been putting in work for years, and this ambush was just another day for him. "I always get lifted before a little gunplay," he admitted.

IG was quiet when something dawned on him. "Yo, where that nigga Killer Mike been?"

The question had them stumped. It felt like a college exam was going down inside Hood's SUV as everyone pondered all the possibilities.

"Word, I ain't seen him in a minute," said Hood.

"He could have gotten jammed up," added Apple.

"Or, he could be plotting," said IG.

"Fuck that nigga," said Apple.

All they saw were hoodies shielding each goon's face as a group of dark figures coolly walked out of the trap house. Apple counted nineteen killers but couldn't distinguish one man from another. The men gave each other dap while they had their backs turned against the curb.

"Tokyo, you ready?" Apple said.

"Hell yeah!"

Apple removed her 9mm and handed Tokyo a .380. She gripped the handle with confidence and knew she had something to prove. IG had his MAC-10 on his lap while Hood had two ninas. Everyone stealthily exited the vehicle, crouching low to catch their prey by surprise. It was easy creeping up on niggas who were about to get caught slipping.

IG let his MAC-10 loose. *Rat-ta-Tat! Tat! Tat! Tat! Tat! Tat! Tat! Tat!* At least four bodies dropped instantly as deafening bursts of gunfire exploded from the automatic weapon. The powerful firearm mowed down half of Queenie's men and tore into Stone's back, pushing him violently forward. Lord opened fire, shattering the glass of several cars on the street.

Bak! Bak! Bak!

A bullet whizzed past Tokyo's shoulder as she ducked for cover. Hovering behind a parked car, she was frozen with fear. Her heart lurched as her assailant zeroed in on her. Tokyo fumbled with the pistol in her hand to defend herself. Lord kept advancing forward, determined to body that young bitch as she hid from his barrage of bullets. Apple noticed and opened fire.

Boom! Boom! Boom! Boom!

Apple ran toward Tokyo and grabbed her up by her collar, shielding Tokyo with her own body. With her arm outstretched, Apple shot her way to safety. Ducked behind an SUV, she gave her protégé instructions. "When I tell you to run, take off down the block. I'll cover you and meet you at home."

"I can't leave you!"

Apple rose up and bucked off her gun again.

Boom! Boom! Boom! Boom!

She turned toward Tokyo and yelled, "Run!" and she took flight like a track star, never looking back.

Boom! Boom! Boom! Boom!

The one-block radius was pure pandemonium. Hood and Rehab were exchanging bullets, trying to take each other's head off, while IG was mowing down soldiers one by one like bowling pins. Peanut's chest cavity was opened up as three rounds slammed through his flesh. His body fell hard on a tricked-out Navigator and dented its exterior.

Neighbors watched the horrific scene from second and third story windows and immediately dialed 9-1-1.

Boom! Boom! Boom! Boom!

Bak! Bak! Bak!

Ra-ta-tat! Tat! Tat! Tat! Tat! Tat!

Two more of Queenie's men went down. Windshield after windshield was shot out, and shards of glass shattered through the air like confetti and blanketed the pavement.

The police sirens blaring in the distance were like a silent whistle to dogs; everyone's ears perked up. Apple glanced over her shoulder, relieved to see that Hood and IG were still alive, but so were Lord and Rehab along with two underlings, Gee and Spanky.

Spanky found himself boxed in. It was raining bullets, and one tore through his shoulder. The blood slid down his arm, making it difficult for him to aim. "Fuck y'all!" he screamed out, shooting wildly, unable to hit his target. Through his peripheral Spanky saw the shadowy figure continuing to advance forward. He tried to steady his Glock, but he had lost feeling in his hand.

Bak! Bak! Bak!

Hood stood firm, both arms outstretched with his ninas, and pumped bullets into Spanky's face and neck. His body instantly dropped to the pavement. Hood walked up and slammed four additional rounds into his face and spat, "Closed casket, nigga!"

Apple wanted Lord. She had been gunning for him since he went after Tokyo. She saw him trying to exit. Lord jumped over a Fiat 500 like it was a milk crate, making a mad dash toward an alleyway.

Apple wanted to give chase, but it was too late. The blue-and-white vehicles had descended on the block, and more gunshots were exchanged as police officers opened fire.

Boom! Boom! Boom! Boom!

Bak! Bak! Bak!

Ra-ta-tat! Tat! Tat! Tat! Tat! Tat!

Enemies had formed an alliance as Hood, IG, Rehab, Gee, and Apple were in a fierce gun battle with NYPD. When IG reloaded his clip and sprayed the cop cars with unrelenting rounds from his MAC-10, the firepower was too overwhelming. The boys in blue took off, running in the opposite direction.

Ra-ta-tat! Tat! Tat! Tat! Tat! Tat!—echoed in the air—*Ra-ta-tat! Tat! Tat! Tat! Tat! Tat!*—he bucked off again.

And then an eerie silence enveloped the block as the assailants made their escapes.

Thirty minutes later, the area was blanketed with SWAT and additional red and blue lights. Within an hour the neighborhood was overrun with men holding brass badges wanting to interview any and everyone who had witnessed the melee. This was a massacre. And to complicate matters, a van full of immigrants was found. No one knew what they were up against.

29

THREE WEEKS LATER

The unknown caller was sent straight to voicemail as Apple and Peaches sat in the custom leather seats at her local nail salon, Susie's Nail Bar. She and her daughter had their feet submerged in bubbly water as the nail techs, Minah and Seohyun, went to work removing old polish and cutting cuticles. The unknown number called again, and Apple promptly hit the ignore button and continued her conversation with Peaches.

"Is that the color you picked out?" Apple asked as she looked at the Barney-purple polish. "I like it."

Peaches nodded. "What's your color, Mommy?" Apple held up a nude colored OPI polish for her approval. "Oh, that's pretty, Mommy."

The phone rang a third time, and curiosity led Apple to say, "Who is this?"

An exasperated Kamel sputtered. "Apple, don't hang up!"

"Kamel?" Apple was heated how her sister had forced her to take her daughter before she was ready. Three weeks ago she had tried to return Peaches back to them, but no one was home. Apple had called both Kola's and Kamel's cell phones repeatedly, but they just ignored her. "That's some foul shit y'all on!"

Apple's anger was inconsequential to him. His questions were rushed, desperation from a caged man. "Are you alone? Can you talk?"

She heard the urgency and panic in his voice and feared something had happened to Kola. Apple put up her index finger to pause her pedicure with her nail tech and then turned toward Peaches. "I'll be back in a sec."

Apple slipped her wet feet into the flimsy flip flops and walked briskly to the front entrance for privacy. "What's happened?"

"Where's your sister?"

Apple sucked her teeth. "You tell me."

"When was the last time you spoke with her?"

Apple heard commotion in the background—gates slamming shut, numerous men shouting, buzzers going off. "Where are you?"

Kamel realized that Apple was in the dark. "I'm locked up, Apple. I've been here for weeks. Your sister just left me here to rot."

"Why? What did you do to her? If you hurt her, I will end you!"

"Shit's fucked up, Apple. I don't know how to tell you this, but there was an accident at the crib, and Junior and Sophia are both dead."

"Dead?" Apple repeated the word but couldn't say much more; it stuck in her throat and choked her up. She fell back against the wall for support. Instantly Apple thought of her daughter. How was she going to explain this to her? "What kind of accident? Swimming?"

"Nah. Gas leaked carbon monoxide from our basement while they were asleep. I had to make a quick run and had to leave them alone. When I came back, it was too late."

Apple knew that lately, Kamel was the responsible parent and would never leave Junior and Sophia alone. He was covering for his wife. "You haven't heard from Kola at all?"

"I haven't seen her since the incident. I've been arraigned, and she didn't come to court, post my bail, hire me a lawyer, nothing."

"Why didn't you call me weeks ago? This would have been handled."

"I was in here racking my brain tryin' to remember numbers. The only cell number I know is my wife's, and she wouldn't pick up."

"That's fucked up."

"Jamel just might be an angel watching over me despite our differences
'cause I was blessed when Monk came through. He knew your number off
his dome. Nigga said he makes it a priority to remember all numbers for
situations such as mine."

"Your brother was a lot of things, but he ain't no angel. I would bet
my life on that," Apple remarked. "But someone was looking out for you
'cause I just saw that nigga Monk last week and gave him my number."

"But, yo, App, find my wife and get me the fuck up outta here. I know
you and I have our issues, but we're still family, and on my life, the only
good thing about this situation is that Peaches was with you that night."

"I got you," she said.

Apple hung up, and unexpectedly, she broke down. Crying was a rare
emotion for her. She placed both hands over her face and screamed into
the palms of her hands for the two children she considered her niece and
nephew, and for how grateful she was that Peaches wasn't there.

"Damn, Kola. Fuck!" she said out loud.

Apple wiped her tear-streaked face and lit up. She pulled on her
Newport as she dissected the situation. Where was Kola? She had no idea
where she would look for her. And where were Junior and Sophia buried,
and why didn't her sister allow her and Peaches to attend the funeral to
say their goodbyes? Apple flicked her cigarette toward the curb and bolted
inside. She had things to do. A crisp hundred was handed to Minah while
Apple scooped up Peaches into her arms.

"Why are we leaving?" Peaches wanted to know.

"We have things to do baby. We have to go and help Uncle Kamel."

Peaches wasn't ecstatic about having to cut her day short to help Uncle
Kamel because her mother had promised to take her to the movies to
see *Avengers: Endgame*. However, a quick stop through McDonald's drive-
thru had silenced her for the moment. Chicken nuggets and fries had

halted the million questions Peaches kept asking and allowed Apple to handle some business.

"Peaches, put on your earphones and listen to some music or YouTube while I make some important phone calls," Apple directed.

Her daughter was too focused on dipping her nugget into her hot mustard sauce to question the command. She simply nodded and did what she was told.

The lawyer, Angelo Scarpetta, was retained with one quick phone call and her Apple Pay cash app. After she had secured counsel for Kamel, she called Hood.

"El Jefe, what's good?"

"Yo, I'm going to keep this short. My sister is missing. Put the word out that there's a hundred large for whoever brings her to my front door—alive."

"This got anything to do wit' Queenie?"

"Nah, this is personal."

"Anything more I can do?" he asked.

"I got it from here."

Apple fought through traffic to arrive at the county jail, where she posted Kamel's bail. It would take hours of idle time and a couple tantrums from Peaches before he was eventually processed and released. Kamel laid grateful eyes on Apple as Peaches ran and jumped into his strong arms. He picked her up in a bear hug and spun her around until she squealed. They were both happy to see one another. She planted a massive kiss on his cheek and wrapped her arms around his neck as he carried her to the car. Kamel tickled Peaches and jostled her around for a few moments until Apple suggested that it was time to go.

Kamel stared out the passenger's window of Apple's luxury vehicle and had a few moments of reflection. He was a free man for now, but this situation was far from over. The assistant district attorney was going hard. He wanted Kamel to leave prison in a pine box. And then there was Kola. She had turned her back on him when he needed her most. As he sat in jail, he wondered if she had discovered his affair. And if so, did it give her provocation to just abandon him even when he had fallen on his sword for her? Kamel had wanted to contact Melinda when Kola fell through so she could post his bail, but he didn't know her number either. He didn't even remember her area code.

Kamel's property was returned to him in the standard manila envelope. His watch, jewels, and cell phone connected him to his former life—his life when he had a wife, two children, a mistress, and hardly any worries. He draped his heavy chains around his neck and put on his Rolex and pinky ring and flipped down the visor mirror. Kamel looked at his reflection and wanted to get dropped off at his barber.

"Are you done?" Apple asked as she watched him with a side eye. "We gotta find Kola and go pay our respects. I want to know where she buried"—she turned to make sure Peaches was still listening to her music— "Junior and Sophia. Damn, I miss my lil' man. And my crybaby Sophia . . . This is so fucked up. They didn't even get a chance to experience life."

"This shit is like a bad dream, Apple. Those kids gave me life . . . I lived for them." He rubbed his beard and shook his head in disbelief. "All the fucked up people walking this earth and God wanna take them?"

Apple noticed that Kamel was laser-focused on reading his text messages. "Any missed calls from Eduardo?"

"Absolutely. Like a hundred."

"What about from Kola?"

He shook his head. "Nah, she don't give a fuck about me."

"Stop whining, nigga!" Apple barked. She cut her eyes over her shoulders at Peaches and then lowered her voice. "Does it not strike you as strange that Kola is missing? What do you think that means?"

"It means that those meds ain't working," he dryly remarked. Now that Kamel was released his mood had shifted; he did a one-eighty right before Apple's eyes. He was no longer humbled and grateful. Kamel was feeling the early stages of bitterness and resentment. He was in this situation because of Kola. Kamel loved his freedom and didn't want to give it up now that he had some alone time to think these past few weeks.

Apple could see he wasn't connecting her dots. "You not worried about Eduardo?"

Kamel blew out air. "I feel for him, but he's just gonna have to handle it. Shit was an accident. I'll call him and tell him that I'm sorry for his loss—"

"Sorry?" *What part of the game is this?* she thought. "You didn't crash his car; you killed his kids."

"Kola killed those kids," he stated.

"Semantics to a drug lord," Apple scoffed. "And if you value your life you better not tell Eduardo they're dead, at least not until we find Kola so y'all can figure this out. She'll know what to do."

Kamel shook his head. The last thing he would do was take orders from the problem child. Apple was back in the game, and she thought she was everyone's boss, dictating orders to underlings. He wasn't on her payroll. Kamel had heard that they were calling her El Jefe, a name held for the top men in the Latin cartels.

"I'ma call Eduardo and tell him straight up, man-to-man, how shit went down. I'll let him know that I left them alone, not Kola."

"You actin' like you can't be touched!" Apple said. "And what about my sister? You're not even worried that Eduardo could already know about Junior and Sophia and my sister could be dead?" She shrugged. "But those texts are important, though."

Kamel was still reading all the angry texts from Melinda spewing her hurt and pain. He was suffocating in the car with Apple, never able to be around her for long. "Drop me off to my truck and let me handle my household."

"You's a stupid muthafucka!"

"Likewise."

Apple and Kamel rode the rest of the drive in silence. She dropped him off to his house, and Kola's car still wasn't there. On the ride back to the city, she called Hood. "I'm going to text you my sister's address. I need you and IG to have eyes on this sneaky nigga. Follow him, see where he goes. Something ain't adding up. Kids are dead, my sister is missing. This muthafucka coulda went Charles Manson on everybody."

"Who's dead?" Hood wanted to know.

"Mind ya business!" Apple snapped. "Information is dispersed on a need-to-know basis."

The sinking feeling in Apple's gut that her sister was dead was solidified when Kamel called the next morning to tell her the incredulous news. Not only had Kola left him to rot in jail, but she didn't claim the bodies of Junior and Sophia, so they were shipped off as indigents to Hart's Island and placed in a mass burial plot. Potter's Field was usually reserved for AIDS victims, the homeless, and indigent inmates. Eduardo Jr. and Sophia were the heirs to one of the richest men in Colombia, and they were resting in a pauper's grave?

"Apple, I'm starting to get worried," Kamel finally admitted. "Kola would have never allowed this to happen. Potter's Field? Back in the day, I heard horror stories about that place."

"You didn't call Eduardo, did you?"

"Nah, I was trying to locate their graves so I could take pictures. I had decided to fly to Colombia with the pictures so he could see their final resting place. I thought the news should come in person."

"Colombia? Nigga, you on bail," Apple reminded him. "My bail!"

"Ain't nobody sweating ya little bail money."

Apple sucked her teeth. It's always funky money, little money, petty money when it's not your money. Borrowed money is the most insulted form of currency.

"I got the streets looking for my sister. When she's not doped up, she's a smart bitch. I'm hoping that the old Kola resurfaced and she went underground. I promise you that Eduardo is gonna put his murder game down hard if he finds out what happened, so I'ma warn you again, keep this shit on the D.L. until we find her. And when we find her, y'all better run. Let him think it's a kidnapping and not a murder." Apple was serious. "And don't sweat any money. I have money stashed, and Kola can have it all."

"You think my baby's still alive?"

"I hope she is, Kamel. I don't feel like I've lost her . . . I still feel our connection."

When Apple said "connection," Kamel instantly got it. He, too, connected with his brother.

"I'm going to work on getting their bodies exhumed and relocated so we can have a proper burial. It's the city, so I was told that there is a lot of red tape. Scarpetta referred me to a lawyer that's going to handle this for us so we good on that, but he said it could take as long as six months," Kamel said.

"I want them buried next to Denise and Nichols. I think Kola would like that."

"Nah, Apple. Eduardo would want something more substantial like a mausoleum, something that represents royalty and lasts for centuries bearing his last name. Anything less than that will be an insult."

"You still hell-bent on telling this man! You're so stubborn, just like your brother. When he got something in his head, he wouldn't give up."

"Eduardo is a reasonable, levelheaded man. He was going to murder Kola and me, but I kicked it, real talk, and he kept it one-hundred. I got this, Apple. All we need to do is find Kola and bury Junior and Sophia in some flashy shit like granite and terracotta stone, maybe have their pictures etched on the wall. I'm telling you I can handle this. The lie would be the mistake, the insult. Trust me, I know how he thinks."

"You think you know him, do you?" she chuckled. "I saw him cut a man that was tied up in his basement in half with a chainsaw and then come out and fuck me with my sister upstairs oblivious to it all."

"I'm a grown man, Apple. I'm not running from no one. I bus' my gun too."

"A'ight, gangsta. I've said my piece."

30

ood and IG sat outside a small bungalow in Yonkers, New York. The white vinyl siding with hunter green shutters was quaint and cookie-cutter cute. They had followed Kamel to this same location two nights in a row. Other than this place, he went to see his lawyer and went down to the county morgue. They both felt it was time to update Apple.

"We got an address for you," Hood said. "I just sent you a text."

Apple pulled up on the block just after midnight—creeping hours. She had left Peaches with Tokyo, so her mind was clear to focus on this situation. She circled a few times and then parked a few blocks over and walked back under the cloak of darkness. She slid in the backseat of Hood's truck.

"What's good? What's going on here?"

Hood said, "He's stayed overnight here twice, so we know there's a bitch inside. She ain't come out all weekend, though. She just in there getting fucked."

"Just how I like 'em." IG snickered.

"How y'all know it's a woman who lives here?" Apple didn't want to believe that Kamel was cheating on her sister. They were married, and that should mean something. Why say the vows if you're going to live like a single man? "This could be a trap house."

"Oh, he trap?"

Apple didn't answer. Kamel had retired years ago. Her silence didn't go unnoticed. IG said, "This ain't no trap house. We laid up on this crib for days, and there's no movement whatsoever. This the smash house."

Apple stared at Kamel's truck indifferently. Her sister was missing, and this nigga was fucking? She laid out on the backseat and said, "Wake me up when he leaves."

Seven hours later, she felt a few taps to her legs. "App, get up. That nigga just left."

Groggily she pulled her eyes open and sat up. She sat up straight and was quiet for a few minutes. Apple yawned and tried to get her bearings. Her tart breath circulated throughout the SUV. It was too early for murder. She wanted a coffee and something sweet to eat.

"I would kill for a Krispy Kreme donut and caramel latte."

They didn't respond. Both were slightly aggravated that she had slept through the stakeout, but she was the boss, El Jefe as she liked to be called.

"You ready?" Hood asked as he looked at her through the rearview.

"Always." Apple checked her .45 Glock—one in the chamber—and they all exited the vehicle and cut through a neighbor's yard and snaked through to the back door of the residence. Their guns were drawn, and Hood did the honors. Hood lifted his knee in the air to give himself some force and propelled his foot forward, slamming against the door with pure power, leveling it. Quickly, they charged inside.

"Oh my god!" Melinda shrieked. "What's happening?"

When Apple saw it was a woman, she bashed her in the face with the butt of her gun. Melinda's head jerked, and she crumbled to the ground. Her body was limp as Apple grabbed a fistful of her hair and dragged her to the living room and told her to "Sit down and shut the fuck up!"

IG and Hood did a preliminary search of the property to make sure there weren't any more people. Melinda was holding the side of her face.

Her lip was split open, heavily bleeding onto her silk shirt. Her eyes searched for understanding at the thugs.

"I have money, jewelry, televisions. Take what you want and leave."

Apple looked closely into the pretty woman's face. She was the exact opposite of her sister. Kola had light skin, she had dark. Kola was petite and curvy, she was tall and thick. Kola's hair was long and layered, her hair was short and natural. The very essence of this woman angered Apple because she was confused. Kamel had a type, so this meant that she wasn't random, a clone to bust a nut in. This said that she had captured his attention, maybe something serious. Was she enough to kill for? Did Kamel murder her sister for this bitch and make it seem like Eduardo had a hand in her disappearance? Apple's eyes scanned her wall, and the photo of her and Kamel boo'd up gave her confirmation.

"We don't want ya shit," Apple said.

Melinda was frozen in fear. If this wasn't a robbery, was it rape? Her eyes darted toward the two thugs, and she began to visibly shake. "Please, God, no . . . don't rape me," she pleaded.

"Bitch, please," IG said, insulted.

Apple grabbed a chair and sat in front of her. "What's your name?"

"My name?" She was so frightened that she blurted out her full government. "Melinda Mary Wilson."

"What's up with you and Kamel?"

"Kola?"

Apple wanted to slap the shit out of her. But she wanted to understand who her brother-in-law was. His wife was missing, presumably dead, and he was fucking this whore?

"Yes. What did Kamel tell you about me?"

"Your beef should be with your husband, not me."

"So he told you we were married?" Apple asked. "You know you're fucking a married man?"

Melinda was beyond frightened. She knew she fucked up. "He said that you two were getting divorced."

"Oh, did he?" Apple said sarcastically. Flashbacks to the Scott and Laci Petterson story felt eerily parallel to this situation. "What else was he supposed to say?"

"I don't know what you mean."

"He showed you divorce papers?"

"Well, no, but—"

"What do you do for a living?"

"What?"

"Don't make me ask you twice or I will knock all your teeth out your mouth. Your whole front row will be Chiclets."

"I'm an investment banker."

"Oh, an educated woman who knows how to make money. Did you buy this house or did my husband?"

"I bought it."

"Listen carefully, and you better not lie to me. How long has this been going on?"

"Nearly a year."

"Since he said we're divorcing, are y'all getting married?"

"Why are you torturing yourself asking these questions? Whatever I say will hurt you, and I don't want to be hurtful. It just happened with us."

"Does he love you?"

She whispered, "Yes."

Apple placed her hand to her ear. "What? I can't hear you? Does my husband love you?"

"I don't know—no, he doesn't. He loves you. So please just go. I promise I'll leave him alone."

"You would do that for me? From today moving forward, you would unfuck my husband?"

Melinda cried hysterically. She didn't know what she had gotten herself into, but she knew that an affair didn't warrant death. The look in the female's eyes was pure evil. Melinda looked at the two henchmen, threateningly giving her hard stares as they clutched the largest weapons she had ever seen.

All her life, Melinda was a good girl, right until she met Kamel. Her mind told her to run the moment he told her he was married, but then he kicked game, so her heart told her to trust him. Give him a chance. Melinda knew he was a bad boy; his swagger was exhilarating. When he would remove his pistol from his shoulder holster and place it on her nightstand, she felt protected, almost invincible. Now, where was he when she needed him? How could he allow this to happen? They had made love all weekend and to prove his love to her he said he would stay overnight. And he did. Melinda thought that Kola was finally out of the picture, that they were getting divorced, and then this happened. She was only starting her thirties. She didn't want to die. Her death would shatter her parents. Melinda begged for her life.

"Please, don't . . . kill . . . me. I'm sorry, Kola. I'm so, so, so, sorry!"

"Shhhhh," Apple said. "I'm not going to kill you."

Melinda wanted to believe her. She searched her assailant's eyes for truth and compassion and thought she had found it. Her wails turned into sobs and then soft whimpers.

Apple nodded, and IG placed a plastic bag over her head and began to smother her while Apple sat inches away. Apple grabbed Melinda's hands as she tried to wiggle free.

"Melinda, stop struggling. You're going to die today, sweetie. But take comfort that Kamel may be joining you soon. Or not—I haven't decided yet."

Apple moved closer as Melinda succumbed to her lack of oxygen. She wanted the last face this bitch saw to be hers. The same face as Kola's.

31

Kamel had been calling Melinda repeatedly, but it kept going to voicemail. With Kola gone, he could rock up to Melinda's whenever he wanted. Tonight he came through earlier than usual to surprise her. He knew he was gambling with his feelings. What if she had another nigga there? Kamel pulled up on the block and her car was there. However, when he knocked, she didn't come to the door. Kamel was territorial and overnight had become possessive over a woman he didn't have a claim to. He pulled his Glock from his waist and crept around back. Kamel didn't know what he would do if he found her fucking another man, but it didn't stop him from moving forward. The broken glass caused his heart to hitch. Instinctively he went in, not sure of what he would find.

Melinda was in her bed under the covers. Kamel gripped his pistol as his eyes darted around her small home. He didn't know if someone was still there or if this was an ambush or a petty burglary, but he couldn't leave without knowing she was okay. He called her name, "Melinda?"

She didn't answer. Kamel's voice echoed throughout her home and came bouncing back to him. Slowly he pulled the covers back, and Melinda was in bed, naked with a steak knife shoved in her vagina. Red lipstick had #2, written on her forehead. Kamel jumped back like he was electrocuted. #2? Who did this? Anger swept over his whole being as he knew it could only be either Kola or Apple or Kola *and* Apple. Maybe Kola wasn't missing after all.

Apple needed her sister. She needed to know that she was all right or that she wasn't. The ambiguity of it all was knocking her off her A-game. Her mind was fractured in two places: Kola and Queenie. She woke up the next morning wanting to call Eduardo to see if she could glean if he knew what was up. Had he hurt Kola? Yesterday morning she had murdered Kamel's mistress, yet she had no qualms about calling him.

"Kamel, what's up?"

"What's good, Apple?"

"Nothing good, my sister is still missing. Listen, give me Eduardo's cell."

Apple could hear that he was driving this early in the morning. "His cell? Why?"

"I want to kick it about some business. You know I'm a working girl—something that's foreign to you—work."

Kamel chuckled and then read off Eduardo's digits. He then asked, "Where you at? You home?"

"Why? You keeping tabs on me and not your wife?"

"I got a feeling she around," he said ominously.

Apple knew that meant that he had found Melinda. "Kola's not around unless that's some code word for spirit. I can't help but think you know more about her whereabouts than you saying."

"Then you and I are on the same page, 'cause you and ya sister be playing mind games. That bitch ain't missing—she hiding!"

"Who you calling a bitch?"

"Say something slick and I'ma put my foot up yo ass when I see you," he threatened.

"On the strength of my sister, you're not a dead man talking. Please don't force me to let my dogs off their leashes," she warned.

Kamel's voice was hoarse from all the built-up angst and trauma he felt over the past few weeks. Finding Melinda's desecrated body just weeks after he walked in to see Junior and Sophia dead had pushed him over to the dark side, a place he hadn't gone since he had killed his brother in cold blood. He was about to spazz out.

Kamel knew that he could never hurt Kola; he was most likely going to go to jail for her. But, Apple? He was ready to blow a cannon-size hole in her muthafuckin' head. He had warned her too often to stop instigating shit and undermining his authority.

"Apple, those little street victories really got you thinking you invincible. I don't fear you, bitch! I never will."

Apple was lying in bed after her argument with Kamel watching NY1 news, and The Huntsman had struck again. She didn't want to hear his latest kill, so she hit the mute button. The day ahead for her was long, mixed with mommy duties and her drug business. She had to take Peaches for an annual checkup way across town by nine, and then hustle back to drop her off to Tokyo so that she, Hood, and IG could oversee two shipments that were coming in today. Apple had fifteen ki's to pick up from the Mingo cartel and two ki's of heroin from Kiqué Helguero. She had also promised to go out with Touch tonight, so she needed to get back early enough to get her hair and nails done.

Apple was exhausted. She didn't know how single moms made it. Peaches demanded a lot of time; always talking, always wanting to do some activity. She wasn't complaining—well, maybe just a little bit. Apple still hadn't told Peaches about Junior and Sophia. It was such a heavy subject, and with no gravesite so her daughter could say goodbye, it seemed pointless. She also wondered if it was time to involve the police and file a missing person's report on Kola. The streets hadn't turned up any leads, and Apple had doubled the reward.

An hour later, Peaches was fed, showered, and dressed for the day. She sported a Gucci dress and jacket, Vans sneakers, and Ray-Ban gold-rimmed shades. She begged Apple to put purple ribbons in her hair even though she was wearing red and green.

"We gonna work on color coordination soon, baby," said Apple.

"What's color coordination?"

Apple took her daughter's hand and brought her to the mirror. "It's not that."

They both burst out laughing. Almost everything Apple said or did Peaches found funny. She loved her mother deeply, and although she loved Auntie Kola, Uncle Kamel, Junior, and Sophia, Peaches didn't want her mother to send her back. She wanted to live with her permanently.

"You still tight about that needle?" Apple asked.

Peaches had her lips poked out, and her tear stains were drying up. She nodded her anger. The only thing to make her feel better was ice cream. That's what she told her mother.

"Okay, you extortionist. I forgot something at home so let's run there first and then we can swing by Cold Stone Creamery before I drop you to Tokyo's." Apple stopped her conversation short when Hood called.

"We just left the doctor's office, but I forgot something at home. I'll meet y'all up top in a couple hours. Be ready," said Apple.

"Chill, Apple. That two hundred large just bought you the intel you needed. You know this shorty named Pilar in building five on my side of the projects?"

"Not at all."

"Well, she's a paralegal and has access to different databases. She found your sister in New Jersey. She said Kola is in the county jail locked up on a petty weed charge."

"Jersey?" Apple was relieved to hear the news. "Yo, come through. Meet me on my block."

"A'ight. You want me to pay shorty?"

"Hell fucking no."

Peaches was left in the car while Apple made a quick run upstairs. Her sister was alive, and that was all that mattered. She had no idea what weed and New Jersey had to do with anything, but those factors were minor. Apple came back downstairs and did the peripheral scan of the block looking for Hood's truck. She pulled out her cell phone to see how long he was gonna keep her waiting. The threat came from her left; she saw movement and was about to react until she saw his face. She exhaled. It was only Kamel. She waved him over so she could tell him about Kola, or maybe he was there to tell her the same news when a bullet whizzed past her head.

"What the fuck!" she yelled and took off running in the opposite direction of her car to protect her daughter. *This nigga crazy*, Apple thought. She grabbed her 9mm and wanted to bus' back, but she knew she couldn't. Her daughter could get hit. Apple had hunched behind a parked car and yelled out, "Kamel! Peaches is in the fucking car!"

Kamel heard the name Peaches and slowed his trigger finger. His arm was outstretched when he looked to his left, and she was standing just inches from him, crying hysterically. Kamel's heart broke. What the fuck had he done?

Hood and IG had pulled up on the block and did a slow trot with their burners gripped in their hands. They both saw Apple's brother-in-law and knew it was a gun battle, but they didn't see Apple. They had only seen Peaches and Kamel. They assumed that Kamel was protecting Apple and her daughter.

Kamel scooped Peaches up in his free arm and began backpedaling toward his vehicle. "Shhhh," he cooed. "We were only playing a game, baby girl. I would never hurt your mommy."

Peaches had her arms tightly wrapped around his neck, and Kamel's eyes darted from Hood to IG.

"Whatchu doin', yo? Where's Apple?" Hood asked.

Apple came running back down the block now in hysterics. "Kamel, don't take my daughter! Whatever beef we got it has nothing to do with her! She loves you, Kamel. Don't do this!"

Now Hood and IG trained their guns on him, ready to take the shot. Apple saw this and commanded, "Put that shit down! That's my daughter!"

She kept walking closer to Kamel as he made his way to his vehicle. Her arms were up in surrender so he could see she wasn't a threat.

"I told her we were playing a game, Apple. Peaches knows I would never hurt you." Kamel was at his driver's side door. "Tell your men to put those things away, and all y'all walk down the block. I'm going to leave my niece right here."

"C'mon, Kamel. Just give her to me now. She's been through enough."

"Apple, I ain't asking twice."

The trio begrudgingly walked down the block with Apple's eyes trained on her daughter. Kamel had violated her in the worst way. When they got to the corner, Kamel leaned over and gave Peaches a big hug and told her to stop crying. He reached in his pocket and pulled out a twenty dollar bill, and she somewhat cheered up.

"I love you, Peaches. You know that, right?"

She nodded.

Kamel slid into his driver's seat and slowly drove away. He had fucked up by not killing Apple today. She would come for him, and he vowed to be ready.

Apple's plans had changed. She couldn't send Peaches to Tokyo's, not after that traumatic experience. And she could no longer deny that she could keep staying at her residence. Her block was hot, and she was foolish to think otherwise. Hood and IG would handle the pickups today, and Apple called Touch and asked if she and Peaches could spend the night.

"What you gonna do about Kola? You want us to go and bail her out?"

"Nah, not right now. Let Kola sit in there until we kill this nigga. With her home, shit will get complicated. There isn't any way Kamel lives after what he pulled here today. As long as I know where she is and that she's safe, I'm good."

32

The two Colombians knocking at his front door was a shock to Kamel. He had spent the night drinking cognac and looking out for Apple and her henchmen. His arsenal of guns was spread out in each room of his house, and he had three on his person—one in his shoulder holster, one tucked in his waist, and one on his ankle. He was ready. Kamel felt he stayed ready.

Cautiously he approached his front door and peered out. Miguel Sánchez and Felix Gómez were patiently waiting to be let in. Their presence gave Kamel pause because they were the big dogs. These men were Eduardo's top enforcers, men who rarely left Colombia. Both stood stiffly and knocked again.

Kamel flung his front door open and exhaled. He would have to deal with this eventually. The shoulder-holstered gun and pistol in his waist didn't go unnoticed by Miguel and Felix.

"May we come in?" said Miguel.

Kamel nodded and moved to the side. They were led into the spacious living room that Eduardo had financed and calmly took a seat. Both men crossed their legs and waited for Kamel to say something . . . anything. He just stood towering over these men with his breath reeking of alcohol and waited for the interrogation.

Miguel looked at his manicured fingertips before he asked, "Where is Eduardo Jr. and Sophia?" His accent was so thick that Kamel almost needed a translator.

"Y'all want something to drink?" Kamel was stalling, and he didn't know why. He had gone over this scenario a thousand times. But he knew now wasn't the right time for full disclosure. Junior and Sophia were still in Potter's Field, and Kola was missing. Kamel wanted all his ducks in a row before he broke the bad news. His mind wrestled with alternate explanations for their whereabouts. If he said that they were with Apple, they would know the truth within twenty-four hours. And he didn't want to say they were with Kola for Eduardo to ultimately learn the truth. It could put her life in danger.

Miguel was polite when he responded, "We want nothing to drink, but thank you. We would like to know where is El Jefe's niños? Please, tell us so we can go."

Finally, Kamel took a seat and explained the events that took the lives of Junior and Sophia. Miguel and Felix listened intently, not interrupting him once. Kamel was emotional as he described finding them that fateful morning. When he was finished, with a calm voice, Miguel said, "Please, I call Eduardo, and you tell him this, sí?"

Kamel nodded agreeably. He wanted this situation to move along, to put it behind him. And at that moment he wanted to call a truce with Apple. She was his sister-in-law, and he had reacted emotionally over Melinda. What he did, trying to assassinate her over his sidepiece, was the second most idiotic thing he had done. Killing his brother was the first. And what about his wife? Where was she? He was so busy feeling resentment toward being left in jail, he never looked at the situation from her end.

While Miguel was trying to get Eduardo on the line, Kamel sent Apple a text.

I FUCKED UP. I WANT 2 FIX THIS. WE'RE FAMILY APPLE & I LOVE YOU. CALL ME SO WE CAN HASH THIS OUT.

Next, he sent Kola a text.

I NEGLECTED YOU WHEN YOU NEEDED ME MOST. I WAS A SELFISH NIGGA & I NEED 2 TELL YOU SOMETHING THAT I'M ASHAMED OF. I HOPE YOU CAN FORGIVE ME. I LOVE YOU BABY GIRL. COME HOME.

Kamel put his phone away when Miguel handed him his cell phone. Eduardo's voice boomed through the line.

"Miguel says there's something you need to explain to me about my children. Is that true?"

"Yes, Eduardo. I don't know how to say this but let me start by saying that I loved them like they were my own children."

"But, they are not yours, Kamel. They are my children, no?"

"Yes, you right. I was just trying to say that I loved them."

"You speak in the past tense and riddles. Why?"

"We had an accident at the house, and carbon monoxide leaked in the house, and Junior and Sophia didn't make it. They passed away, and I'm sorry."

Kamel tried to break it to Eduardo gently. He looked at Miguel and Felix and still felt no threat.

"Where's Kola?"

"I honestly don't know. She's been gone for over a month. Kola wasn't here when it happened; that's on me."

"Over a month, you say? Is that when this happened? This accident, as you say?"

"Yeah, it happened last month, but—"

"I need to go now and mourn my children. I have to call their mothers. Kamel, you tell my men where my children are buried. I will have them brought back to Colombia. This is their home with me."

All Kola wanted to do was go home, take a shower, and get in her bed. She hadn't seen or spoken to anyone since she was arrested last month. She was worried sick over Junior and Sophia and hoped that Kamel and Apple had handled their burials. She couldn't even think about what this tragedy would do to Eduardo.

Kamel's truck was outside, but he wasn't home when she got there. Kola hadn't been on her meds since she was locked up, so she instantly felt every ounce of panic. Was Kamel still in jail? Her cell phone was dead when she had gotten it from intake, and she didn't have a car charger, so she made the journey home without contact.

Kola showered from head to toe, scrubbing the filthy residue of the jail off of her. The honey scented shampoo felt like a luxury to the jailbird. Naked, she opened the refrigerator, and Kamel's decapitated head was staring directly at her. His eyes were pulled out with a dull spoon, and someone had performed a Colombian necktie. Kola had seen this once before; it's where you slice the throat, and the tongue is pulled through the open wound. Kola ran to the sink and heaved up water and the banana she had just eaten. Her stomach contracted repeatedly, causing her pain. And then she saw a finger lying on a plate. Kola backed away and noticed what she had just recently overlooked. Kamel's body was intricately cut into thirty-seven pieces and placed randomly around her home.

Everything went dark.

The police cruiser sounded his siren a couple times as he rode slowly behind the woman moving down the street like a zombie. Neighbors had reported a naked female who must have had a mental breakdown, and he was there to take her in. His eyes lingered on her backside just a few seconds too long before he parked his cruiser and got out. He removed his police jacket and approached.

"Ma'am? Are you all right?" he asked. "I'm going to need you to come with me." Officer Lake placed his large jacket over Kola's petite frame and led her to his car and sat her down. He called for an ambulance and then asked what her name was.

Kola just stared blankly ahead. He waved his hands in front of her face, and she didn't blink. She looked spaced out, and he figured she was tripping off some bad opioid. By the time Kola was admitted into the hospital and placed on a seventy-two-hour psychiatric hold, several neighbors had called in and gave her address. Five hours later, the news broke.

"A local man's body was found dismembered into nearly forty pieces and strewn around the home he shared with his wife in what police are calling a drug execution. His fingers, toes, genitals, limbs, and all internal organs were removed. His head was found in the couple's refrigerator with what's described as a Colombian necktie, a calling card from drug cartels. What makes this equally strange is that the couple's adopted children were found dead in the home last month due to carbon monoxide poisoning and the father, Kamel Carmichael, had been charged with negligent homicide and was out on bail awaiting trial. His wife, Kola Carmichael, was picked up today roaming the streets naked from what's reported as a mental breakdown. She's being held at St. Vincent's hospital on a psychiatric hold. As soon as we learn more about this bizarre story, we will update the public."

33

The next morning, Apple woke up to her ringing cell phone. It was Cartier calling. Baffled by the sudden phone call, she answered, "What's this about, Cartier? You all right?"

"You haven't heard?"

"Heard what?"

"Kola's man was just found dead. It's all over the news. They said it's cartel-style murder."

The news hit Apple with a brief silence. She was bewildered and showed indifference to the report, but asked, "What happened to him?"

"It's gross, Apple. The journalist could hardly hold her composure as she reported that shit. They left his body like the game Operation. They removed every damn thing. All his fingers, toes, tongue, teeth, genitals, and even his eyeballs."

"Got fuckin' damn! I told that stupid, hardheaded muthafucka this would happen!"

"There's more," Cartier said. "The reporter said his wife was found wandering the streets near her home naked."

"Kola?" Apple was confused. "I thought she was locked up."

"Nope. She's being held in a psych ward on a seventy-two-hour hold. Apparently, she found his body. That shit must have hit her hard."

"Ain't this some shit?"

"You know I'd be there for you and Kola, but right now I'm going through my own shit. My house ain't in order so I gotta send love from Brooklyn."

"You don't even have to explain. Hold yours down and holla if you need me. One."

"Thanks."

Cartier ended the call. Apple wanted to tell Cartier about Junior and Sophia, but now wasn't the time. Her friend was going through some shit too, so why compound matters? Apple lingered in her bed, still feeling indifferent with a little remorse for Kamel. He was a dead man walking. If it wasn't Eduardo, then she would see him dead for trying to murder her over his sidepiece. Melinda's hot box had her brother-in-law fucked up. He forgot who he held allegiance to. But life went on. People lived and they died. She had more pressing matters about the land of the living. It was now the perfect time to call Eduardo. Apple needed to know that her sister would be safe.

He answered, "Cómo está?"

"What have you done?"

"Who is this?"

"It's Apple."

"Then you know what I've done! That piece of shit, that puta—I wish I could resurrect him so he could be killed again. And you!"

Apple gasped. "Me?"

"You don't call to send your condolences, you call in support of that murderer. You take his side over mine? After everything that I've done for you and your sister, you treat me this way?"

Apple knew he still had anger and rage to dole out, and she didn't plan to be on the receiving end of his grief. "I am calling to give you my condolences, and for the record, I just got your telephone number. You know you and I aren't on speaking terms, and it should go without saying, I loved Junior and Sophia just as much as you did."

"Everyone loved them. Kamel, Kola, you, but they are still dead. My question to you is why is Peaches still alive and my son and daughter are not?"

Those words were Apple's worst nightmare. "Are you threatening her?"

"It's a legitimate question. Peaches lived there, no? If it were carbon monoxide as Kamel said and not an execution then Peaches would be dead too, sí?"

"Eduardo, don't make this about my daughter. She's innocent in all of this. She wasn't there because she was with me, her mother. Kola and I had already started to transition her to living with me full time. It's that simple; no conspiracy. And if you're thinking anything sinister about my sister, she had nothing to do with Kamel's negligence. The police here did a full investigation, and it was all his fault. *Only* his fault. He was charged with negligent homicide. He was out on bail awaiting trial."

Eduardo snorted. This was news he hadn't known. "Well, they cannot try him now. He is dead."

His sarcasm didn't go over Apple's head. She needed to get through to him before the conversation ended. "Eduardo, I didn't call you to defend Kamel. Fuck 'im. I called to know why you would do him like that and leave him for my sister to find? She just lost her children—"

"My children!" he screamed.

Apple was navigating through the torrential, emotional territory. She tried to pull at his emotional strings. "Eduardo, Kola was admitted to a psych ward. They're holding her for three days. I don't think there's much more she can take."

"What do I care? She's always been cra-zy," he concluded. The way he rolled his tongue when he said crazy almost made her chuckle. "Everybody's got to pay!"

"Don't toss threats!"

"It's no threat," Eduardo said assuredly. "I am a man of my word."

"Eduardo, both Kola and Peaches love you! I'm begging you, don't do this."

"You think I am a monster? Peaches is my daughter. She is safe."

"Your daughter?"

"Sí, yes, of course. I am her Poppo. I was her father before you were her mother. Do not forget that, Apple. Because of me, my daughter isn't wasting away in Mexico."

Apple thought, *Why argue?* This man is rotting away in a Colombian prison. "What about Kola?"

"Send her to me."

"Come again?"

"Kola needs to be here with me, in Colombia. This is where she belongs. I only allowed her to go to the United States to watch over Eduardo and Sophia. They are no longer alive, so she must fulfill her original duties as head of my household. She will be treated like royalty, so this is far better than a death sentence."

"You know I can't make Kola do anything."

"Oh, well, then she dies," he said. "And, Apple, Miguel will get in touch with you so he could make arrangements to have my children exhumed and flown here. Kamel wouldn't give up where they were buried. They need to rest in peace on their native land, on my estate."

"Kamel wouldn't tell me either! I've been begging him so that Peaches could say her goodbyes."

"You better find out, or so help me, I will kill everybody! Do you fuckin' understand, puta? Find my niños!"

Queenie had buried two more of her men, Stone and Nerd, both viciously struck down by her nemesis, Apple. She was quickly losing the war she had waged and needed to go to her many religions for assistance in conquering this battle, because right now she felt like a confederate soldier in a war they couldn't win.

At her altar in her living room, she bent down on her knees and prayed for vengeance. Queenie lit a blue candle for clarity, a black candle for protection, and a white candle for victory over her enemies. She sprinkled ginger, which helped make her words that much more powerful, and chanted. Anecdotal phrases were pieced together as she spewed her hatred toward Apple as a testimony to the spirits that would assist her. After a long prayer session, Queenie's body quaked, and she stood up and jerked rapidly, then twirled around in circles before ultimately falling out flat on her floor. She had felt a surge of dark energy take over her body so powerful the hair on her arms stood up, and she knew her prayers were answered.

Apple was a dead bitch.

The fist smashing upside her head brought Apple down on one knee. Her hand went up instantly to address the throbbing pain when she was met with another fierce blow to her cheek. The pain coursing throughout her body was almost debilitating as she tried to recover. Dazed, Apple swung wildly into the air, and her fists missed their intended target. She locked eyes with an unknown assailant—a female—short, stocky, and overflowing with rage. The sneak attack had momentarily knocked Apple off her A-game.

When the woman charged her again, Apple crouched low, and with one arm under the female's vagina and the other around her neck, she lifted her adversary up and body-slammed her on to the ground. The girl popped back up like a jack-in-the-box toy and charged at her again. Apple punched the female repeatedly in the face until her hands were bloody. They were in the project's courtyard, and her men patrolling the rooftop had peeped the scuffle and were already coming to their boss's defense.

Apple swung the woman around by her hair and tossed her across the ground. Once again, she sprang up, refusing to stay down.

When she screamed, "You better give me my fuckin' money 'fore I kill you, bitch!" Apple added a name to the face. Pilar had given up the information regarding Kola and wanted what was promised to her. When she screamed her threat, Pilar had meant every word. Two-hundred-thousand dollars was worth going to jail over, but was it worth dying for? Once Apple realized this shit could take all day, she pulled out her 9mm and squeezed.

Bak!

The bullet hit its intended target, which was Pilar's leg. Apple wasn't trying to kill her.

Bak!

She hit her other leg, and Pilar fell to the ground, grabbing her ankle and calf and screaming in pain.

Apple leaned down and said, "Bitch, if you ever put your fuckin' hands on me again, you're dead. If you ever utter my name again, your family's dead. If you ever even glance my way, both you and your family are dead. Choose your next actions wisely!" Apple grabbed the back of Pilar's collar and dragged her across the ground, through patches of grass, over broken glass, cigarette butts, and dog urine until she arrived at the curb where she was left like trash.

Apple's soldiers, including her two lieutenants, came barreling out of the building like army troops invading enemy territory. Guns were drawn, and the adrenaline was high as they flooded the courtyard, their presence even intimidating members of the Lincoln Ova Everything gang, who once had control over Lincoln Houses. Apple's henchmen formed a protective barrier around their boss and the bleeding Pilar, not knowing how to react. Apple placed her pistol back in her waistband and said, "I'm good. Y'all go back to your posts."

As everyone walked back to take their respective positions, Apple made eye contact with a familiar face. She was the female Tokyo had sliced up with her razor. She, too, felt Apple owed her promised money, and until that very moment, she had entertained confronting Apple with her fists. Her grandiose idea was quickly snuffed out as the young girl decided that she could very well live with a checkered face, as long as she lived.

Walking back to the building, Apple's senses were heightened. She had come to Lincoln Houses for a specific reason. She needed to speak to Tokyo. Apple was a few steps from entering the building when something pulled her attention. She looked over her shoulder and saw a figure, a male dressed in a black sweatsuit. His hoodie was pulled protectively over his face, and she couldn't make out his features. He had watched everything unfold. Had the figure lingered longer, she would have sent Hood and IG over to check him. But he quickly exited toward the avenue, so she moved on.

Apple gave Peaches the biggest hug she could and kissed her face repeatedly until her daughter begged her to stop. "Stop it, Mommy," Peaches said through giggles, trying to push Apple away.

"Make me," she said and picked her up in a bear hug. Peaches wrapped her legs around her mother's waist, and her arms were clasped tightly around Apple's neck. Apple walked Peaches to a back room where two of Tokyo's younger cousins were playing *Minecraft*. The children were building their 3D world and were only interrupted when Apple came.

"You having a good time?" Apple asked her daughter.

She nodded her approval of how her morning was unfolding and sat back down to help her fellow teammates gather resources and explore.

Apple left Peaches and went back to have a quick chat with Tokyo in her bedroom, who was trying on outfits for a date she had tonight. She only wore catsuits, so it was more about picking the right accessories to make her stand out. Since Tokyo's rise in the drug game, her popularity amongst the young hustlers had multiplied. She was the new it-girl, and all the little niggas wanted to smash. Tokyo paused when her boss walked in. She smiled wide.

Apple was blunt. "Look, you're dead weight on my team, so you're out."

The words floored Tokyo and her eyes quickly filled with tears. She tried to hold them back, but she couldn't. The tears flowed fast and heavy, and her body reacted; her chest heaved up and down in dramatic fashion. Tokyo knew this was about the shootout she hadn't participated in. The moment the battle started, she bitched up, ran, and left her team one man down.

"I'm . . . sorry," she choked out. "I . . . can do much better next time."

Tokyo looked pitiful, but the tears would not sway Apple's decision. She had a lot on her plate with buttoning up her beef with L.E.S. Crips, The Huntsman killing her workers, Kola in the psych ward, Kamel's murder, and now Eduardo's threat. Apple didn't want to be the one to tell Eduardo that his children were in Potter's Field, and she knew there wasn't any way her sister was going to willingly get on a flight to live the rest of her life under Eduardo's thumb in Colombia, where her days would be filled by visiting him in jail.

Apple felt protective over Tokyo, and that wasn't good. She couldn't add the young girl to her list of things to fret over. Tokyo could handle herself in hand-to-hand combat. She was a street chick who knew how to survive, but that was a far cry from drug distribution, murder, and intense shootouts. Tokyo wasn't about that life, and Apple no longer wanted to indoctrinate her to thrive on that level. You either had it, or you didn't.

"You know how I feel about these displays of emotion, Tokyo," Apple snapped. "It feels awkward for me to see you like this. You're like a little sis"—Apple stopped short because that wasn't true. No one could ever feel like or replace her little sister, Nichols. "You're like family, and I want you safe. I have a job for you if you want it where you can continue to earn a salary. Not what you're making now, but it's decent."

Tokyo wiped her tears. "What job? I'll do anything."

Her need to please Apple wasn't flattering. It was vexing. Apple was brimming with anger from Eduardo's threats, Kola's predicament, and getting punched in the head just a short while ago, so her temper was on ten. "Have some respect, Tokyo. If you'd do anything for money, then that makes you my enemy. It means you can be bought!"

Tokyo's eyes widened. "I would never hurt you! For any amount of money and that's on my life. You've done more for me than my own mother, and I'll never forget that. I love you, Apple, and would die for you."

Apple gave her a break. She nodded. "Peaches and I are moving into a three-bedroom. The extra bedroom won't be occupied by the intended party, so I wanted to know if you wanted a job as my live-in nanny and assistant. You could watch Peaches there while I handle business, and that way I'd know that my baby was safe."

Tokyo thought she had hit the lottery. She would live with her idol, Apple, in a fancy apartment and get paid to watch Peaches? That didn't feel like a job because she was manageable. The little girl was low maintenance. Tokyo squealed her delight and then hugged Apple before being pushed off.

Apple scribbled on a piece of paper and pulled out thirty grand. "Here's the address. The apartment is empty. I want you to go food shopping, stop by Cellini's and order you and Peaches bedroom sets and televisions. Her favorite color is purple. If you get there now, they said they can have the furniture delivered by three this afternoon. Contact the cable company and get all that shit set up. I probably won't go there tonight. I have a lot to take care of and will spend the night at my apartment." Apple handed her the keys, and Tokyo's smile faded.

"What's the problem?"

"I have a date tonight," Tokyo explained.

"Cancel it."

Apple made the unscheduled visit to Dannemora so she could receive counsel from Corey. They had less than an hour left for visiting hours when she arrived. Corey walked out quickly; his rushed steps made Apple feel important. To her, his urgency embodied unspoken feelings; he cared about her wellbeing.

Corey dragged his chair from under the table, and it made a screeching sound before he sat down. The OG stared at the ingénue and asked, "What's up, young blood?"

"I have an issue."

"Lower Eastside more formidable than you anticipated?"

"Queenie?" Apple sucked her teeth. "She's not even in the top five of past opponents."

"Then what's this about?"

Apple sat silently for a few seconds, weighing her situation, and pulled out her most pressing dilemmas. She said, "Have you seen coverage on The Huntsman?"

"Yeah, the vigilante. He and I started terrorizing our neighborhoods around the same time. Evidently, he's had more success than me."

Apple's ears perked up. "You know who he is?"

"Wouldn't that be the million-dollar answer?" Corey chuckled. "Nah, young blood. When I started pushing dope through Harlem, as the crack epidemic grew, The Huntsman made his first kill." Corey slowly shook his head because the fact that someone had murdered over two-dozen people, all newsworthy events, and not been caught was astounding. Everyone was impressed.

"Well, he's still killing, and now it's spilling into my business. Two of my block huggers were murdered, and if he targets more, it'll be that much more difficult to find young soldiers to push my products. I've put a bounty on his head, but nothing."

Corey smirked. "What do you want me to say?"

"How can I catch him?"

"You can't," Corey explained. "Someone like The Huntsman knew from the gate what my son learned. Murder is to be done alone. This man doesn't have anyone that can snitch on him, give him up for reward money, or turn him in for moral reasons because he's a ghost. He will only get caught if he's sloppy, and that he is not. He can probably kill in his sleep. He's seasoned, older, and wiser and most likely has great patience. Let it go and be glad you're not on his radar."

Apple agreed he was a ghost. She then opened up and explained the Kamel, Kola, and Eduardo situation in great detail—the children dying from carbon monoxide poisoning, Kamel's dismemberment, Kola's nude catwalk, and finally Eduardo's threats. Corey listened, filtering each fact through his lens of wisdom.

"Miguel has to die in the same fashion as Kamel. You need to send a message to Eduardo and the streets that you're not to be fucked with."

Her eyes widened. Apple wasn't expecting this response. She wasn't sure what his advice would be, but she was convinced that it wasn't going to be that.

"If I did that, murdered Miguel, Eduardo would just keep sending more men at me. Besides, this isn't my beef. I really don't got shit to do with this. I didn't kill those kids, so why go to war with a Colombian drug lord who has nothing to lose but countless bodies of men on his payroll? He's in jail for life, and his children are dead. I don't want to start something I can't finish."

"You're thinking small," Corey scolded. "If you don't put your murder game down with the Colombian cartel and the Crips, it won't be long before your whole organization crumbles. For you to even show fear about going up against Eduardo proves you're no Queen of New York. You're in bed with the Mingo and Helguero cartels—Eduardo could end that for you with one phone call! You need to kill him, kill them. Find someone inside his Colombian prison and pay a guard to take him out. You have money, lots of it. Put it to work for you. I wouldn't tell you all of this if I thought you'd fail. You're like a daughter to me, could have been my daughter-in-law, so I wouldn't steer you wrong."

Apple listened to Corey's monologue, and her eyes were now open. How could she have ever thought they could have had something real?

She left the visit promising retribution and murder, and those were commitments she vowed to keep.

Queenie sat with Rehab and Lord, going over her books. Her organization's finances had taken a considerable dip due to this war, and things were getting strained. Her product wasn't flipping, as sales began to dwindle thanks to *Queen of New York* and the most recent dope, *Kiss the Ring*. Queenie had enormous payroll expenses—shooters, block huggers, funeral expenses, lawyers, bail, housing, transportation, insurance—a host of bills that were getting harder to pay.

"Y'all niggas realize that Apple has crippled our organization and she's still breathing, right?"

Lord couldn't let this go unchecked. "But do you realize that I was the one who advised that we let this shit go?"

Queenie glared. "Stone, Mike, and Nerd are all dead. We owe it to them to get retribution. We can point fingers once we lullaby the female formerly known as the baddest chick!"

34

Apple felt guilty for not rushing to see Kola right after her ordeal when she knew her sister needed her most. But she was there now, and to her, that was all that mattered. St. Vincent's wasn't as bad as she had envisioned. Kola was in a small, private room monitored every hour by a nurse to make sure she wouldn't attempt suicide. Her sister was on mild sedatives, and her treating psychiatrist had been notified. Detectives Rothman and Brown had come by to question Kola on who she thought had a motive to chop her husband up into pieces, but she refused to talk and they were promptly escorted out via the hospital staff.

"Hey, sis," Apple said as she slowly inched toward Kola's hospital bed. Kola smiled weakly and reached her hand out toward Apple. The two held hands and Apple kissed her sister's forehead. "I can't keep coming to visit you in hospitals."

A tear slid down the side of Kola's face and Apple wiped it away. "I know it's a lot, Kola, but we're going to get through it together. I'm sorry I wasn't there for you. It's all my fault—everything. Junior, and Sophia . . . they should have been with me."

The honesty of her words said out loud for the first time pierced Apple's heart, and the preponderance of guilt now weighed heavily on her shoulders. Apple cried, and Kola moved over. Apple squeezed into the small twin bed, and the twins just cuddled in silence. Kola still hadn't said one word. An hour later, and Apple was still there.

Apple finally said, "We have to deal with Eduardo, Kola. He's making threats, says he wants you to move back to Colombia. Tell me what to do to help you."

"How was the funeral?" she asked, not ready to deal with Eduardo's demands. "What did you pick out for Sophia to wear? I hope not a dress; you know she hated girlie things."

Apple sat up straight in bed and faced Kola. She knew she would need to lend her sister her strength because this news was sanity shattering, but it couldn't be avoided.

"I didn't find out about them until last week. They're buried in Potter's Field, and I'm afraid to tell Eduardo, afraid of what he'll do," she paused and stared Kola in her eyes, "to you."

Kola closed her eyes, and the tears flowed like running water. Why was she even alive and all of her babies were dead? She didn't care if Eduardo sent his hit squad after her. What did she have to live for? Finally, she whispered, "Call him."

Her voice was so fragile and strained; it sounded like a light wind could shatter her into a million pieces. She repeated, "Call Eduardo and pass me the phone."

Apple nodded and got Eduardo on Kola's phone. When Kola told him the cruel fate of his children, Apple stepped out of the room to give them their privacy. Touch had called earlier, but she had her phone on Do Not Disturb. She called him back.

"Where you at?" he wanted to know.

"I'm in Westchester visiting my sister."

"Come through when you're finished," he suggested. "I miss you, Apple. A nigga gotta beg for your time."

Apple thought about his uncomfortable apartment with his bare white walls, hard mattress, and depressing vibe and suggested this: "Come to my place instead, around ten."

"Oh, word? A booty call?" Touch chuckled. "That's what's up."

"It'll be our last rendezvous there."

"What you mean by that?"

"I'll explain later. I gotta go."

When Apple came back into the room, Kola kept a couple things about her conversation from her sister. Eduardo said that Miguel and Felix would see to getting Junior and Sophia's bodies exhumed and brought back to Colombia, but he also threatened that if Kola didn't voluntarily join him by next month, then he would kill Peaches—a child's life for his children's lives. That was the Colombian way. Kola knew it was an idle threat, but still, she didn't like it.

"I don't want you worrying about me, Apple. Give Peaches a big hug from me and tell her that I love and miss her. Does she know about what's happened?"

Apple shook her head. "I haven't told her because there's no finality without gravesites. When you get better, we should buy some plots next to Denise and Nichols, and I'll tell her then."

Kola thought about that and then quickly agreed. "Apple, if you haven't thought about this, and I'm sure you haven't, but I think it's time you got out the game. For good. My spirit told me to say this to you and I'll leave it there."

Apple wasn't anywhere near her exodus. She had only to kill her enemies, and then things would settle down. She nodded, though, so her sister could acknowledge that she had heard her request. She changed the subject. "I met someone."

"A man?"

"What else, bitch?"

"Who? And don't say Caesar Mingo."

"That fat fuck?" She chuckled. "Nah, he's a professional poker player. His name is Touch, but his real name is Malcolm Xavier Nuñez."

"That's interesting."

"And Peaches likes him."

This gave Kola pause. Sometimes she questioned her sister's parenting skills. "He's already met my niece?"

"Yeah, we had an incident, so it was an emergency, but he's cool. He adores Peaches."

"You don't even know this nigga!"

"Kola, don't start. I'm trying to cheer you up. You should be happy that I'm finally moving on and it's with a legit guy."

"He's a gambler, Apple. That's hardly a long-term occupation. And they have addiction issues; he could be smoking crack or addicted to porn or will blow all of your money down a slot machine."

There she was again. The lecturer had resurfaced, and that was Apple's cue to get ghost. She kissed Kola on her forehead again and gave her a quick squeeze. "Love you, sis. Take your meds, and I'll bring Peaches with me to see you on Thursday."

Kola sighed. Apple always had to learn things the hard way. Kola turned over and kept one last secret. Tomorrow she would voluntarily admit herself into the psychiatric hospital under the care of her physician. This was her only way out from under Eduardo's controlling thumb.

From Westchester, Apple drove to Lincoln Houses and held an emergency meeting with her men. There she explained that she was now giving the green light to hit Queenie, Lord, and Rehab and whatever other L.E.S. Crips were around when they struck.

"I've allowed her to live long enough to know that it was me who took everything from her. As her money and empire have dwindled, she's had to face the fact that her short run is now over. That bitch tried to take my crown—erase my name from the streets I've bled on? Let me make myself clear. I want Queenie dead."

Apple was speaking to a small cluster of her best shooters inside the project apartment she had taken over. And as an afterthought, she addressed Hood. "When Drac calls, tell him to move forward against Corey Davis. I want these hits wrapped up before the weekend."

Apple's men were amped to go up against the Lower Eastside Crips, and Hood and IG were understandably shocked that after all this time, after all their bitching, she was finally ready to stop fucking around. They didn't know what forced Apple's hand, but they both suspected that it had a lot to do with her brother-in-law getting his body dismembered like pork on a hibachi grill. People in the drug game weren't fucking around, and the longer she allowed this beef with Queenie to fester, the more significant an advantage Queenie could obtain over them.

Apple left her men with specific orders and rushed home so she could get ready for her date. On her drive back to her old residence, she called Tokyo to tell her she wouldn't be home again tonight. Tokyo sounded disappointed but cheered up when Apple promised to take them fall shopping for clothing. It was like she had two children.

Apple circled her block three times before pulling into a parking space at her old apartment in SoHo. She had less than two weeks before she had to vacate the apartment and she hadn't even packed. She was always a procrastinator. The police cruiser did its nightly routine and slowly passed by her, slowing down to peer in her car. When he saw a woman, he sped up and continued on his local routes. Apple strutted toward her building when she saw him, the slender man in the black sweatsuit and hoodie. He was at the corner of her block and had stepped out of the shadows. Apple grabbed her 9mm and took off running. She gave chase to the unknown assailant, and when she bent the corner, he was gone. Her eyes darted left and right, but she didn't see him. As a precaution, she called Tokyo back and told her to be on alert and then called Hood to warn him and her crew that Queenie was possibly planning something and for everyone to be on alert.

"Fuck Queenie!" Hood yelled. "As soon as we finish up here, me and IG gonna go down to the Lower Eastside and hunt that bitch. We heard that they like to hang out at this pool joint."

"Bring a few shooters. Y'all see that bitch, one-eight-seven her!"

Apple lit candles and soaked in a long bath, readying her body for Touch. He had the magic stick, and his lovemaking had her open. She thought about him daily and had to force herself to focus on business and her safety or else, if she had her way, she would spend every waking moment in his strong arms.

Touch arrived looking very handsome and smelling exceptionally good with his muscular body, chiseled jawbone, and Spanish Harlem swag. He wore a Gucci knit sweater, knit hat, jeans, socks, and sneakers. Gucci down to his socks.

Touch smiled from ear to ear as his eyes scanned Apple up and down. She wore a one-piece sheer bodysuit with a jeweled thong and pasties. Her body was tight and toned, and she knew how to seductively sway her hips when she walked. "You look so sexy, Apple," he said to her.

"Thank you," she said.

Apple stepped aside, allowing him to walk into her cozy home. It smelled like vanilla throughout, and he spotted fresh flowers on her dining room table. Her apartment looked professionally decorated and lived in.

Touch leaned in and planted a kiss on her juicy lips, and they both smiled.

"You want something to drink?" she asked.

"What you got?"

She grinned. "Ginger beer and whiskey shots."

"Of course . . . five stars everything."

Apple fixed their drinks, and they sat down and sipped. Touch looked around and asked, "You moving?"

"I've moved. I got a place in Tribeca for my daughter and me."

He smirked. "What's wrong with this apartment? This makes my place look like a homeless shelter."

"Too many people know where I live."

Touch took another swig of his drink and got comfortable. Her perfume, the dim lights, and her silhouette had him aroused. He wanted her to sit on his face, grind her hips, and come in his mouth, but it seemed she wanted to talk. "Like who?"

"I know you got a thing wit' that Crips bitch Queenie, but if you didn't know, that bitch got issues."

"What thing I got with Queenie and why y'all got beef?"

Apple sipped more and wanted to know why she always sounded like an insecure, jealous thot when she was with him. "I really can't give you a definitive answer on why she doesn't like me 'cause I'm not in that bitch's head. It probably has something to do with you." Apple was fishing for answers. Did he fuck Queenie before? Had her archenemy sampled Touch's good dick?

"Nah, this ain't about me, but whatever it's about you should just let it go. I know Queenie; I know how she moves." Touch clenched his jaw and gritted his teeth. "If she ever hurt you—if they hurt you . . ."

He didn't finish his sentence. Apple cocked her head to one side and filtered his words through her street lens. There was something ominous and dark in his eyes and his voice. His words were reserved—weighty but straightforward. What was unspoken spoke loud and clear. Touch had just inferred a threat toward Queenie, and Apple believed him. How had her corny poker player given her pause? Who was he? What was he really about? Was Touch a body snatcher like Nicholas Davis?

Apple pressed on. "She ain't gonna do shit but keep watching me from afar. Queenie got stalker tendencies, and my heart skips no beats for her shenanigans. Lately, she got someone following me, spying, but that's about it."

"Following you? What you mean?" Touch's eyes went from murderous to concern. The look of fear in his eyes was trippy. Apple didn't know what was going on.

"Yeah, some guy. I know it's not any of her henchmen, but she likes to play these types of games. I came in tonight, and the same guy in a hoodie was hiding in the shadows."

"What he look like?"

Apple shook her head. "I dunno."

"Think!" he snapped. "Was he young, old, fat? Tell me, Apple."

"Fuck is your problem?" she snapped back. "Who you yelling at?"

Touch exhaled. He inched closer and caressed the side of her face. His thumb brushed slowly up against her bottom lip, and he could feel her body relax. "I'm sorry, Apple. You got a nigga worried for your safety. You think we should go to the police?"

Apple burst out into hysterical laughter, tossing her head back and showing her straight teeth. She realized he didn't know who she was or what she was capable of. His concern made her feel all warm and fuzzy inside. Her laughter caused him to giggle too.

"Fuck is so funny?" he said with a chuckle.

"You." Apple laughed even louder. "One second you had me thinkin' you might have bodied a nigga or two in your past, and then you say shit like let's go to five-oh, and I realize that you're really a poker player."

"I told you I was."

"Yeah, well now I believe you." Apple swallowed the rest of her drink and said, "I want you."

Touch followed Apple into her bedroom, watching her plump ass hypnotize him with each step. He pulled off his sweater and t-shirt and tossed them to the floor. As Apple stood in the room, Touch approached her from behind and gently wrapped his strong arms around her slim waist and pulled her into his half-naked frame. Touch kissed the side of Apple's neck affectionately, hungrily touching her breasts. The muscles in his chest flexed against Apple's back, and she twirled her hips, helping his erection grow.

"Damn, I missed you," he whispered into her ear.

Touch continued kissing the side of her long, slender neck and softly touching her erogenous zones. He inhaled her skin; her scent was feminine and flowery. "Damn, you're so sexy," he murmured.

He continued loving on her, removing her clothing. He couldn't take his eyes off of Apple. Everything about her was perfect. Touch was a lucky man to have her in his life, in any capacity, but he wanted more.

They kissed passionately, their tongues twirling around, exploring one another. Apple got lost in his kisses, his touch. He was making her forget the last man.

Touch scooped Apple into his strong arms and she straddled him in the air. He cupped her butt and carried her to her bed, laid her on her back, and continued tonguing her down while removing his jeans and boxers. His dick swung freely, brushing up against Apple's stomach.

Touch grabbed a condom, and Apple took it from him. She wasn't done with foreplay. They switched positions, and Apple placed Touch on his back. She buried her sweet box in his face and leaned over to sixty-nine. Apple sucked his pre-cum off his mushroom tip while her hands ran up and down his shaft. She lathered up his magic stick with her saliva as she deep-throated his massive penis. He was impressed. Apple didn't gag as her head moved, skillfully handling his manhood, her hips grinding on his face as Touch's tongue licked and sucked her juices.

"Damn, ma . . . shit," he murmured, unable to control the nut peaking. "I'm about to come."

She was about to come too. They both exploded, swimming in pleasure and a heightened sense of eroticism. Apple turned around to face Touch and rolled a condom onto his still brick dick. She lowered herself on top of him and began a slow grind as her nails dug into his chest.

"You feel so good, baby. Ah . . . Oh shit, your pussy feels so good," Touch moaned with his eyes closed as he pushed into her more and more. "Oh shit! Damn, Apple!"

Apple arched her body as waves of bliss washed over her.

"Oh, fuck me!" she cried out.

The couple twisted into position after position—reverse cowgirl, doggy-style, and sideways. Touch hit it in multiple positions, enjoying every inch, and every second, he made love to her. He wanted this forever.

"Come for me."

"I'm gonna come in your tight pussy," he said breathlessly.

And when he came, she came—their bodies connecting on so many levels.

"Damn, Apple, what you doing to me?"

The SUV slowed to nearly a crawl, like a low-rider cruising in Compton ready to do a drive-by. But Queenie didn't want a brief drive-by. She wanted the chaos she was about to implement tonight to linger. She wanted bodies to drop, the streets washed red in blood, and Apple's reign of terror to finally be buried six feet deep.

Apple's men, per her orders, had finished a day of cooking up coke and bagging up dope and were now ready for war. The click-clacking of guns could be heard throughout the apartment as the shooters checked clips, chambers, and ammunition before going to hunt their target—the L.E.S. Crips and their HBIC at the rumored pool spot. Hood, IG, and four other triggermen rode in the elevator in silence, all focused on the task ahead of them.

The fall air was cold but not brisk as they filed out of the building, all checking their surroundings as they walked toward Hood's truck. No one gave the burgundy Nissan Murano a second glance as it crept down the block. The windows rolled down, and two shooters, Lord and Rehab, leaned out of the curbside windows. Queenie could be heard screaming from the driver's seat, "Murda dem!"

Her triggermen lifted their guns, aimed at the crowd with a merciless purpose, and heatedly opened fire.

Boom! Boom! Boom! Boom! Boom! Boom! Boom!
Bak! Bak! Bak! Bak! Bak! Bak! Bak! Bak!

Instantly, IG was grazed in his face. He spun around like a fidget spinner and then hit the ground. Hood saw this and reached in his waistband and pulled out his ninas. He outstretched both arms and bucked back. Glass shattered wildly, and a gun battle ensued. Hood took two hits; a shotgun blast entered his elbow, nearly splitting his arm into two pieces, and another bullet lodged into his thigh just a couple inches away from his groin. Hood buckled over in pain.

IG recovered, and he and his team chased the SUV a couple blocks until all they saw were brake lights.

35

Apple lay in Touch's arms stroking his chest as she initiated pillow talk. She could tell something was on his mind. He was distracted.

"Tell me about your relationship with your mother," she said.

Touch's mood soured. His mother, Nancy, was off-limits. He remained silent, not wanting to address the question in any capacity, but she pushed.

"Whatever it is, you can trust me."

Touch exhaled. Could he? Telling secrets was the most idiotic thing a person could do. The secret allowed someone to weaponize the embarrassing fact and later use it against you in any capacity they chose. It left you wide open and susceptible to manipulation, revenge, or blackmail depending on how tawdry the details were. However, if it brought him closer to Apple, he would take that chance. Touch spoke openly of his mother's betrayal, the shame and humiliation of her act, and how it left him feeling insecure.

"I think it's time you forgave her and got to know your siblings."

Touch smirked. "Not gonna happen."

"You should at least start the process of forgiving her because once she's gone, you'll regret not making things right."

He snapped, "You don't know anything about it, Apple, so drop it."

"Why don't I? My mother paid a crackhead to toss acid in my face," she said softly. And just in case he didn't glean what she'd just said, she repeated, "Acid. And I wanted her murdered, but when she was, I lost a part of myself. I'd give anything for her to still be here, for you to meet her. And, I guess, I want to meet your moms too."

Touch lifted his eyebrow. "You do?"

"Of course I do. She's your mother; she gave birth to *you*. I would like to meet the woman who helped co-create all of this," Apple said and stroked his penis, which instantly responded. Touch smiled wide, and the two lovers went for round three.

Apple played sleep when Touch snuck back into her bedroom at six in the morning, got dressed, kissed her on her forehead, and left. Where the fuck was he going? She wanted to cook breakfast, maybe do something with Peaches this morning, all of them like a family. All types of thoughts bombarded her as she lay in bed. Was he married? Was he sneaking around like Kamel had done to Kola? Was his plain-Jane apartment really his smash house? Apple stared up at her ceiling for hours feeling insecure, and then she got angry. She hopped out of bed, showered, dressed in her best garments, and went to confront Touch on his territory with her 9mm tucked snugly in her clutch.

Touch needed to speak with his father alone, so he called and asked Jorge to come to his house.

"What do you want, Malcolm?" Jorge asked. "You know I hate traveling to your apartment. It takes forever on mass transit."

"Take a cab, Pops," he suggested. "You know it's not a problem for me to pay the fare."

"No! No," Jorge opposed. "That won't be necessary. I don't know where your money comes from. I'll take the train."

"Here we go again," Touch admonished. "Just hurry up."

Jorge arrived at his son's apartment, dressed down in his leisure sportswear, two hours later. He was in a foul mood from being summoned, but he showed up, because that's what they did. Both father and son always showed up for each other.

"You want something to drink?" Touch asked.

"I do not."

Touch nodded and got to the point. "I know who you are, and I know what you've done, and I want you to stop."

Jorge snorted. "What is it that you know, son?"

"Don't make me say it out loud. Just stop, Pops. Stop what you're doing and grow old. You've been doing this shit for too long."

Jorge turned the tables. He took a few steps closer to his son. His eyes were pools of darkness, his voice laced with outrage and embarrassment. "I can say the same about you. My very own son—a bottom feeder. You have no code. You have no honor. You're just like them."

Touch was visibly shocked. What did Jorge know? "What are you talking about, old man? This shit ain't about me! It's about how a thirteen-year-old kid followed his father one day and found out that the man he loved and trusted was The Huntsman."

Jorge shrugged nonchalantly. He removed the hood from his head and appeared to stand up straighter. "I'd rather be a vigilante than an assassin working for assassins. You're a lowlife, the exact type of individual that usually meets the tip of my knife. You better be grateful that you're my son or—"

"Or what?"

"Don't fuck with me, Malcolm! Or would you rather I call you Touch? Your assassin's name!"

"I don't know what you're talking about," Touch lied. "All I know is that you better stop stalking Apple. I know it's you and I ain't fuckin' around. I love that woman, and I'd do anything to keep her safe."

"You know she's behind the dope that's killing our people, and you take her side over mine?" Jorge was incredulous.

"I don't know what she's done or hasn't done. All I know is that you better not lay a muthafuckin' finger on her! Stop your menacing, stalking, killing, insanity 'fore I stop you."

Jorge snorted, and then chuckled, and finally let out a hearty laugh. He was amused. Years of murdering without reproach had made him cocky. He turned his back toward his son and walked to the front door. "I won't hurt her, but The Huntsman will kill that bitch!"

Jorge unlocked the front door and proceeded to leave when Touch reached out and grabbed his father by his collar. Jorge was yanked two steps backward when he spun around and stabbed his son repeatedly in his gut. Jorge's movements were lightning-fast and deliberate.

The blows had taken Touch by surprise; his eyes widened in shock and fear. He released his grip from his father's collar, and his hand instantly touched his open wound. Touch looked at his hand now covered in blood and pushed his father away.

Jorge rebounded and charged his son, and they both stumbled and fell on the hardwood floor. With Touch laying face up, Jorge straddled him and brought his survival knife as far back as possible. With force he slammed it down, aiming for his son's eyes. Jorge needed to gouge out his son's eyes so the world would know that he was a menace to society, just like his other kills. Touch blocked the blow, and the knife lodged in his wrist bone.

With his free hand, Touch pulled his burner from his waist and fired once. *Poot!* The bullet slammed into Jorge's temple and he keeled over, collapsing on his side. Touch needed his cell phone to call for help, but he was quickly losing consciousness. He grasped his phone, and before he could make a call, everything went dark.

Apple arrived at Touch's apartment ready to confront him and whatever jump-off he was with. She felt slutted out, walking to his front door still feeling the pressure from their lovemaking between her legs. Apple went to bang on the door and noticed that it was slightly ajar. Instantly she pulled out her gun and slowly stepped farther inside to a horrific scene.

Touch was bleeding out on his living room floor with an older male dead, shot once in the head. Girlie was lying by Touch's head whimpering. Her feet had trampled in the blood and she was visibly upset. Apple paused only to take in the situation and then immediately sprang into action. She locked his door and ran to her man. Apple pulled off his belt and grabbed a couple rags. She placed the rags over his abdomen and tightened the cloths with his belt to slow the bleeding. Next, she pulled out the knife that was wedged into his wrist and tied a cloth around that wound too. She was about to call an ambulance when she noticed the gun was only inches from Touch. Fuck, he would do time for murder.

Apple didn't know what to do. He was running out of time. She needed to get him away from the body and into a hospital. Her brain wasn't functioning with her man dying in front of her.

"God, please, don't let me lose him too," she prayed. "Help me!"

Apple was about to call Hood when Touch opened his eyes. He thought he was seeing an angel.

"Touch, stay with me, baby," Apple cried. "I'm gonna call for help."

"No," he whispered when Apple pulled out her cell phone. "Pass me my phone."

Apple handed him his phone and listened intently as he spoke to someone on the other line in code. When he hung up, he said, "I hope I can trust you."

Apple nodded.

"Unlock the front door, sit in a chair facing the wall with your hands behind your back in plain sight. If you have a weapon on you, remove it. Place a blindfold over your face and don't move until you're told to do so. Don't ask any questions. Stay silent until we're alone."

"What's—"

"Now, Apple. I need you."

Apple nodded again.

"If I don't make it out of this alive, I want you to know that I love you."

IG tried contacting Apple all night to no avail. He needed her to know what had happened at Lincoln Houses and also for her to be alert. Right now, he was in the hospital, getting his face stitched up and also waiting to hear how his man was doing. Hood's right arm looked chewed up; it appeared to be attached by skin and veins. The screams coming from Hood as they rushed to the hospital were ear-piercing sounds of pain.

IG felt fucked up. He could still see the smirks on Rehab's and Lord's smug faces as they let those things go—bullets mercilessly ripping into them. He left one more voice message for Apple.

"El Jefe, we got hit tonight. Hood took two rounds, but he'll live. He's getting stitched up. Hit me back when you get this. One."

With Apple not returning his calls and Hood in surgery for the next few hours, IG felt he was left in charge. He would not let this shit linger.

If the bullet meant for his head had drifted an eighth of an inch to the right, he would be dead. The thought of being outlined in white chalk on his territory had him seething. With two carloads of the most thorough killers Harlem knew, he set out to end L.E.S Crips's reign once and for all.

36

Apple sat with her back facing the door feeling the most vulnerable she had in years. She had put her life and trust in a man she barely knew; the dead man and pistol lying at Touch's side were a testament to that fact. The blindfold had heightened her senses, and she heard and felt everything—the front door creaking open, footsteps, the clanking of items, and an overwhelming presence filling the room. Antiseptic smells mixed with cleaning products wafted throughout the apartment. Apple heard wheels being pulled and felt someone brush past her repeatedly. If she had to guess, she'd say there was more than one person who had entered the apartment. The front door opened frequently, and yet no one had said one word. Hours passed. Apple had to use the bathroom but adhered to her man's strict instructions: stay blindfolded, don't move, and don't turn around until told to do so.

Sporadically, Girlie would sit at her feet comforting her, and Apple could tell that someone had walked her more than once. She could hear her feet pitter-patter across the floor to exit and enter.

She knew that the sun had long ago faded, and Apple estimated that she had been sitting in the same position pushing thirteen hours. Her body had stiffened, her back felt sore, and her legs had fallen asleep throughout the day, but she was still alive.

Apple drifted off to sleep and only realized this when her body tilted and she slid off the chair, crashing to the floor. The pain jolted through her body and instant anger surged through her veins. Apple no longer cared about rules, threats, or compliance. She ripped the blindfold from her eyes, ready to confront the unknown. It took a few seconds for her eyes to adjust to the lighting. The living room was dark; only the moonlight filtered through the blinds. Apple could make out that she was alone. She looked to her left where Touch and the unknown dead body had lain, and both were gone.

Apple ran and turned on the lights, and all signs of a struggle—blood, gun, knife, bodies, were gone. She panicked. This was a total mind fuck. Where was he? Did they take him, and if so, who were they?

Apple ran into the bedroom and walked into a fully equipped hospital room. Touch was lying in his bed, hooked up to machines and an I.V. Several bottles of medication were on the nightstand, and his stab wounds had been stitched up and dressed with gauze. Apple stepped farther into the room, looking to see if they were alone; they were. She picked up the medicine, and the bottles were nameless. Apple read off words like Vicodin, Percocet, and Penicillin. There were also typed instructions left for her, which included changing his I.V., making sure he took his pain medication, and cleaning his wounds.

Whatever Touch was into, Apple knew this right here was uncharted territory for her. Her mouth was gaped open in awe—mind blown from this level of sophistication and organization. Her poker player had some explaining to do.

IG and his three carloads of henchmen laid in the cut on a side block adjacent the twenty-four-hour pool hall. It was a long shot but all they had. IG knew how killers think—he was one. After most kills, they either wanted to go out to be seen for potential alibis or go out to celebrate the successful murder they had just committed. It was nearing dawn when Lord's Range came to a rolling stop with Rehab in the passenger's seat. As Lord placed the ignition in reverse so he could parallel park, IG exited his Range and nodded toward his men. Each goon had smirks on their faces that personified their inner thoughts—death and destruction.

Time had stopped ticking for Alonzo "Lord" Bivens and Sean "Rehab" Jackson. IG sprayed the front of the SUV with an onslaught of hollow-point bullets from his automatic weapon. Their bodies popped up and down like popcorn as each bullet smashed through their flesh. When the other L.E.S. Crips gang members heard the commotion, they came out, only to be mowed down by Apple's triggermen.

IG and his soldiers took flight, racing back to their vehicles to evade capture. IG figured that most of the gang members wouldn't survive their injuries and those that did make it would be out of commission for a long time.

Apple slept a few hours before she was up attending to Touch's situation. He kept going in and out of consciousness, and her biggest fear was that his wounds would get infected. Apple monitored him closely for fever and kept a keen eye on his stitches, making sure there were no irregularities or telltale signs of infection like pus or swelling.

To compound matters, she finally had a moment to call IG back. He explained that Hood had gotten shot but that he had finally put Lord and Rehab to sleep. Apple wished that Queenie was inside that vehicle, but the fact that she wasn't told Apple that Queenie was hers to kill. It started with these two women, and she would end it. Just not right now. Touch was her current priority, and Apple would put her house in order once she was sure his condition had stabilized.

Tokyo was called upon to do all of Apple's errands, which included bringing Peaches to see her and bringing Apple some groceries and takeout. Peaches and Tokyo hung out in the living room of Touch's apartment for hours with Apple each day because Apple wasn't going anywhere anytime soon. Before Tokyo left, Apple would give her the same spiel.

Apple was emphatic. "My daughter's life is in your hands. Be fucking careful, and use your head. That bitch Queenie is still out there. She's lost all her men, so she's gonna want payback. You, me, IG, Hood, and especially my daughter are targets. Don't fuck up."

Tokyo was tired of hearing the same warning, but she would never say so. She convinced her boss she could be trusted and would return the next day.

IG snuck a bottle of Ace of Spades into Hood's hospital room. His man was laid up recuperating. Hood had gone through nearly fourteen hours of surgery as his surgeons tried to save his arm that ultimately had to be amputated from the elbow. The white bandage was like a magnet that pulled your eyes to his missing limb and made everyone feel uncomfortable. It's impolite to stare, but it was hard not to.

"What up, Nubs?" IG said, bringing levity to the situation.

"Oh, you got jokes?" Hood smiled and lifted his arms in surrender.

"Always." IG pulled out the champagne and gave Hood dap. "We celebrating."

Hood was down for whatever. He needed to get fucked up, considering what he'd been through. "What's the occasion?"

"We bodied them niggas for you." IG popped the cork and poured the champagne into two small plastic cups. "We wiped out most of L.E.S., and I personally got Rehab and Lord. Put them niggas right to sleep."

Hood grinned. "My man."

"That bitch still out there, though."

Hood nodded. "She gonna get hers."

"Apple had me leave three hundred stacks at your crib."

The large amount of money almost made Hood tear up. Most men bosses would have never blessed him in such a way. Whatever injuries you got during battle were charged to the game.

"This is why I fucks wit' her. She's a real one. And, yo, tell her that I spoke to Drac. He gonna handle that for her."

IG nodded. He'd pass on the message.

37

Yo, shorty, why a nigga gotta keep begging to see you? We was
'posed to been hook up. Another nigga must got your attention."

"It's not even like that," Tokyo tried to explain. "I'm babysitting."

"Babysitting?" He chuckled. "You can't be serious. You could be
chilling wit' me and you'd rather be watching someone's brat? Tell that
bitch to watch her own kid. She got you watching her child while she out
getting dicked down. That's foul."

Tokyo exhaled. She was on the phone with Vance, someone she had
been trying to get with for a while. Her allegiance to Apple was interfering
with her love life. Apple's issues were cock-blocking, and right now, she
wanted some dick. Vance was highly sought after. Every chick in the hood
wanted him and he was checking for her.

"She's not foul," Tokyo whined. "It's a situation, but in a few days I
should be able to come and see you. Maybe we can go to the movies?"

"A few ddddays," he hollered, sounding like Soulja Boy. "You got me
fucked up. I ain't gonna keep chasing you. Lose my number."

Tokyo panicked. "Wait, hold up. Let me see if I can get a sitter."

"You ain't gotta do all that. Text me your address where you at."

Tokyo thought for a split second. "I can't."

"So come to me. You can bring the kid."

"I can?"

"No doubt. I'll have some things lined up for her to do when you get here."

Vance texted his address and asked, "How long before you get here?"

"Forty-five minutes."

"See you soon, sexy."

The morning count was complete at Clinton Correctional Facility, and the heavy, iron gates in cellblock B were opened for breakfast. It was seven in the morning, and Corey had woken up with an appetite. The OG exited his cell and stood in line before the corrections officer gave the command to move forward to chow. As the inmates exited an open area, there was a small, congested area that inmates needed to pass through that was out of view from guards. The moment Corey Davis entered, Drac's muscular forearm wrapped around his neck and pulled. The icepick repeatedly slammed into Corey's kidney until his body went limp.

Drac handed the weapon off to Bee, who wrapped it in a towel and stuffed it down his pants. The killers went in separate directions, and all other inmates scattered. By the time the corrections officers noticed the body of Corey Davis on the floor, he was dead.

"Peaches, please, hurry up and get dressed," Tokyo said, as she rushed around beautifying herself for her date.

"I'm trying," she replied, sitting on the floor tying her shoelaces.

Tokyo ran into the bathroom and gave herself a birdbath; she took a rag and wiped her vagina and under her arms and quickly brushed her teeth. Tokyo ruminated over whether she should wear heels with her catsuit or keep it casual and put on a pair of high top sneakers. She settled on sneakers because she was bringing a child with her on a date.

Tokyo leaned down and said to Peaches at the front door, "We're not gonna tell your mom where we went okay?"

"Why?"

"Because I'm asking you to keep this our secret."

Peaches thought for a moment. "I don't wanna keep it a secret from Mommy."

Tokyo exhaled. Peaches was a goody-goody. She'd work on swearing her to secrecy later. Tokyo grabbed Peaches's hand and practically pulled her down the hallway and up the block to where she was parked. They got in, and Tokyo was already peeling out before the little girl had buckled her seatbelt. Tokyo's Lexus weaved in and out of traffic in a race to make it uptown within a reasonable amount of time when she slammed on her brakes mid-block.

What the fuck was she doing? Suddenly, dread washed over her and she trembled. Horns blared behind her and the drivers cursed their anger as they drove around the stalled vehicle. Tokyo placed her car back in drive, made two right turns, and returned back to Apple's feeling she had literally dodged a bullet.

While Touch was recuperating, two things happened: Apple found his gun collection and also a frantic, white male came banging on his front door calling out his name. Apple snuck to the door and took a peek, but she didn't open it the first two times he showed up. But the third time he arrived, she thought it best to stop his visits.

"May I help you?" she asked the surprised gentleman.

"Oh," he said and took two steps back. "Who are you?"

"I'm Apple, Touch's girlfriend."

Gabriel raised an eyebrow. Touch hadn't mentioned he was seeing anyone, but he'd never mentioned a female in all the years Gabriel had known him. Touch was secretive, an introvert. He said, "I'm his stepfather. Is he here?"

"He's not. He's in Vegas at a tournament. Did you call him?"

"I've been calling him, but he hasn't answered."

Apple nodded. "He hasn't answered for me either; I was starting to feel insecure like he was fucking some bitch."

Gabriel clutched imaginary pearls. How uncouth was she? "Well, should my son call, please tell him that his father is missing. He hasn't come home in days. I've already gone to the police."

"Oh my god. Is there anything I can do?"

Gabriel snapped, "You can give him my message."

Apple nodded and closed the door. "Bitch," she mumbled. So the dead man was Touch's father, perhaps? If so, what on earth could have transpired to push father and son to become adversaries and end in murder?

It took some time, but Touch had eventually gathered his strength. Apple had doted over him for days, feeding him, giving him his medication, and nursing him back to good health. She did this without one question regarding the shit-storm she had walked into. Touch was a grown man, and he knew that he owed her an explanation and didn't want her to have to beg for it.

"C'mere," he said.

Apple had just gotten out of the shower and had put on one of his t-shirts. Her hair was freshly washed and conditioned, and she had some personal matters of her own. Her world didn't stop, and her beefs weren't placed on pause because her man had gotten stabbed up. Apple still had threats, her sister was still dealing with mental illness, and most importantly, she had a child to raise she had been neglecting. This weighed heavily on her. She tried to compartmentalize her time, but divvying up hours per day still left things overlooked.

"I'm wet," she protested.

"C'mere," he repeated and motioned toward one side of the bed.

Apple crawled into his strong arm and snuggled. She kissed the side of his face and waited to hear what she knew he wanted to say.

"Where do I begin?" he asked. He felt Apple shrug under him. "I never lied when I said that I played professional poker. All that's true. But, I did omit a truth about myself that I'm not particularly proud of. For over a decade, I've been a hired gun for an organization. I can't tell you the name of that organization because, well, they'd kill us."

Apple nodded. "They saved your life, didn't they? Was that who you called?"

"You saved my life. Had you not come to my home, I would be dead."

Apple was intrigued. "They have doctors on staff too, and to do all of this—this equipment, this level of infrastructure—is impressive."

"Very. They're all of that but so much more. This agency is not to be fucked with."

Touch inhaled deeply, and it felt like his stitches would burst. He grimaced from the uncomfortable pain and continued. "The man that was dead . . . that—" Touch choked up. He couldn't finish his sentence because he sobbed uncontrollably. A deep, guttural wail escaped as he was hit with the realization that his father was dead and he had killed him. Jorge was all that Touch had known, and no matter how mentally fucked up they both were, they needed each other. And now he was gone. Touch felt like an orphan.

Apple held her man in her arms and caressed him until he let it all out. The anguish and pain needed to escape, and she was glad he was releasing it with her.

Finally, she finished his sentence. "That was your father?"

Touch got himself together and needed to explain the logistics. He didn't want to seem like a monster, a sociopath so heartless that he could not only murder strangers for money but even his own father.

"My pops wasn't who most people thought he was. On the surface, he was an aging gay man in frail health that had his heart broken by the only woman he loved. Some of that was true, but he was also The Huntsman, the vigilante who started killing before I was born."

Apple sat straight up in bed like she had gotten struck by a bolt of lightning. This was popcorn-at-a-movie gossip-worthy. "Your father was The Huntsman?"

"He was. I've known since I was thirteen," he explained. "When he came out of retirement, I thought that I could watch him—stop him before he murdered someone else—but he was slick. He was probably watching more of me than I was of him. Anyway, I started reading about that dope, *Queen of New York*, and suspected that Queenie was behind it. I knew my pops would go after her, so I told him in so many words to let it go."

Apple shifted in bed because he mentioned her enemy and because he had no clue that it was her dope.

"Did he? Did he promise to leave Queenie alone?"

"Queenie was safe because he figured out what I didn't know, which was you were pushing that dope. When you told me that you were being followed, I asked him to come over and begged him to not harm you."

Apple was speechless. She not only looked like a liar—flashbacks of the conversation about income flooded her mind—but, more important, did he just say he murdered his father for her?

"You didn't—"

His deep, baritone voice was emphatic. "Nah, I could never. That was my pops, I couldn't kill him over you. He came at me and nearly took me out. I fired my gun reflexively. It was muscle memory, a fight for survival."

Bullshit, Apple thought. She wanted to believe that he had killed for her just as Nicholas had.

"Gabriel came by."

The name was painful to hear. How would Touch and Gabriel move on without Jorge? "I'll handle him. I'll call him tomorrow and prepare him for the worst. At some point, my father's body will turn up so we can put him to rest, have a burial."

"How can you be certain that you'll get that chance? They could have dumped him in an ocean. Gabriel might not ever get closure."

Touch shook his head. "I'm certain because Jorge was my father and they know this. He'll turn up soon, a victim of some sort of robbery."

Apple fell asleep in Touch's arms and was awakened in the morning by arm movements and a chant. He was sitting up in bed praying to Allah.

And he was Muslim.

As the sun filtered through the room and landed on the multidimensional man, Apple knew that Touch had touched her heart, differently.

"Call that bitch again," Queenie demanded.

"I did. Shorty not picking up."

"Mi thought you said you could get Tokyo over here with Apple's daughter."

Vance shrugged. "Something must have happened 'cause I know she's wanted to hook up for a while now." Vance licked his lips and gave a cocky grin. He was sitting on his couch with a blunt pinched between his two fingers.

Queenie had sat impatiently in his foul-smelling apartment for the one chance to capture, torture, and murder Apple's child and her protégé.

Most of her men were now dead, and this pretty boy Vance thought she was fucking around.

Bak!

The gunshot to his abdomen caught Vance off guard. The pain exploded throughout his whole body, and his eyes popped open in wonderment. Why would she do this to him? His hands clutched his open wound, and he perspired. The sweat trickled down his forehead, and he puffed air in and out of his mouth dramatically, trying to stay awake. The rise and fall of his cheeks would not resuscitate the young man. The close-range gunshot had done too much damage. He'd lost too much blood, too quickly. Vance's eyes closed and they would never reopen.

38

Apple softly kissed Touch's lips and promised she would be back in the morning, but it was time for her to go. She'd put her life on hold for him, and today she would walk out his door and back into reality. Corey Davis was dead, IG was holding down her operation, and they had put out a new stamp of heroin, *Bow Down*.

"Hold up," Touch called from his room as she approached the front door. "Come back for a moment."

Apple exhaled. She had shit to do. But she returned with a broad smile, not showing her underlying annoyance. "What's up?"

"Sit down," he asked.

"Touch, why? I got a lot to do today."

"I know," he agreed. "Humor me. Sit down."

Apple sat on the side of his bed and watched as Touch struggled to get up. He clutched his stomach where the knife had gone in and winced. He took slow, deliberate steps to where she was seated and bent down in front of her on one knee. Touch grabbed the white cloth first aid tape and tore off about two inches. He took Apple's hand into his.

"What are you doin'?"

"Shhhh," he said. Touch wrapped the tape around Apple's ring finger and asked, "Apple Evans, will you marry me? I know we haven't known each other for long, but let's do life together. I'll learn from you, and you can learn all about me. I've never given my heart to a woman, and you can have it all, my whole heart in the palm of your hands. I can take care of you. I have savings, and I'll go legit. I'll quit the business—anything to make a life with you and Peaches. Just say yes."

Apple looked deeply into his eyes and then down at her makeshift ring and said, "You gonna have to start spending some money on me, 'cause right now, you're playing me cheap."

"You want a million-dollar ring? You got it. Just say yes."

Apple thought for a moment. She knew what she was feeling, but saying yes right now when they'd both just experienced such trauma wouldn't be wise.

"I can't," she replied.

"You still in love with your ex?"

She searched her feelings and answered honestly. Apple had held onto Nick's memory long enough. It was time to let him go. "I'm not, and I care deeply for you, but not enough to commit to forever."

"A'ight," he said and took the news like a champ. "Once I get better, I'ma make you fall in love. I got some work to do. You motivate me to get better that much quicker."

Apple leaned in and gave him a passionate kiss. "I think I already love you," she said and finally left.

The quarter of a million dollars was about two hundred grand more than she needed to pay the landlord. He would have given her access to Queenie's apartment for fifty thousand, but the additional funds were enough for the sixty-plus-year-old to plan for early retirement. The condo board had strict rules that spare keys be left in the office in case emergencies occur. For years, Queenie refused to give her key until they sent a letter from their attorney. This posh building wasn't up for Queenie's shenanigans. Spare keys were needed for plumbing issues, burst pipes, fires, and any other unforeseeable events. The superintendent allowed Apple to go up the block and make a spare key and then he promptly went to bed. He didn't care at all what the female would do. He knew Queenie was a criminal with her tattooed teardrop that represented murder. She was low class. The whole building despised her. She was mean, rude, and never tipped.

As far as he was concerned, he was doing a bad thing to get something good done.

Apple opened the door cautiously. If an alarm went off, she would turn around and quickly exit. A couple steps into Queenie's apartment, and Apple was set upon by numerous cats. The stench of cat urine assaulted her nostrils when she entered the premises. Apple was aghast but not surprised that the weird drug queenpin would live like this. The biggest challenge that Apple had was to not take all those cats into the bathroom and drown them. They needed to be alive when their owner entered or else she would know something was amiss. Apple stopped at Queenie's altar and shook her head. Apple didn't know who she had been dealing with all this time. Was she mentally unstable? What Apple stared at wasn't normal by anyone's stretch of the imagination.

She wasn't in Queenie's apartment for long before she heard keys jangling. Apple crouched low behind one of the massive pieces of furniture and screwed the silencer on her gun. From her position, she saw Queenie enter the apartment, lean down and pat one of her cats on the head, and toss her keys on a side table. Queenie clicked on her lights, kicked off her shoes, and placed her coat and pocketbook in the hallway closet, oblivious that she wasn't alone.

Apple had to steady her breathing. Her anger was palpable, and a massive mountain of hate was about to finally erupt. Queenie walked and stood before her altar, and with her right hand, she did an air cross. The gun smashing into the back of her head pushed Queenie forward. She fell into her altar and candles, statues, and other religious artifacts came crashing to the floor—broken glass flew everywhere. Queenie spun around to face her assailant and instantly locked eyes with Apple.

"Who let you—"

Apple smashed the gun into Queenie's face once again, wanting to inflict pain before she ended their ongoing feud. Queenie slipped on the glass, cutting up her bare feet, and fell into Apple. Queenie's weight caused Apple to take a couple steps back, and subsequently, she tripped over the coffee table in the cluttered apartment. Apple's pistol fell, and Queenie saw an opening and lunged for it. The two struggled in the deathmatch for dominance. Pound for pound, punches were exchanged as the females tussled on the ground in a fight for their lives. Apple quickly regained control of her adversary. With her knee pressed firmly into Queenie's chest, Apple repeatedly smashed her fists into her face until she was unrecognizable. Apple was winded, but Queenie still wasn't beaten. She wiggled under Apple, struggling to free herself from Apple's grasp. Apple saw her gun about five feet away and contemplated how she wanted to finally end this when her hands instinctually wrapped around Queenie's neck and squeezed.

As Apple's grip tightened, Queenie tried to pull Apple's hands off of her, but she had little strength left. Angry eyes bored into frightened eyes as Apple watched the life slip away, once and for good, from Queenie. The head of the L.E.S. Crips was finally dead.

Apple pushed herself off of Queenie and took several minutes to calm down. Her breathing was erratic, and both her hands were swollen and in immense pain. The cats that had run away and hidden while the battle ensued had now come back into the living room and brushed their bodies up against their dead owner, sensing her fate.

Apple gathered her breath and her gun and quietly left the residence. She could now exhale. All her enemies were now dead, and she could resume her life without having to look over her shoulders.

39

FORTY-FIVE DAYS LATER

I t was shortly after six in the morning, and Apple had just hung up FaceTime with Touch. Her man was in Vegas, making a killing. Touch had recovered from his injuries, buried his father once police located and identified his body as a victim of an apparent robbery, and retired from his agency. Touch was now fully committed to poker, but he couldn't seem to persuade Apple to let go of her illegal empire.

The morning was quiet as Apple fixed herself a pot of coffee and put food down for Girlie, who had become a constant fixture at her home when Touch was out of town. Peaches and Tokyo were asleep in their respective rooms, so she figured she had at least another hour of solitude.

The hard knock on her front door sounded familiar, but Apple was sure there had to be some mistake. It couldn't be. And then again, there was a thunderous, consistent bang followed by, "Police! Open up!"

Apple instantly worried about Kola hiding out in a nuthouse. Did she do something to herself? Was she dead? Had Eduardo killed her? So many thoughts entered her mind as she walked to open the door. Apple trembled with fear of hearing the news. She couldn't lose another sister.

"Apple Evans?"

"Yes."

"You're under arrest for the first-degree murder of Queenie Inga Grimes."

Apple gasped. "What?"

"Turn around and place your hands behind your back. You have the right to remain silent . . .," the detective spewed.

"Just take me, please. I don't want my daughter to see this shit."

The detectives had no intention of wrapping this up. They wanted to make this as painful, embarrassing, and humiliating as they could. There needed to be a spectacle for what was done to Queenie Grimes. Her position as the head of the L.E.S. Crips was a nonfactor to them.

Tokyo heard the commotion and sprung into action. Apple had two guns in the house, her 9mm and a .45 she kept in Tokyo's room away from Peaches. Tokyo wiped the guns down and in a plastic bag dropped them out her window which faced the back courtyard. And then she groggily came out of the room rubbing her eyes.

"What's going on?"

The two detectives, Whitehouse and Bennett, were shocked to see another female; she wasn't on the lease. Startled, Bennett removed his holstered gun and pointed it toward Tokyo. He screamed, "Get the fuck over here now!"

"Oh my god, what are you doing!" Apple screamed. "My daughter's here. Why you got your gun out?"

Tokyo threw her hands up to surrender and was quickly detained and manhandled. She, too, was handcuffed, and she and Apple were thrown on the couch. Apple shot Tokyo a worried glance and relived the event that led to her arrest. How was she caught? She wore gloves, so no fingerprints. She had paid off the superintendent who had given her access to the apartment. Apple was sure that he wouldn't implicate himself, and he didn't know who she was. And, most important, she had checked for an alarm system.

Apple pleaded again. "Can you take me to the precinct so I can be processed and charged? I said my daughter is in her room asleep."

Detective Whitehouse pulled a warrant from out of his back pocket. "I don't give a fuck what you want. We have a warrant to search the premises, so this won't be buttoned up on your timeline." He glared at Apple with contempt and then added, "You should have thought about your daughter before you murdered a woman in cold blood."

Apple felt fucked. She knew they would find her weapons, and both had bodies on them, especially her 9mm. It was the same one she had in South Beach. Apple knew better than to keep dirty guns. It was a cardinal rule that she had disregarded.

Another hard bang on her door and a squad of uniformed police officers were let in carrying coffee cups and scowls. They were there to help with the search warrant. Everyone shot dirty looks at the suspects as Tokyo sat handcuffed, wondering why she was being treated like a criminal.

Law enforcement conversed with themselves about how to effectively execute the warrant when all voices came to a halt. Peaches came walking out of her room on her tippy-toes like a ballerina, something she had recently started doing, looking for her mother with Girlie by her side. With wide eyes, she looked into everyone's face and asked, "Where's my mommy?"

"Peaches," Apple called out. "I'm here."

Peaches tried to walk toward her mother's voice when an overzealous officer stepped in front of her, blocking her path. He looked to Whitehouse, who was in charge, and Whitehouse said, "Let her through."

Peaches squeezed on the couch, wedged herself between her mother and Tokyo, and called Girlie over. Girlie growled low, barked a few times at the unknown men, and then happily came and lay under Peaches's feet.

"Some guard dog you are," Apple said, and Peaches just laughed.

Eventually, Apple and Tokyo—both still handcuffed—along with Peaches and Girlie were placed outside Apple's apartment on the floor under the watchful eyes of an officer. This act embarrassed them as neighbors came out of their apartments on their way to work to see this spectacle. Apple had just moved in, and it appeared she would be moving out.

Finally, Tokyo whispered and told Apple what she had done with the guns. Apple was so relieved that she knew she would bless her financially for thinking on her feet. Even if the officers found the guns outside, the chain of custody had been broken. They could never pin them on Apple.

Three hours later, the search warrant turned up fruitless. Tokyo was released from detainment, and Apple was arrested on first-degree murder charges.

40

ONE YEAR LATER

Apple had fought the biggest fight of her life trying to beat this murder charge. She hired a dream team, a gaggle of lawyers with a combined two hundred years of experience, hoping to get acquitted. Touch had proven himself to be a winner. He was the rock she needed and the glue that helped keep her together when she wanted to fall apart. The thought of going to jail for the rest of her life and only seeing Peaches on jailhouse visits had frightened the woman with the lion's heart.

Kola had signed herself out of the custody of the state so she could be there for her sister. When Apple called to tell her she was arrested for murder, she could hear the panic in her voice, and the victim was the same woman that Kola had begged Apple to not pursue. However, Kola didn't come with the "I told you so." Instead she did whatever she could, attended each meeting Apple had with her attorneys, and was a beacon of positivity feeding her sister strength and optimism even though the circumstance seemed bleak.

Cartier was also there for Apple with her new baby, Caviar, and a new relationship on full display with Caesar Mingo. She had gone through a lot with Harlem, a younger female who Cartier had taken in off the streets and who eventually had an affair with Cartier's husband. Head was recently laid to rest, yet Cartier still unselfishly put her issues aside to support her friend. Cartier was a treasure trove of wisdom, having been in

Apple's position when she was still a teenager.

The Mingo and Helguero cartels also kept a close eye on Apple. A person in her position facing life behind bars could have an inclination that snitching for a better deal was an option. But their men assured them that Apple had made no deals. She was a standup soldier and was handling her situation like a real gangstress.

Turns out that Nerd and Queenie reached from beyond the grave and had the last laugh. Nerd had his parents' home hard-wired with surveillance cameras, but Queenie was a clever one, and she had Nerd connect a wireless camera system that was inconspicuously placed around her house, hidden in places such as her altar. The footage showed Apple enter the apartment with a key. The police couldn't disprove that Queenie hadn't given the key to Apple, which Apple's attorney had alleged. The cameras also showed Apple lying in wait for Queenie to arrive. The last piece of clear footage was Apple hitting Queenie on the head with a gun before a fight ensued. When the altar was knocked over the actual murder wasn't captured. Finally, it showed Apple exiting the residence.

If she took this case to trial, Apple's dream team would argue self-defense. They would be hard-pressed to prove it, so when a twenty-year plea deal was offered, Apple jumped at the chance to plead guilty. With good time she could be out in fourteen years. She would be approximately early forties, still young enough to have a good life.

Touch promised to do the time with her and also help Kola take care of Peaches, but Apple knew those were the words of today. Tomorrow would be another story.

There wasn't a dry eye inside the small room that Apple, Kola, Peaches, Touch, Cartier, Tokyo, Hood, and IG sat in. Apple had about thirty minutes before she would go before the judge and get sentenced. Her lawyers were already inside the courtroom doing preliminary paperwork with the prosecutors so Apple's transfer into state custody could go smoothly.

Kola needed alone time with her sister and requested that everyone meet them inside the courtroom. Apple gave everyone tight embraces and quick kisses on their cheeks. Peaches got the most affection, but the small child didn't understand much of what was happening.

Apple took one last look at everyone and said, "See y'all in twenty thirty-three."

EPILOGUE

Apple stood in front of the judge and read the statement that her attorney had prepared for her. In it, she apologized for her actions and confessed her guilt. But she also announced that she was a better person now, and would work on rehabilitation while doing her time and vowed to do acts of benevolence upon her release. The judge scowled down at her. He belittled and reprimanded her. There was no excuse for her actions—for murder, especially of that brutality. She was sentenced to twenty years, and the bailiffs were ordered to immediately take her into custody.

Apple was sentenced, but unbeknownst to the court and everyone else except Peaches, Kola was handcuffed and led away to do her sister's time. When Kola asked everyone to leave the room, she broached the subject of trading places. Apple was vehemently against allowing Kola to do time for a crime she had done, but her sister was aggressive with her stance.

"I'm not gonna keep explaining why we need to do this," Kola griped. "Think of your daughter. Peaches needs you—not me. If you say no, then I'm returning back to my psychiatric facility because you know the only other option is Eduardo and I'd die before I ever go back to Colombia. Look, I want the best for my niece, and with Touch by your side—and if you promise to leave the streets alone—then Peaches has a chance to live the life that we never did. If you keep up this lifestyle, then I promise Peaches will follow in your footsteps. You'll have raised a street bitch, and you'll only have yourself to blame!"

Apple was still resisting.

"I wouldn't do this if I didn't think I could handle it. And I'll work on my mental health while I'm in there. Just promise to visit and bring my niece at least once a month. Can you handle my demands?"

Apple nodded.

"Say it, Apple. Say you'll get out of the game!"

Apple thought about what her sister was sacrificing and said, "I will. I'll get out of the game starting today. I won't let you down, Kola. My hand up to God, I'll go legit."

The twins switched clothing, and Apple took her bun down while Kola styled her loose hair correctly. Apple called everyone back into the room so they could all walk out in a crowd to help camouflage the switch. When everyone filed into the waiting area, Peaches had the most quizzical look on her face when Kola bent down and scooped her up, pretending to be Apple.

As they walked into the courtroom, Peaches whispered in Kola's ear, "Auntie Kola, we playing a game?"

Kola nodded and put her index finger to her lips for secrecy.

Kola standing as Apple was sentenced and led away as the real Apple cried real tears for her sister's sacrifice and departure. Kola was stoic as she was led away with her head up. Anything for family.

With a new lease on life, Apple said to her protégé, "Tokyo, pack ya shit!"

After everything Cartier had gone through with having two women living under her roof with her man, Apple wouldn't repeat that same mistake. Apple was who she'd always be: heartless, vindictive, petty, strong, sensitive, loving, loyal, cheap, generous. She was the Queen of New York—Harlem's baddest chick—but she'd never be the chick who put her man in the position to fuck the next bitch.

With her career in drugs on hold for the next decade, at least until Kola came home, Apple and Touch decided to take Peaches on a long Disney cruise as they continued to bond as a family. The couple was inside Touch's bland apartment waiting on their Uber to take them to the airport when Apple said, "C'mere."

Touch walked over to his woman, and she wrapped white first aid tape around his ring finger.

He smiled. "What's this?"

"This is me askin' you to become Malcolm Xavier Evans."

"Evans, huh? If I say yes, you need to know that it's forever. I don't believe in divorce."

Apple grinned. "I invented till death do us part."

Allergic to Broke

I'M DOPE. I DON'T SELL IT.

Statement Hoodie Order Below!

www.melodramabooks.com

Cheapiana

$AVE.
INVE$T.
BLE$$ED

Cheap Over Broke

GETTING LUCKY

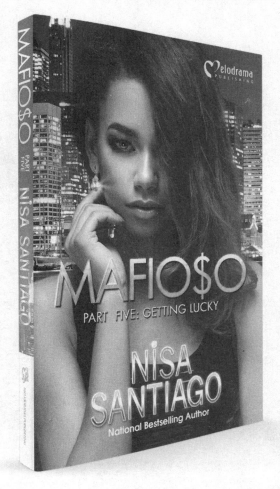

The stunning acquittals of Scott and Layla West resonate throughout the justice system, and the powerful cartels take notice.

The Wests were untouchable and their drug empire is still intact, but family ties begin to unravel.

New mom Lucky has a lot on her shoulders as she continues to deceive the head of the Juarez cartel. Partnering with her twin brothers, Lucky lines up the pieces on the chessboard, but she underestimates the king and queen.

BROOKLYN
Bombshells

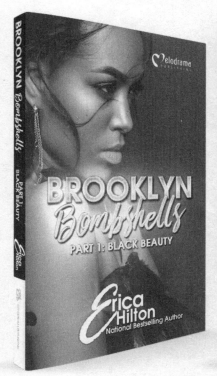

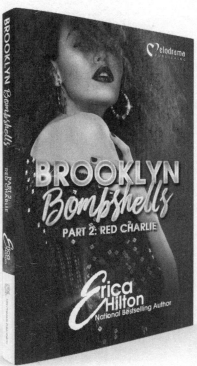

THE SERIES BY